WELCOME TO
HAPPY-LAND

Tom Kiske

This book is a work of fiction. Places, events, and situations in the story are purely fictional. Any resemblance to actual persons, living or dead, is coincidental.

"Welcome to Happy-Land," by Tom Kiske.ISBN 978-1-62137-760-3 (Softcover).

Published 2015 by Virtualbookworm.com Publishing Inc., P.O. Box 9949, College Station, TX , 77842, US.

Also by Tom Kiske

Time Has Its Own Terms

Tales in Ordinary Time

ACKNOWLEDGMENTS

Many people contributed to this book through encouragement, suggestions or just through their lives. It would be impossible to list them all, however a few deserve special mention and thanks: my wife for her continuing support of my writing, my son for pushing me to get this book done, the Wancho Gang and other long-time friends for being the inspiration behind the story, Don George for permitting me to cut and paste some of his teenage love life onto Tom Bonner, Bobby Bernshausen and Virtualbookworm.com Publishing (VBW Publishing), and all those who lived through the tumultuous Fifties and Sixties. Thank you all.

For McKinley Goldbugs and Happy-Landers.

For Kathy, Chris, Lauren, Michael, Sofi and Nico.

and for Bryan.

PREFACE

T he mid-Twentieth Century was a time of great upheaval in the so-called "rust belt" cities, and none felt the rapidly changing environment more than St. Louis. Between 1950 and 1960 the old city lost more than 100,000 residents. The following decade saw another 100,000 flee to suburbs that were seen as newer, cleaner and safer than the central core, which continued to decay.

City leaders knew St. Louis - once the nation's 4th largest city - was in trouble, and they were determined to take action to halt the decline. Their solutions took the form of several ambitious and costly projects categorized under the headings of "urban renewal" or more ominously, "slum clearance." At the same time, efforts were underway to alleviate the traffic congestion resulting from suburban office workers commuting to downtown businesses.

Ground was broken for The Jefferson National Expansion Memorial along the downtown riverfront, occupying a 90 acre site that had been cleared of hundreds of old brick warehouses and factories. This would be where the towering Gateway Arch - the gleaming new emblem of St. Louis - would rise. Further extensive demolition provided routes for the new interstate highways, I-55 to the south and I-44 to the southwest.

Critical decisions that would forever alter the face of the city and the lives of thousands of St. Louisans were being made, and being made by a mere handful of people. The Land Clearance for Redevelopment Authority (LCRA), for example, was governed by a board of only five members. In 1958 the LCRA Five finalized their Urban Renewal Plan targeting the Kosciusko district, a 221 acre area partly adjacent to the historic Soulard neighborhood. Kosciusko included 70 blocks of what was termed a ". . . somewhat rundown assembly of 19th century brick commercial buildings and tenements." The housing stock, according to the plan, was "substandard" despite being architecturally similar to the nearby Soulard area, where greater foresight afforded priority to preservation.

Powerful corporate interests located in or near Kosciusko craved room for expansion - a craving blocked by those pesky "substandard" houses. Three thousand men, women and children lived in those houses, but as they were "predominantly poor" in the words of the Urban Renewal Plan they didn't get a say about what was about to happen to them – never mind that many of them supplied the labor for the very industries that were forcing them out of their homes. No voice either for the owners of the little mom-and-pop shops in the path of the wrecking ball. The juggernaut of slum clearance was on the move and there was no stopping it. Not for historical considerations or architectural preservation and certainly not for a bunch of predominantly poor people. Just shuffle those "worker-bees" off to hives that came to be known as the The Projects - public housing monstrosities like Pruitt-Igoe and Darst-Webbe. Or let them fend for themselves, push into adjacent neighborhoods - and who cares what they think, what the people in those neighborhoods think, or what tensions and troubling unintended consequences might follow? For the poorest of the poor the last refuge was the riverfront shanty town known variously as Hooverville, Chicken Town or Happy-Land.

Welcome to Happy-Land is a novel built around this place and time. It is entirely a work of fiction. The characters are fictional and any resemblance to actual persons living or dead is unintentional. The spirit and mood of the inner city circa 1960 is authentic.

I've seen fire and I've seen rain
I've seen sunny days that I thought would never end
I've seen lonely times when I could not find a friend . . .

James Taylor

ONE

*"Every segment of the people has a stake in St. Louis's choice
between progress and decay. Progress means more . . . of the
things that mark a city of character."*
Richard G. Baumhoff, St. Louis Post-Dispatch
editorial "Progress or Decay? St. Louis must
choose." March 5, 1950

". . . the city's dyin' and we don't know why . . ."
Randy Newman

I t wasn't much of a clubhouse, and for sure not much of a gang
headquarters. It was one dingy room in the basement of an 1880's
era brick four-family flat at Eleventh and Victor streets in an old
St. Louis neighborhood. It was just another slum in an old city that was
rotting away and falling apart. The foundation and basement walls of
the flat, like most in the area, were of rubblestone inside and out. We
had whitewashed the inside walls to mask the grime, but already it had
begun to bleed back through the thin covering and it looked bad.

The floor was dirt, but because the basement had been used for
decades to store coal for the fireplaces, once the house's only source of
heat, a fine layer of black coal dust had been ground into the dirt and
mixed with it to form some new compound not normally present in
nature, but common in subterranean St. Louis.

In the center of the basement room one bare light bulb dangled
from a frayed cord mended and re-mended with black electrical tape.

1

There was no window, and the flickering bulb cast only a dim glow that hardly made it to the corners of the room.

The gang's furniture consisted of a tattered sofa along one wall, a stained and sagging mattress flopped on the floor in the middle of the room, and two galvanized washtubs we used as makeshift chairs. You plopped your butt in the tub, your arms and legs dangling out. Real comfortable. A cork dartboard hung on the basement door.

The gang was Bryan, Jeffrey, Ronnie, Diane, Cathy and me, Tom Bonner. It wasn't much of a gang. Didn't even have a name. The gang across the street - the bad guys - didn't have a name either. Only the big gangs had names - gangs like The Aces AC. Those guys even had these cool jackets with Aces AC spelled out across the back over a cartoonish ace of spades. AC stood for Athletic Club. For some reason, all the big gangs on the South Side of St. Louis called themselves athletic clubs. They hung out at the South Broadway Athletic Club, down at Broadway and Shenandoah. That was a real athletic club with a gym and everything. Some of the AC's actually did something athletic once in a while, cork ball or bottle tops or bowling or, more often, kicking the crap out of each other.

The two rival gangs up on Eleventh Street weren't in the AC category, but we wanted to be. Each gang revolved around one really tough guy. The other gang had Freddie. We had Bryan.

I'd known Bryan forever - for as far back as I could remember, which was before Kindergarten - and he had always been tough. He was almost two years older than me and had always been bigger and stronger, but it was more than that. Everybody knew Bryan was a tough kid. He wasn't a real tall guy, in fact I'd already caught up to him in height. He didn't have those gigantic body-builder muscles, either. It was just that he was strong. His biceps were as solid as the cobblestones in the streets. You could poke at his muscles with your finger and they wouldn't even push in - not at all. He had this big vein that stuck out like a rope under the skin, starting high on his chest and then running out along the inside of the bicep of each arm, pulsing and throbbing like he was all ready for action. You know what I mean.

In those days we all had to wear our t-shirts with the sleeves rolled up exactly twice and anybody who saw those biceps of Bryan's sticking out knew he wasn't a guy you messed with. And because everybody knew Bryan and I were best friends, nobody much messed with me, either. At least not until the neighborhood started changing and the damn hoosiers started moving in.

2

At first, when I was a kid, the gangs and the problems were mostly down below Broadway or on the North Side. If you stayed out of certain areas you were okay. Then the city did some kind of urban renewal thing down there, tore down all the houses to make room for factories and warehouses and stuff. People who used to live down there were supposed to relocate into The Projects, but lots of them just moved right up the hill into our neighborhood. Most of them were OK, but some weren't. They brought trouble along with them. The nice folks who used to live in our neighborhood and kept up their houses and were nice to talk to, they all moved out to the county and so the neighborhood turned to crap.

One especially nasty family of eight or so, the Rindles, moved in right across the street from my folks house. The oldest kid, Jay Rindle, and some of his cronies got together a gang and started screwing around, so my buddies and I had to have one, too. I don't guess I ever thought that much about what it meant, being in a gang, and I sure as hell didn't know how much trouble we'd all end up in, or I wouldn't have gotten involved in the first place. But crap, we were just kids, having a little fun, protecting ourselves from the punks and hoods and hoosiers and trying to act like we were cool. It wasn't a real big change, anyway, going from just a bunch of guys who hung around together to being a gang.

So there we were one summer afternoon in our crummy whitewashed basement clubhouse. There was no air conditioning back then, so a basement wasn't a bad place to be. The earth and the thick stone walls kept out some of the heat. Diane and I were sitting on the mattress in the middle of the room.

"Wanna smoke?" Diane asked, holding out her cigarette.

"Nah, I don't think so," I mumbled back. Damn little fourteen year old. Shouldn't be smoking herself, let alone passing around cigarettes to everybody.

"Go on, try it," she teased, "It won't hurt you."

She was kinda poking the cigarette in my face and grinning like because she smokes she's in on something I don't know about. I was trying to be cool, but feeling my face starting to flush. I pulled away to keep the cigarette out of my face. Damn little fourteen year old.

"Hey, leave him alone," Bryan chimed in, "It will hurt him. He's an athlete."

That's just what I needed, Bryan defending me from this little girl. And athlete? Me? Where'd that come from? High school basketball didn't seem like enough to make me an athlete. I sure didn't feel like an athlete.

Anyway, because Bryan said so, Diane let me off the hook.

"Oh, okay," she said, dangling the cigarette in her fingertips like she was Lauren Bacall or somebody. Me, I silently cussed myself for getting so flustered. I just still wasn't too comfortable around girls, even little fourteen year old twerps like Diane.

First of all I didn't like that she was always hanging around me. Like coming over and sitting right next to me on that mattress. I mean she was cute and all, with that short-cropped blonde hair and funny just-learning-to-be-sexy ways, but hell, she was just fourteen and Jeffrey's little sister. Nothing was going to happen there - ever!

Now, Cathy, that was something else. She was Jeffrey's sister, too, but at sixteen she was fully developed and ready for...well, ready. But of course she was with Bryan. All the girls liked Bryan. It wasn't just the muscles. Mostly it was the hair. First, he had a lot of it. Thick, black hair. Second, it was naturally wavy. He wore it long and combed back at the sides with plenty of Brylcreme into a nice Elvis-type ducktail. It wasn't an extreme ducktail though, the kind where you make that little crease right at the back. A crease would make it look too much like what we all figured the actual crack of a duck's ass must look like. That would not be cool. Bryan had a DA, but without the crack. I'd heard more than one girl talk about how she'd like to get her fingers in Bryan's hair.

I had this plain old brown hair, cut short, no DA. Nobody was wanting to run their fingers through my stupid hair. Well, maybe Diane, but even she'd rather be in Bryan's DA.

Too bad for her, though, because Bryan was back there on the sofa with Cathy. They weren't making out or anything, just kinda sitting close together. Being close together. Everybody knew what was going on between the two of them. Even Jeffrey. He didn't mind though, because it was Bryan. I mean who wouldn't want their sister going out with him?

Jeffrey had this pocketknife and he was throwing it at the door, trying out different kinds of tosses - overhand, underhand, throwing it by the handle one time and by the blade the next. He was pretty good at it and the blade stuck in the door with a nice "thung" every time.

"So what we gonna do about them jerks across the street?" he asked between tosses. Actually, I figured Jeffrey was kind of a jerk himself. His old man was some kind of Golden Gloves champ and

Jeffrey'd done some boxing himself. The guy always wanted to be fighting somebody.

"What do you want to do about them?" Bryan asked.

"I say we go over and rumble."

Another thing about Jeffrey is that he was always trying to sound cool by saying stuff like "rumble." I guess maybe we all did that. It felt funny for me, though. I mean like if I'd said that, I'd have thought the word "fight" first, and then had to mentally translate it to "rumble" before I said it. At least I did that some of the time. It seemed kinda phony, though, like acting or something. A lot of the way we did stuff was probably because of the movies. Blackboard Jungle. Rebel Without a Cause.

"Man, how come you always wantin' to rumble? Bryan asked.

"Well," Jeffrey said, "I'm just not taking no crap off nobody. I mean we gonna do it or not?" He gave the knife a really good toss and it chunked hard into the door, which was getting pretty chewed up.

"Listen," Bryan said, "There's enough damn rumblin' goin on around here already. We don't need to be startin' nothin' up. Those guys ain't done nothin' yet. If they do - when they do - then we'll be ready."

Bryan could talk that way because everybody knew he wasn't afraid to fight. He'd been around enough though that he'd just as soon have a good reason for going after somebody.

"Crap," said Jeffrey, "At least you all know how I feel."

"Well, I'm thinkin' we need to get some weights or something," I said.

"What? Weights?" Jeff snarled, "Whatdya mean weights?"

"You know, like barbells and weight-lifting stuff," I explained.

"Aw, crap," Jeff decided. Mr. Golden Gloves would rather diddle with his knife.

"No, that ain't a bad idea," Ronnie chimed in, "I been over to those guys place and they got a bunch of that junk."

"You been over to their place?" Bryan asked.

"Yeah. You know, just to check it out."

Ronnie was the kind of guy who could just as easily have hung out with the gang across the street as with us. He was a big guy, but pretty easy-going. A guy who never took anything too seriously, got along with everybody. I think he only hung out with us because his sister and Bryan's sister, Rose, hung out together down at the White Castle on Chouteau Avenue. I guess something like that gives you something in

5

common, even though neither of them ever talked about their older sisters. Not even Bryan. Not as long as I'd known him.

"So, what kinda stuff they got?" Jeff asked.

"I dunno - just like Tom said, barbells and junk. Freddie's always screwin' around with em."

I could see Bryan's interest perk up when Freddie's name was mentioned. The way everybody saw it in our neighborhood was that Bryan could probably beat the crap out of anybody except maybe Freddie, and Freddie could beat up anybody except Bryan. I don't know how Freddie's buddies felt, but even as Bryan's best friend, I wasn't too sure if he could take Freddie. For one thing, Freddie was a heck of a lot bigger than Bryan. I'd never seen Bryan lose a fight, but Freddie...well, Freddie was pretty stout.

"I think it'd be real cool if you guys started lifting weights," Diane said.

At this, Bryan went over and grabbed her up off the floor and started tickling her.

"Why'd we be liftin' weights when we could be liftin' you?" he joked.

"Quit it. Quit it. Put me down," Diane squealed. She was yelling and wriggling around like she was trying to get loose, but you could tell she really loved it. The attention and all.

Finally Bryan hauled her skinny little butt over and tossed her down on the couch next to Cathy and she was all sputtering and red in the face and straightening out her clothes, like she was real embarrassed.

Jeffrey interrupted the festivities with a snort.

"Listen, if you guys really wanna do this, I think my old man still has some weights, maybe even a training bag. I don't know where we're gonna put all that stuff in this crappy little room, though."

"Nah," Ronnie said, "There's plenty of room, we could get rid of that lousy-ass mattress and maybe just get a coupla real chairs or something instead of them washtubs. How much room would it take for some barbells and junk? It's just - would your old man let us take that stuff?"

"Who knows? Who knows anything about their old man? All I could do is ask the old bastard - I mean, if you guys want me to."

We all looked at Bryan for a decision. He thought about it a minute. "Yeah," he said after a little bit, "Go ahead and see if we can use it for a while, anyways." Then he yawned and stretched. "Listen," he added, "I'm gonna have to bug out pretty soon. What do you guys wanna do tonight?"

Nobody said anything for a while, then Ronnie's face lit up.

"Hey, I think the Holy Rollers are gonna be there tonite. Wanna go by for a while?"

Watching the Holy Rollers had become a source of entertainment in the neighborhood ever since their church had moved into what used to be Phil's Tavern at the corner of Eleventh and Barton. There was a small window at the back of the building where we could peek in without being seen. The church had a fiery minister who regularly worked his flock into a frenzy of tears and confession and I guess what you call talking in tongues. I felt a little funny about it, but crouching together at the rear window watching folks jerking around in the throes of hellfire and damnation was a lot more fun than sitting home with the family watching Ed Sullivan or Red Skelton on TV.

Jeffrey wasn't too keen on the idea, mostly because his mother had started going to the church from time to time, but since he wasn't able to come up with a better idea for the evening, he said he'd come along. The girls, though, never really saw the fun in this activity.

"We're gonna skip it," Kathy said, "Diane and I both have homework tonite."

Schoolwork was something that never got talked about much in our gang. School was just something you had to do. You went whenever you couldn't figure out a good excuse not to, got done as quick as you could and got back home to hang out, which was where the important stuff happened. Nobody saw a whole lot of point in what had happened to a bunch of Greeks or Romans a thousand years ago or how to solve an equation for "x." For me, I did pretty well in school and my folks made a big deal of it, so I took a fair amount of crap from some of the guys..

"How 'bout you, Bonner," Jeffrey sneered, "You got homework, too?"

"Hey, I'll be there," I snapped, "Don't worry about it."

Bryan glanced over at me. He was funny about school. He'd done real well in grade school and his teachers had urged him to go on. High school was still kind of optional in those days and Bryan's folks clearly didn't give a damn one way or the other if he went, so it was pretty easy for him to drop out, which he'd done after less than a year. He'd been around my parents enough, though, to hear them harp on getting an education, so he felt guilty about quitting and decided to give it another try when I started high school. By then, he was a couple of years older than most of the kids in his classes, which was kinda embarrassing for him so he was skipping out again. By that time, too, he was working at the butcher shop and living with his grandma, who was real old and needed a lot of care. I knew he probably was about to drop out again but he always told me to finish up and graduate. It was like he was my Dad or something when it came to school, or even more, it was almost like me finishing high school was doing something for him, too.

"Maybe you need to worry about your own crap, Jeffrey," Bryan said, "Instead of everybody else's."

Jeffrey just looked away and went back to fiddling with his knife, throwing it down to stick in the floor.

"Hey," Diane piped up, "How 'bout some ice cream everybody?"

Jeffrey and Kathy and Diane's parents owned the little confectionary on the corner, right upstairs from our club. It had been Horton's tavern until they took it over and turned it into what you'd think of today as a convenience store. The closest supermarket in our area was the A&P store way over at Eighteenth and Russell, so Deem's Confectionary was where most folks bought their day-to-day groceries. Every once in a while Kathy or Diane could sneak something out for us, mostly ice creams or cokes. Jeffrey either couldn't or wouldn't grab stuff for us like that, I think because his old man had caught him once too often and had threatened to beat the tar out of him next time. The old man liked to beat him up anyway, just to teach him to be tough. Jeffrey wasn't about to give him another excuse to do so.

We all decided an ice cream would taste pretty good and Bryan said he'd stick around a few minutes longer, so Diane scurried out after something cold for the bunch of us.

She'd only been gone a few minutes when somebody started pounding on the door. Before anybody could answer, instead of Diane, in sauntered Freddie and his gang.

"Hi, guys," shouted Jay Rindle with this smirk smeared all over his ugly mug, "We just thought we'd stop by and see your new place."

Up to this point, we'd never really got into it with any of these guys, so we were still sorta friends, or at least not yet straight out enemies, so everybody was playing it cool.

There were six of them and they all slunk in and started looking around and touching stuff and saying how nice the place looked, but we knew it was all bullcrap and they were just screwing with us.

"Gee," one of the assholes chirped, "What a great mattress."

8

"Yeah, and what did you do, like paint the walls or something?" another one chimed in, acting like a goddam fairy.

Meanwhile Freddie had gone straight over to Bryan and just stood there next to him, watching while the rest of the jerks poked around at our stuff. I saw Freddie lean over and say something to Bryan, but I couldn't hear what it was. I don't think Bryan said anything back.

Standing together like that, I could see Freddie was a lot bigger than Bryan. More than I'd thought. Not taller, just broader and bigger around, and I could see again how much bigger his arms were than Bryan's. Worse, it was clear he wasn't afraid of Bryan and though he showed him some respect just by going over there and standing by him, bringing his gang over like this meant he thought they were ready to take us on. More, it meant he figured he was ready for Bryan. You could see it in the way he was standing, sorta moving in on Bryan's space. But Bryan never budged, just stood there with this cool Elvis-type semi-sneer, semi-smile I'd seen him use before.

"Ain't you guys got no radio?" old Jay asked, knowing damn well we didn't, "We're gettin this great hi-fi from my old man's furniture store."

It was funny how Freddie was definitely the leader of their gang, but he hardly ever said anything. Instead, it was that little jerk Jay whose mouth was always running off.

"Radios are for wimps," Jeffrey threw back at them.

Cathy could tell things were getting a little tense and decided to bug out before they got worse.

"I better go check on Diane," she said and headed for the door.

"Aw, Cathy, come on, don't go," Jay pleaded in this mock sugary tone, "Don't go just onna counta us bein' here."

She didn't say anything or even turn around, but just closed the door behind her. I could see Jeffrey's face getting redder and redder. Jay was messin' with his sister.

Ronnie could see what was going on. I guess he knew what it was like to have somebody ragging on your sister, because his sister Barb was kind of a whore, so he just sort moseyed over real slow like and kinda put himself in between Jeffrey and Jay to keep them apart.

"So," Ronnie said real cheerful like, "When're you guys gettin the hi-fi?"

It took Jay a minute to change gears from thinking about Cathy and about maybe fighting Jeffrey.

"Uh, I don't know, but pretty soon. We're definitely getting it and its gonna be cool."

Then he did manage to shift gears and figured maybe he'd work on Ronnie's allegiances a bit.

"Yeah, listen, Ronnie," he said ignoring the rest of us, "When we get it why doncha come by and check it out?"

"Sure," Ronnie answered, "Lemme know."

Meanwhile, Jeffrey had gotten himself back under control enough to toss out a zinger.

"Yeah, maybe we'll all come over and dance with you ladies."

"You could try it," Jay barked back.

All this time Freddie had just been standing there next to Bryan, those huge arms of his folded across his chest like some kind of goddam Indian or something, not saying a word, just watching everything with no expression at all on his face. Finally, he pulled himself up off the laundry tubs he and Bryan had both been leaning against.

"Let's go" he grunted.

With that, all his crew started strolling towards the door, like they owned the joint and were only leaving because they got bored or something. Jay couldn't resist a parting shot.

"Hey, what's this crap on the floor, man? It's got all over my shoes. What is that, coal or something? Geez, I hope we don't get it all over the carpet back at our place."

Freddie was standing at the door, sorta herding the jerks out. Bryan, who hadn't moved since they came in, slowly walked over, grinned and grabbed Freddie by the arm, right on the bicep. I'd seen Bryan do this with other guys before. He'd done it to me and I knew what it felt like. Bryan could squeeze your bicep so hard that it hurt like hell and you had to beg him to quit. He didn't do it very often and I think mostly it was a way to check a guy out and see how strong or how tough he might be.

It didn't seem like it was hurting Freddie much, but I don't know how hard Bryan was squeezing. I did see that his bicep gave some under Bryan's grasp, though, and I could also see that Bryan was saying something to Freddie. But I wasn't close enough to hear it. Freddie's ears looked pretty red as he walked out the door, though.

After they left, nobody said anything for a while.

"Well," I finally mumbled, "That seemed to go well."

"Those dirty bastards!" Jeffrey steamed, then he glared over at me. "Listen, Bonner, you better get something straight. You better put away your goddam books. You're gonna have to decide if you're gonna be a school boy or one of us. You try doin' both and you're gonna get hurt, or get somebody else bad hurt."

"Shut up, Jeffrey," Bryan snapped, "Tom's in this with the rest of us and you know it."

Ronnie was just standing there like the whole thing was maybe a little funny. The rest of us didn't quite see it that way, though. We were all kinda looking to Bryan to see how we ought to handle this. I didn't know what to think, myself. I'd never been in anything like this, but I could see from how Bryan's eyes were narrowed that he was thinking it over pretty hard and what he was thinking probably wasn't very good.

Finally, he spoke, real calm and slow, almost a whisper.

"Looks like you get your wish, Jeffrey."

"Huh?" I said, hoping I didn't know what he meant.

"Those guys had no business here," Bryan said in that ominous tone, "We got to go after them."

"YES!" Jeffrey proclaimed, chunking his knife deep into the wooden door.

We never did get our ice cream.

TWO

I t was a short walk home from the clubhouse. Just one house away, but I had to stop and say hello to Boozer. Old Booze was a black mutt - mostly German Shepherd, I think - that lived in the basement of the flat between my house and the club. Some hoosiers had moved into one side of the flat a couple of years earlier and kept Boozer in the back basement room. There was one window and that was all Booze ever got to see of the world. The glass was busted out and the hoosiers had put up some chicken wire, so whenever I'd cut across their back yard Boozer would run up to the window and press his muzzle into the chicken wire and whine and whine until I had to stop and stick my hand through to pet him a little. Then his tail would go nuts and he'd slobber and make happy dog sounds until I left and he'd go back to whining. Most of the neighborhood kids knew Boozer and would stop once in a while like me to pet him and give him a little company.

I guess the hoosiers fed the dog and gave him water, but they never let him out of that crappy basement room. I could see in from the window that it was just like all the other basements, with that black coal dust all over. I don't know, maybe Boozer wasn't even a black dog. It might have been he was just covered in all that soot. Not much of a way for a dog to have to live. I figured if Boozer stayed down there long enough he'd probably go mad. I couldn't understand why hoosiers would want a dog if all they were gonna do was keep him down in a lousy basement like that. Maybe that's just the way hoosiers are.

Anyway, I said goodbye to the Booze and headed on home. When I walked in the back door I could see I was in trouble because my Mom and Dad were already at the kitchen table eating dinner. Like always, they each had a section of the Post-Dispatch propped up in front of them.

My Old Man looked up from the paper. He wasn't happy.

"About time you got here," he growled, "Go wash your hands."

I was in luck. He must have been in the middle of a good article or he'd have started chewing on my ass about not being home for supper right at 5:30.

The Old Man worked in the safe deposit department downtown at Mercantile Commerce Bank. Every day he left work at exactly 5:00 pm, caught the Carondelet bus for a twenty minute ride home and expected supper on the table promptly at 5:30. More, what he expected was supper on the table and his family around the table. Being late or - God forbid - absent, was a sign of disrespect. He liked to point out that when he was a boy that meant that by God you went without.

I washed my hands, filled my plate with Polish Sausage and sauerkraut from the skillet on the stove and slid quietly into my usual spot across from the Old Man.

"Bread?" my Mom asked, pushing the cellophane-wrapped loaf of Wonder Bread (Builds Strong Bodies 8 Ways!) in my direction.

"Aw, Hell, look what the damn fools are up to now," the Old Man fumed, rustling the paper in front of him, "Do we need another goddam highway in St. Louis?"

"A highway?" Mom asked.

"Yeah, here's another story about that new highway they're building right alongside the Express Highway. How much sense does that make?"

At the time, St. Louis had exactly one freeway. It was a narrow four lane that ran from Skinker, out by Washington U., east along the south side of Forest Park and ended, as far as I knew, at Chouteau avenue, just west of Grand. I think another section might have gone on towards downtown, but the only times we were ever on it we always got off at Chouteau.

The Old Man calling it the Express Highway was a major bow to progress. I guess when it was built it was called the Red Feather Expressway. For my Dad, that was - goddamn it - its name! No matter everyone else in the city called it the Express Highway, it was the Red Feather Expressway and that's what it ought to be called. Change, to my Old Man, was never good.

"As if they haven't screwed this city up enough already," the Old Man continued, "There won't be a goddam thing here but highways and housing projects and warehouses. Then they can turn the keys over to the damn hoosiers."

"Well, dear, maybe we do need more roads," my Mom interjected, trying to calm Dad down, "You know, more and more people are moving out to the county."

Oh man, was that a bad move! Mentioning "The County" to my old man was like waving a red flag at a bull.

"The county! The county!" the old man sputtered as his face reddened, "Yeah, let's just tear the whole damn city down so the rich folks out in the county can get to work five minutes faster."

The City of St. Louis had withdrawn from St. Louis County about a hundred years earlier, but to my Old Man there was still some sort of civil war going on. The poor, downtrodden city folks versus the lousy snobs who lived out in the county and who were all rich. The fact that I had aunts and uncles who lived in various parts of St. Louis County and who weren't a whole lot different from us never caused so much as a hairline crack in my Dad's rock solid view of the economic and social class struggle between City and County. My mom had violated one of the principle tenets of the Bonner Catechism: County Bad, City Good (except for hoosiers and certain other minorities).

"Well, no, we certainly can't have that," Mom backpedalled, realizing her error, "How about some more sausage?"

"You're goddam right we can't!" he thundered, passing his plate her way, "They're already tearing down folks houses down below Broadway with that Kosciusko slum clearance thing. Slums my ass. Next they'll say THIS is a slum, too!"

Aside from the faux pas of mentioning the County, my Mom was normally adept at defusing the Old Man's tirades. It was almost an art form or maybe a science with her. In this case she was employing the food distraction technique. It was one of a few I recognized. How many other little tricks she had I could only guess at. She'd had practically a lifetime of honing her skills in this area, as she'd accepted early on that her primary mission in life was calming the Old Man down whenever something set him off.

Unfortunately for her, it was a thankless and nearly impossible task. First, because practically anything could light my Dad's fuse. You might learn some of the triggers, but you'd never know all of them because he kept adding to the list. Besides, his philosophy and personality were pretty much a hundred and eighty degrees out from my Mom's. He enjoyed steaming and fuming at things. He believed it was his right and duty to get pissed off as much as possible and to be as loud about it as he could. He thought that by screaming and shouting about stuff, he was keeping himself healthy and preventing a stroke or heart attack.

"I don't keep it in," he used to brag to my Mom, "I let it out. You keep it in. That's why you'll wind up with a heart attack someday, but not me. No sir."

The Old Man went back to the offending article in the newspaper and read on, simmering in silence for a few minutes.

"Well, there's one good thing about this damned road," he finally admitted.

"There is?" Mom piped up hopefully.

"Yeah. The way they've got it coming in, it looks like it's gonna cut the city in half. Maybe that'll keep the bad element up on the North Side."

My Dad may have been prejudiced, but he sure as hell didn't discriminate. He tossed around racial and ethnic slurs with equanimity towards all. Italians were dagos or wops, Hispanics were spics, Jews were sheenies, Blacks were any number of derogatory terms and any outsider who moved into our neighborhood, especially from a rural background, was a hoosier. It wasn't that the Old Man hated, or even disliked these people. I think he was vaguely aware that the terms he used might be offensive. He just didn't give a damn.

I kind of understood how he got that way. When he grew up, people in the city pretty much stayed in their own neighborhood. Polacks and Krautheads and Micks knew what they were and where they belonged. Go too far outside your area and you got your ass kicked. Just like with the Red Feather Expressway, he saw no reason why that ought to change.

"Pop," I said, "What's going on over on Dago Hill?"

St. Louis had two Dago Hills. The main one, the one everyone knew about and which was already changing into a more bland "The Hill," was an Italian neighborhood up around Southwest Avenue, centered around St. Ambrose Parish. The other, smaller Dago Hill known only to those of us who lived nearby, was a vacant lot taking up most of a whole block between Sidney and Victor Streets. One of St. Louis's many breweries had once stood there but it had exploded and burned to the ground fifty years earlier. The only sign Dago'd ever been anything but a vacant lot was a concrete slab in the middle of the block and two sections of stone wall along Victor Street. That was all that was left of the brewery. That and a sinkhole that opened up every once in a while near the Sidney Street side. Some folks said the hole lead down into storage vaults for the brewery's beer. A couple of times each year the city had to fill in the sink hole after a collapse, but it always opened up again.

Aside from the intrigue of the sinkhole, the lot itself was a great playground for neighborhood kids. There were plenty of hills and valleys where a kid could roam around and play cowboy or soldier. There wasn't a park in our area, but we made do with Dago. For kids it was even better than a park because the weeds and giant sunflowers that grew each summer made a jungle for the neighborhood Tarzans, a kind of botanical laboratory for budding scientists, and for all kids, a place to get away from the grownup world. There was no-one to tell you that you couldn't dig a foxhole in the soft brown soil if you felt like it. My buddies and I had played war there many times when we were younger. But now something odd was happening on Dago. Something I'd never seen there before.

The Old Man peered at me over the top of his newspaper.

"Like what, what's goin' on at Dago?"

"Well, I don't know. They're putting up little flags and stuff all over."

Dad thought for a minute.

"Hmmmm, sounds like survey work. You know, I think I read somewhere that they were thinking about putting up a Boys Club or something there."

"A boy's club?"

"Yeah, you know, there's one off Twelfth Street down by The Projects - a gym and stuff for the colored kids. Jesus, that's all we need is a Boys Club here. Every goddam hoosier from Godknowswhere will be moving into the neighborhood."

17

Then a puzzled look crossed his face.

"Funny," he said, "I didn't think they could ever build over there with the sink holes and all."

I wasn't sure how I felt about something being built on Dago. I'd learned to pretty much disregard the Old Man's rants, so it wasn't that I was worried about the neighborhood being overrun with hoosiers. Besides, that was kinda happening anyway, people moving in and out left and right. Some folks wanting to sell couldn't find a buyer at any decent price so they just left. There were more and more abandoned houses every week. Sometimes they'd get torched. For the insurance money, my dad said. But Dago had been Dago for as long as I could remember and I'd never thought it might ever be anything else. I didn't go over there hardly at all anymore, but it was part of the neighborhood. I liked knowing that old lot, liked knowing everything about my neighborhood. Didn't like that it was changing.

Damn! I was turning into my old man.

"How long does it take to build something like that?" I asked.

"Well, if they're just flagging the lot, it's probably gonna be at least a year."

I made a mental note to spend some time at Dago while it was still there. I was too old to be playing soldier, but there was still a lot of nifty stuff to discover roaming around up there.

We finished dinner, then cleared the table and began washing the dishes. The Old Man didn't mind pitching in. Since Mom cooked, it was up to him and me to do the dishes. He washed, I dried.

"You still hanging around with that crowd next door?" the Old Man asked. He could see the gang thing starting up and he didn't much like it.

"Well, yeah, I guess."

"I'm tellin' ya son, those kids are gonna wind up with their asses in a sling. You keep hanging out with 'em and yours will be right in there too."

"Aw, Dad," I said, "They're okay. We're not doin' anything."

"You oughta be concentrating on your schoolwork, son. Make something of yourself. Get ahead in the world."

Oh man, it was going to be one of those. I didn't get this kind of lecture too often, but when the Old Man started on this tack, it was usually good for ten or fifteen minutes. I tried to cut it off at the pass.

"Hey, I'm doing okay. Remember, all "A's" except two "B's" on the last report card."

"Yes," he interjected, "No reason for those 'B's' is there?"

That was exactly the way it was with the Old Man. No matter what the hell I did, it wasn't good enough. I guess he was trying to motivate me to do better or something, but you know, after hearing that kinda crap long enough, it sorta starts to piss you off. I mean if nothing's ever good enough, why the hell try anything?

"Well, Dad, I heard they're gonna be starting an honors program with an 'H' grade that'll be above an 'A' so I guess I'll really be in the toilet then."

The Old Man glowered at me.

"Don't say 'toilet' in front of your Mother," he warned.

That was another thing that was kind of goofy. The Old Man's conversation was littered with profanity - granted, just the everyday garden variety of hells and craps and goddams and never the dreaded F-word - but for me to say "toilet" was out of bounds. I could never take a piss or even a pee around my folks, just "go to the bathroom."

To make it even funnier, in our little three room flat the bathroom was right next to the kitchen and there was a high open window between the two. I couldn't say the word, but by golly when I was in there, anyone in the kitchen could sure as hell hear me churning up the water in the bowl. To me, that was a lot worse, a lot more embarrassing than saying a word that for some reason was "bad." But what the hell did I know?

We were just about finished with the dishes when Mom hit us with a big one. She'd been scurrying about putting away the pots and pans and had just sit back down at the table and started to pick up the newspaper when she remembered what the really big news was.

"Petersons are moving," she announced.

That hit the Old Man like a ton of bricks. He forgot about the dishes and his head spun around to look at Mom.

"What?" was all he could muster.

"Yeah, Em told me they've sold the house and are moving out someplace on Chippewa."

Emily and Ade Peterson were fixtures in the neighborhood. They'd lived there longer even than we had. They lived two houses down from us in the only one story house on the block. Ade worked for the city as some kind of mechanic or something in the trash department. It was a good, steady, fairly high-paying job compared with most people in the neighborhood. He and my Old Man were friends and spent a good amount of time together evenings and weekends -

drank some beer together and complained together about what was happening to the neighborhood. He called my Old Man the Mayor of Eleventh Street and my Dad called Ade the Treasurer and said he'd rather be Treasurer than Mayor. It was a standing joke and pretty much the way they always greeted each other.

People were leaving the neighborhood just about every week, moving further out to the western edge of the city or to the - gasp! - county. The Old Man didn't pay a whole lot of attention to most of them, but losing Ade was a blow.

"Where are they going?" he asked.

"Someplace out on Chippewa," my Mom repeated, "Out near St. Louis Hills, I think."

"Oh," Dad replied, kind of vacantly.

St. Louis Hills (not to be confused with "The" Hill) was one of the few really nice parts of the city. It was newer than most areas, with substantial, well-maintained brick single family homes. In the Old Man's view, it was another place for rich people. It did have two good things going for it in his mind, though. First, it was on the South Side, and second, at least it wasn't The County.

"Well, I bet they don't like it out there," the Old Man grumbled, "I bet they wish they were back here before long."

Then another, even bleaker thought crossed his mind.

"They didn't sell to coloreds did they?"

The worst fear among those of us left behind in the great urban flight was that the neighborhood would "turn black." The place could go to hell before our eyes, which was obviously happening but that was okay as long as black people didn't move in.

"Well, I don't know who they sold to, dear, but I'm sure they wouldn't do that."

"No," the Old Man agreed, "I don't think Ade would do that."

He was still standing there at the sink with the dishrag slung over one shoulder and a kind of lost look in his eyes, trying to puzzle out how Ade Peterson could desert him, desert the neighborhood like that, when Mom asked The Evening Question.

"Well, you want to sit out a while?"

It was a rhetorical question. Sitting Out was a ritual, and had been for many years. Not just for our family, but for everyone in our neighborhood and in neighborhoods like ours around the city and, I guess, in most cities. It went back to before there was television and all people had to entertain themselves was, well, themselves.

"Yeah, maybe for a little bit," the Old Man replied.

I knew my part. We headed off together for the side yard to fetch the lawn chairs. The two of us carried the heavy metal chairs to the sidewalk at the front of the house and set them up along the fence by the sidewalk. Everbody had their own chair and they were always set up the same way. If Mamie and Stanley Cush, our upstairs neighbors, weren't already out, we knew that unless something really unusual was going one, they'd soon be joining us. The seating order was fixed: my Dad and Stanley, my Mom, Mamie and my Aunt Katherine.

Aunt Katherine, my Dad's sister and a widow, lived upstairs in the other half of the four family flat. Ten years earlier, she'd helped my Dad buy his half of the building. He'd told me the story many times - how it was the only time in his life he'd been in debt to anyone.

The house we lived in, the four family flat, had been legally divided into two halves, God knows how long ago. My Aunt Katherine and her husband had bought the north half of the building and then later the south half became available. My Dad thought it might be a good idea to buy it and have a place our family could live without paying rent.

Because the Old Man had little cash and either didn't know about or didn't trust banks and mortgages, he borrowed the three thousand dollars he needed for our half of the building from my Aunt. In his way, he created his own unique financial instrument to secure the loan.

From a large sheet of paper, he cut out thirty small slips. On each he wrote out by hand, "I owe you $100.00." He signed his name on each slip. Then he gave all the slips to Aunt Katherine. He set aside part of each paycheck in cash and whenever he had accumulated a hundred dollars he would take it to Katherine. She'd give him back one of the IOU slips and he'd tear it up. In this way, over several years, he repaid the loan, ripping up one $100 slip at a time.

That was the way the Old Man did things.

And Aunt Katherine, well, she'd gotten kind of old and doddering, but she was part of the family, part of us, and we took care of her, and that included making her welcome as part of our evening Sitting Out.

There was one indispensable fixture that lubricated the social aspects of Sitting Out: the Beer Bucket. My Dad had one, Stanley had one, and I'm sure every adult male on Eleventh Street had one. My Dad's was aluminum, with a tight lid to prevent spills. It was thoroughly dented and dinged, commemorating many years of happy beer drinking.

Two or three times over the course of an evening, my Old Man and Stanley would grab their buckets and head down the block towards the tavern on the next corner, stopping for a few minutes at each house along the way to pass the time of day with whomever happened to be Sitting Out that night. I remembered tagging along with the Old Man as a kid, picking up other kids as we went down the block.

Kids weren't allowed inside the tavern, so we'd hang around outside the screen door, peek in at the colored lights and the polished wooden bar, inhaling the musky beerish smell that even then seemed to beckon to us as well as to our fathers.

Their buckets filled, my Dad and Stanley would wander back home to rejoin the families, drink beer from the buckets and talk into the evening.

Once in a while my Mom would take a sip from Dad's bucket, but neither she nor any of the other women on the block ever went to the tavern. They would stroll down the street and visit with one another or sometimes take a kid to the confectionary for an ice cream cone, but it wouldn't be right for a woman to go into a bar.

That's the way it had been - the way it used to be, back when folks in the neighborhood were all pretty much just like us. Now, things weren't so good. Not so many people sat out anymore. There was TV now and I guess maybe it wasn't quite so nice or even so safe to sit out like that. My folks and the Cushes upstairs, of course, would be the last to give up this dying ritual. Another damn change.

As I was helping the Old Man bring out the chairs, I was remembering the way it used to be, seemed not so long ago. Mom and Dad would be Sitting Out and all the kids in the neighborhood would be running around playing. We didn't need any parks or playgrounds, the sidewalk worked fine for us. You could draw a hopscotch grid on a brick sidewalk and play on it just as good or better than on one painted on a concrete playground. And there was always somebody's big brother or sister or Mom or Dad or cousin or uncle nearby to play along, to teach new games or to show how they used to do it.

Yeah, it was okay back then, but now it was just different. I didn't sit out much with Mom and Dad anymore.

Still, the Old Man had to ask, "Gonna sit out tonite, son?"

"Nah, I think I'll just go downstairs."

Because I didn't have my own room in our little three room flat, I'd made my own room down in the basement. It wasn't a room to sleep in - you wouldn't want to do that down there - just a place to hang out and be by myself if I wanted.

Our basement was better than most. About a third of it had a concrete floor. Then there was a wooden partition wall and the rest of it was the usual dirt/coal dust floor. The dirt floor part was partitioned off into storage compartments, sorta like cages. A door opened into this part of the basement and a kind of hallway led past two of the little cages, then made a hard left turn into two more compartments. The last two places were along the front of the house and had been where the coal used to be delivered. The first compartment had always been the Cushes, because they'd lived in the house since before my folks bought it. The second was where I built my room.

I didn't want to have a dirt floor because it was messy and got too cold down there to be able to use the room in the winter. I was lucky because my Uncle Fred was a carpenter. He found out I was building the room and brought me some fire damaged tongue-and-groove flooring he'd salvaged out of a house he was working on rebuilding. He showed me how to lay the flooring. Some of it was a little charred and smelled kinda bad, but it was a lot better than anything else I might have found.

For the walls of the place I just nailed cardboard over the two by fours and painted it. It probably violated about a hundred fire codes, but I didn't know. I was just a kid. More important to me was finding the right color to paint it. I chose light purple.

For the ceiling of the place, I found some sheet plastic stuff and tacked it up with a staple gun. After it was up, to make it look better, I soaked an old sponge in red paint and dabbed it around the plastic. It didn't look too bad if you didn't look too close, and so I had my own goddam room, just like the rich kids. Just like St. Louis Hills or out in the county.

So that's where I went in the evenings, when my folks were sitting out and there wasn't anything else to do. I went down to my own private place.

I liked to go down to the room I'd made for myself and work on my projects. I had a lot of projects. I had my collection of stuff I'd read and written down to remember. Wrote them on these bright white cardboard things my Mom brought home from the laundry where she worked. I don't know why I did this, or why I wrote them on those cardboard things. It was just that I guess they meant something to me at the time and that was the most permanent way I had of putting them down to keep. I don't know, it seemed important at the time.

One of the things I wrote down on was this: "Life can only be understood backwards, but it must be lived forwards. by Soren Kirkegard."

I still think maybe that is true, and a good saying that helps explain some things. It helps you understand why you can't understand some stuff.

Another thing I did down in my basement room was to do experiments. For example, one thing I was working on was building a transistor radio.

Transistors had just come out and you could buy a decent transistor radio for about thirty dollars, but I'd read this article in *Popular Science* where you could build your own transistor radio for a lot less than that.

So, Mom and Dad were sitting out and I was down in my room trying to read the directions and figure out how to hook up my transistor radio. I had the parts all laid out the way they showed in the magazine and with wires just kind of twisted together, I got it to kinda work from time to time. A lot of static, but you could kinda make out what they were saying and hear the music.

There was one little window in my basement room, looking out to the alleyway between our house and the house next door. Because it was summer, I had that window open and that meant I could hear pretty much everything that went on out where my folks were sitting out.

I wasn't paying that much attention. I was mostly concerned about figuring out how to make my transistor radio work. Then I heard it.

I heard them going off and I knew what it was and I ran up to the window in my stupidass little basement room to see.

I could see the firecrackers going off, and I could see that son of a bitch Freddie's gang. Freddie wasn't there, of course. He was too smart to be the one who'd actually do something like this. But I saw Jay and some of the others high tailing it around the corner, up Victor towards Twelfth street. The lousy bastards had tossed firecrackers at my folks and the others sitting out on the sidewalk, and I could see them running and laughing their asses off.

My Old Man had gotten up and was starting to chase them, but he was too late and too slow. He had too big a gut and had drunk too many beers, and so when he saw he wasn't going to catch them, all he could do was stop and shake his fist and shout after them. I saw for the first time that my Dad was getting old, that he was too old to take on these guys.

And I saw that it was going to have to be me who evened up the score. Me and Bryan. Me and the guys. Me and my gang.

THREE

"Go lightly, simply. Too much seriousness clouds the soul. Just go, and follow the flowing moment."
Frederick Lehrman

I got up the next morning still thinking about the firecracker incident, but it was a school day and so there wasn't much I could do but get ready and go. I folded up the hide-a-bed sofa I slept on in the front room, threw the cushions back in place and headed into the can, where the waterfall effect of my first stop announced "good morning" to everyone.

Washing up was a tricky chore, too, in that little bathroom. When the house was built there was no such thing as a hot water heater. Up to a couple of years earlier when you wanted to take a bath you had to go down to the basement, light the gas under the galvanized tank and wait a half hour or so for it to heat up, then be sure to go back down and turn it off before it blew up. When the old tank finally rusted out and sprung a leak, the Old Man reluctantly had to buy one of those new automatic jobs, but only because they no longer made the manual kind. So now we had hot water on demand, but there was still a problem.

The little porcelain sink had two separate faucets, a tall brass one for cold water and another, shorter faucet that was nickel plated or something for the hot water. It probably seems like you ought to be able to just turn them both on and kind of mix the hot and cold together in your hands to make a decent warm water for washing your face, but believe me, it doesn't work that way. It's always either way too hot and you're scalding yourself or too damn cold and you're freezing. I guess you could fill up the basin and make it okay, but hell, that would take too long and besides, then you wouldn't have anything to bitch about.

It never seemed to bother my Mom or Dad, but then maybe they just were used to it. Actually, they didn't complain about much of anything. I wasn't going to get used to it, though.

"Hey, Pop," I yelled into the kitchen, "When we gonna do something about these faucets?"

"I dunno," he yelled back, "Maybe when you get a plumber's union card."

It's hard arguing with a guy who still believes just having hot water is a luxury and maybe a little too fancy for the likes of us.

I finished getting cleaned up and dressed, gulped down some scrambled eggs and toast, grabbed my books and headed out the back door. Before I could start for school, though, I had to stop by and see Boozer. My Mom had given me some sausage left over from the night before to feed him. He must have smelled it as I came up to his window because man that tail was going more nuts than usual even and the whining almost made you want to cry.

I fed the poor dog the sausage and got my hand all gommy from him licking me to make sure he had every last scrap of the stuff. I don't know if those damn hoosiers ever fed the dog. I think maybe they didn't, or if they did, it wasn't much, because that mutt was always hungry. Hungry and alone and stuck in a goddam dark basement. What a life for an animal. Man, I felt sorry for old Booze. I had to get going, though, so I gave him one last muzzle rub thru the chicken wire and headed off for school.

The Old Man was leaving for work at the same time and so we walked together up to the bus stop at Twelfth and Barton. On the way we passed by the Spanglers house. Boy, that was a crew! Old Alice Spangler had a smoker's cough. She'd come out on her little balcony and start coughing and coughing. Couldn't stop. You'd swear she was gonna cough up a lung. She'd cough 'til her face got red as fire and then keep on until she finally just ran out of air to cough with.

Her brother and his family lived in the same house. He was weird as hell. A few Sundays back I saw him starting out to take the family out for a drive. They came back like twenty minutes later.

"Back already?" I asked as Alice got out of the car.

"The goofy bastard," she said, "He won't go through an underpass. Says it's bad luck."

An odd family, but then there were lots of those in the neighborhood.

Anyway, my dad and me got up to the bus stop and he asked, "You get your homework done last night?"

"Sure, Pop, I always get it done, don't I?"

"Just keep up your studies, son," the Old Guy counseled, "Then you won't hafta take no crap from nobody. You won't have to kiss nobody's ass."

I don't know, he had kind of a funny look on his face, then, and I could see how maybe he was going off to work where maybe he was going to have to take a daily ration of crap and kiss some ass just to keep food on the table for me and Mom. Guess he wanted something better for me.

"I will, Pop," I said, "Don't worry. See ya tonite."

I left him standing there waiting for the bus and headed off up Twelfth Street to pick up Mick.

I guess Mick was my best school bud, at least since me and Steve had sorta gotten into it over that Janet girl. Every morning for the past few years, I'd stop on the way to school to pick up Mick. Funny how you get into these little habit patterns of doing things. Every goddam morning I went the same way - up to Twelfth, over to three blocks to Ann Avenue to Mick's, and then straight up Ann seven blocks to school and in the same side door every morning. We could have walked over another block to Russell and gone in the main entrance, but we never did. Never once, just always the same exact route. It sounds kinda boring when you say it that way, but really it was just, I guess, a comfortable way of easing into the day.

Mick lived upstairs in a two-family flat. I walked up the front stoop to his door and rang the bell. That was always the same, too. He was never sitting waiting for me, or looking out the upstairs window. I rang the bell, and just like always, it took a couple minutes for him to come lumbering down the steps. Always seemed like he was still half asleep.

"You get your physics done?" Mick asked.

"Yeah, I think so."

"I couldn't figure out that vector crap," Mick said.

"Aw, it's not so tough. I'll show you when we get to school."

Mick and I and most of the guys we hung out with were in second semester physics and mostly just enjoying the hell out of it. I don't know if it was the subject - the idea of learning stuff about how things around you work, or the teacher, Mr. Zukin. He was pretty cool. A short little balding guy, but you could tell he liked what he was doing. It rubbed off on us. We didn't even screw around that much in his class. Some of us were trying to get the school to add a third semester of physics as part of the honors program they were talking about.

"You have to bring it home this time, or finish it up in school as usual?" Mick asked.

"Well, I had some time in study hall."

Mick was about the only guy I'd tell that I'd actually finished homework in school. It wasn't exactly cool to be too smart or to actually care about schoolwork. Mick and I had hung out enough though that I knew he wouldn't give me any crap about it or spread any stories. Besides, he was pretty good in school, too.

I was lucky. I didn't have to do that much homework. Mostly, if I just halfway paid attention in class I could figure things out well enough to ace most of the exams, so it was just the required stuff I had to do - stuff that counted for credit and where just taking the exam wasn't enough - you know, like essays and projects and stuff. That and the math. Didn't care too much for math. Geometry was okay because it was mostly just logical stuff, but this algebra with quadratic equations and crap - that was stuff I had to actually take home and work on in the evening. It was almost hard.

"Do anything last night, Mick?" I asked.

"Not too much. Worked on that physics a little and watched Dobie Gillis. Wanted to listen to some records, but Mr. Gerovich was home."

Mick's last name was Keaton, but his old man was Mr. Gerovich. That was all Mick ever called him, not Dad or John or Fred or whatever the hell his first name might have been, just Mr. Gerovich. Divorce wasn't commonplace back then. It seemed odd for a kid and his dad to have different last names. Seemed a little weird. And Mick's old man was definitely weird anyway. Mick hated the guy. I mean, my old man got on my nerves sometimes, but Mick *hated* his old man.

"What, he doesn't like music?" I asked.

"Ah, the old dork said he was gonna bust up my record player if I kept playin' it."

"You have it up real loud or something?"

"Nah, he's just an asshole. All he wants to do is ogle those girlie magazines of his."

30

I'd never actually met Mick's dad. In fact, I'd never been inside Mick's house. With most of the rest of the guys I hung out with, we'd at least come in each others house for a few minutes here and there and at least knew each other's parents enough to say hi to. But not with Mick. I'd talked to his Mom a few times and she seemed okay, but I'd never been past that doorbell I rang each school morning. It was because of Mr. Gerovich. Mick had told me about the girlie magazines once or twice before, just like spitting the words out.

I mean, with most guys, if they'd said something about their old man having some Playboys or something, you'd just laugh and say, well, can you sneak 'em out? But with Mick, there was something pretty serious going on and you wouldn't joke around about something like that. I don't know, I think maybe that was just the tip of the iceberg. Maybe the old man went around the house naked or something. I'd heard of stuff like that going on. Or maybe he liked to knock Mick and his Mom around. That kind of crap went on a lot, I knew. But Mick was a big boy. At six feet he was my height and outweighed me by thirty pounds or so. Seemed like he could have taken care of himself. But then who wants to fight your old man, even if he's not really your old man and even if he's a creep?

"Anyway," Mick said, "I got some extra copies of a record. Want one?"

"What is it?"

"Little Darlin' - that new one by The Diamonds."

"How come you got extras?" I asked.

"I dunno," Mick said, "I just like it so I bought three copies so maybe it'll be in the Top Forty."

I thought that sounded kinda dopey, but Mick was my buddy, so I kept my mouth shut.

We got to school, went in our usual side entrance, joined the throng of kids inside and headed down the hall towards our lockers, reaching out automatically as we passed the lobby for a lucky rub on the nose of the bronze bust of William McKinley.

McKinley High School was a three story stone and brick castle at Russell and Missouri Avenue. I don't know how long it had been there, but it was a long time. My Old Man had even gone there. He never graduated, but went there for a while anyway. I guess maybe a lot of kids in that area had a mom or dad or uncle or somebody who'd gone to McKinley and now they were there. It was weird to think maybe someday me and Mick might marry somebody, have our own kids that might go there, too.

Mick and I fiddled around at our lockers a while, then grabbed the stuff we'd need and headed off to home room together. McKinley had just started with this track stuff and we were both in a Track One home room.

You know, the people who run schools are really full of crap. I mean, when they first announced all this track stuff they made this big deal about how it didn't have anything to do with how smart you were or anything and how it was supposed to be based on your "likely future career choices" and crap like that. They thought kids were stupid enough to fall for that kind of bull. All you had to do was look around and see who was in Track One and who was in Two or Three and you could see what the deal was.

It wasn't like anybody gave a damn, or anything. Wasn't as if nobody knew beforehand who the smart kids were or pretty much exactly where they stood in the brains department. It was just another example of teacher bullcrap, which was just one sorta specialized category of adult bullcrap. We all knew it, we all expected it, and for the most part, it didn't bother us too much.

In some ways, it was kinda funny. Like here they set up these tracks, split off home rooms by track and then here in this Track One homeroom they give us a homeroom teacher like Mr. Smith.

I mean, Smith was okay and all. His family lived down near Bryan's grandma on Tenth street. He coached something or other, taught drivers ed and some history classes. He was a big guy. A young guy, too. Not many McKinley teachers were less than about eighty years old. Old buzzards, that's who taught us. The main thing about Smith, though, was that if you could pick the last guy you'd think would be teaching Track One kids, it would be him. I don't mean to put the guy down, because maybe he was foreign or something, the way he talked. Not that there's anything wrong with being foreign. Hell, McKinley pretty much had nothing but kids whose folks were Syrian or Lebanese or Polish or Greek or who knows what. Too many kinds of foreign to keep track of. Too many to give a damn about. With Smith, though, the way he talked made it seem like he wasn't too bright. He had this way of dropping consonants that made him sound, well, dopey.

"Okay, kids," Mr. Smith said, raising his arms to quiet the home room, "We go-a hava 'nouncement."

Go-a. That's the way he said it. I mean none of us were speech perfectionists. There were lots of accents at McKinley. Besides, nobody would have said "going to." For most of us it would have come out "gonna." But for Smith, it was "go-a," and for that he got singled out. Kids are funny. It's not cool to be too smart, but you can't be a dunce either. Mostly, too, you can't talk differently. Better or worse.

"Today there go-a be a special aud session fer some a youse," Mr. Smith continued, oblivious to the oddity of his diction and the way us smartass high school kids snickered at it.

"Dose a ya whose names I read report to the aud after home room fer a special session."

Then Mr. Smith read off a list of about ten names. Mick and I were on the list. So was Steve.

Steve was one of these guys who can't shut up. He'd been a really good friend when I first started high school and it was through him that I'd met Mick and a bunch of other kids. I was pretty shy back then, but Steve had the same kind of goofy sense of humor I had and we got along real well from the first class we met each other in, the first hour of the first day of school. He was a lot more outgoing than me. More popular.

It was in our sophomore year that we both got interested in the same girl, Janet Ellring. For a while we took turns walking her home from school. I guess she was sorta my first girlfriend in high school, but it didn't last very long. I could see that Steve was getting pretty competitive. I really liked the girl but figured being friends with Steve came first. So basically, I gave her to him. I quit seeing her, quit walking her home. I think that she was maybe having a little fun, both of us chasing her and all. I kinda figured maybe I had the upper hand, that she might've liked me more than Steve, but I was probably wrong about that - me with my dorky hair. Still, it was a notion to hold onto. You can never be sure what a girl's thinking anyway. They'll never come right out and say hey I like you. You gotta guess and I was no good at that. So I bowed out of the competition. Kept a friend, maybe lost a girlfriend. I mean I still saw Janet around, we still talked, but it wasn't the same. I don't think Steve had a clue about what had really happened. He thought he'd won.

The funny thing was that it wasn't too long afterwards that Steve and I weren't such good friends anymore. Part of it, of course, was that he was spending time with Janet. I don't know, maybe part of it was that I wasn't spending time with Janet. I mean, I don't think I was jealous, but, hell, maybe there was some of that. Some regret. She was a pretty girl. Anyway, I know I got kinda tired of him talking all the time, especially since most of his chatter was about how he'd done something great. It started getting on my nerves. After a while I figured out that there are people like Steve who basically think out loud, or who always have to be telling you how wonderful they are.

Some of the other kids' opinions of Steve were even less kind.

"The son-of-a-bitch talks to hear his head rattle," Mick used to say.

So, naturally, it was Steve who piped up in class.

"Hey, Mr. Smith, what's the aud about?"

Smith's brow furrowed as if he were contemplating some deep philosophical question.

"It's a special aud," he managed, "Just fer some a youse."

"Oh," Steve mimicked, "You mean we're go-a have an aud?"

The slam went right over Old Smith's head. "Yeah," he said, "But just those a youse whose names I called."

I was starting to get pissed at Steve for making fun of the poor bastard and I gave him a kinda nasty look, but the bell rang anyway about that time and we all jumped up and mashed together through the door into the hall.

Mick and I walked together down to the auditorium and found seats about halfway down, behind a couple of pretty decent looking girls. One of them turned around and looked at me kinda funny.

"Hey, aren't you Tom Bonner?"

"Yep," I replied, raising one brow in my best James Dean/Marlon Brando look, "Who're you?"

"Didn't you used to go with Janet Ellring?"

"Well, I knew her, yeah."

She turned and whispered something to her girlfriend and then the two of them just giggled like something was just too goddam funny, their little ponytails jiggling back and forth like silly little mops.

"Well, what's so goddam funny about me knowin' Janet?" I snarled, switching to an Elvis sneer.

They quieted down then, and I could see their cheeks getting red, too. I didn't have to take crap off anyone, and especially not these two little ponytails.

By then the aud had pretty much filled up and just a few stragglers were rushing in to find seats. There were maybe about a hundred of us altogether. Maybe not even that many.

Old Man Conklin walked across the stage to the microphone. He was Assistant Principal and in charge of discipline, among other things. I think he was also supposed to be some sort of counselor, but from what I heard, the kind of counseling he did was limited to ass-chewing and maybe a whack in the head if you got out of line. Nobody screwed around much with Mr. Conklin.

"Today we're here to announce the beginning of a new program at McKinley," Conklin intoned in that big, serious voice he had, "It's a special program for special students."

There were three other people on the stage behind Mr. Conklin, sitting all stiff and stuffy in their suits and hardly ever smiling, except when Conklin would turn and look at them. Then his face would be changed with that grimace of his that passed for a smile and these three suit and tie guys would grimace back at him. As soon as he turned back around to face us, the three stooges' smiles faded and they turned back into stooge zombies.

Conklin droned on about this new program for fifteen minutes or so.

"Our world is changing rapidly, students, he said, " It's a world that needs scientists. The Russians, sworn enemies of America and of democracy, have launched a Sputnik, a little moon up in space, which is the same as declaring war on us. Who is going to help us face this frightening new challenge?"

He turned and exchanged a brief grimace with the three zombies, then swung dramatically back to face his audience.

"You are, that's who," he thundered, "Tomorrow's Scientists and Technicians!"

T.S.T. That was the name of the new program Conklin and the three dorks had evidently dreamed up together. Maybe just the three jerks had done it. Nobody knew who the hell they were. They sure as hell weren't from McKinley. Probably some central administration goons and Conklin was showing off for them.

He rambled on and on and on, screeching at us about the Commies and the Chinese and about what a wonderful new program TST was going to be, without ever really telling us a goddam thing about what the program was going to do, when it was going to start, or how it was going to work.

It was more teacher bull. But we were getting kinda used to it. We got a new program about once a month. We had that track crap, of course, and then it was only a month or so back we'd all had to sit through an aud just like this one announcing the "Superior And Talented Students" Program. That was the one I'd given my Old Man some crap about earlier - where you could be in special classes and get an "H" grade that was higher than an "A."

"Hey, Mick," I whispered while Conklin droned on, "First we got STS and now we got TST. Know what that makes us?"

"What?"

"STSTST."

Mick started laughing and I thought we were going to get kicked out, but Conklin was too involved with his own speechifying to notice anything going on in his audience.

"What do you think that stands for, Mick?"

"I dunno," he chuckled, "What?"

"I think it's 'Suck This, Suck This, Suck This!'"

Mick was laughing so hard and at the same time trying to keep it under control and not make any noise, that his eyes were watering and his face was getting really red. I thought he was going to crap in his pants.

Still, Conklin never noticed. He was winding up for his big closer.

"Yes, students, this is a wonderful new opportunity for each and every one of you. A chance to excel and to make a name for McKinley High School."

Here his eyes narrowed and he let his gaze slowly cross the auditorium from side to side.

"But," he concluded, reverting back to a more threatening tone, "Don't any of you think for a minute that this makes you special."

After Conklin wrapped up his inspirational message, Mick and I left the aud together. His next class was upstairs, so we said adios and he went one way and I went the other. I was walking down the hall by myself just kinda mentally reviewing the aud session and thinking to myself that the best part of it was getting Mick to laugh like that. It made me laugh to myself to think about him sputtering and trying to keep it in. I think it's a cool thing to make somebody laugh. Makes them forget about crap like what a creep their old man is. Even makes you forget about crap like the gang across the street from your house and what you're going to do about them.

I was walking along like that with my mind a long way off when around the corner just almost right in front of me came Elaine and a couple of her friends.

Elaine. Wow.

Talk about special. You know how some girls are just special? Here's how special Elaine was. She lived up near Steve and one time over summer vacation I go up to his house and all over his bike - his brand-new shiny black bike - he's painted "Elaine" over and over and over in white paint. As many times as he could find places on the fenders and frame to fit it in. Well, of course, I thought he was nuts. Especially since he'd only got that bike like two weeks before for his birthday. So, I'm giving him a big ration of crap and all he does is kinda smile and say, "Oh, yeah? Wait til you see her."

Steve was right. Elaine was a year younger than us, but she was something. Knew it first time I saw her. I started going by Steve's just in hopes of running across Elaine. Once we actually met I used to try to find stuff to tease her about. She'd act miffed, but I thought that really, she kinda liked it. Maybe even liked me.

Elaine was the cutest girl I'd ever seen. She had these neat little ways about her. You know, funny little expressions and stuff like that, that I could call up and picture in my mind, like at night when I was laying in bed, before I fell asleep.

Yes, I liked Elaine. I liked her a lot. The funny thing, though, was that ever since that summer, I hadn't been able to talk to her. I guess maybe it was only after the summer was over and I didn't get to see her so much that I realized I missed her and that I did like her as much as I did. I couldn't talk to anybody about it, though, and she was a year younger and all. So I just liked her and thought about her and kept it to myself. Liking somebody like that was kind of embarrassing and not cool. It wasn't like with Janet. Somehow, Elaine was a lot more.

As we passed each other in the hall, I did what I always did with her, which was to kind of nod and half-smile and give her a little "Hi." Our eyes met like they always seemed to and it was like we were reaching out for each other with our eyes, but I had to just keep on walking. That was the way it always happened whenever we saw each other at school, and since Steve and I weren't such good friends anymore, that was the only place we ever saw each other.

This time, though, after we'd taken a few steps past each other, I heard Elaine call out my name. I turned and she walked back to me, leaving her two friends behind.

"Tom," she said, "Can I ask you something?"

"Yeah, sure, Elaine."

She looked down at the floor, then right in my eyes.

"Well, how come whenever we see each other at school like this, you never stop and talk with me?"

I didn't know what to say. I didn't expect her to come right out and ask something like that. It's funny, too, when you've kept something to yourself for so long it seems like maybe its just imaginary. Like you've made it up or something and maybe there really isn't a real Elaine, or at least not one like you've made up. I know that sounds a little weird, but that's the way it seemed. Like a dream or a movie or something had all of a sudden come to life in front of you.

I was looking for some way to answer, something to say.

"Uh, I don't know, you've always got your friends around you and all," I mumbled.

She looked at me really funny and this cute little frown flashed across her face.

"Oh," she said, "Well, my friends can just....go."

Then she looked right in my eyes again and the little frown turned into this huge smile. I could feel my heart thumping away in my chest, could feel my face starting to get warm.

"Okay?" she said.

"Uh, yeah, alright."

"So, you'll talk to me?"

"Well, sure, of course."

She just stood there for a moment looking at me and keeping that big smile glowing at me.

"That's great, Tom," she said finally, then turned and rejoined her friends, giving me one last look over her shoulder and one last smile as they walked off down the hall.

I just stood there for what seemed like a really long time, watching them walk away. Watching her walk away. Asking myself, is this real? Could it be this girl - this *pretty* girl - might actually like me?

I went on to class after that, but I really never stopped thinking about it the whole day. I kept replaying the scene in my mind, kept seeing that smile of hers. And I wondered about how things might be going to change between Elaine and me and what that would mean.

It seemed like things were changing every day. Not just little things, either, but big, major, important things. Things that could make a difference in the way your life went. It gave me a real funny feeling, like being happy and sad at the same time. It was hard to make sense of a feeling like that.

I was still trying to figure it out when the final bell rang for the day.

FOUR

*" . . . I said, 'Boy this is going to be one terrific day, so you better
live it up, 'cause tomorrow you'll be nothing.'"*
James Dean's character in <u>Rebel Without a Cause</u>.

I 'd already grabbed my books and stuff from my locker and was
headed for the door when I heard a familiar voice behind me.
Crap!

"Hey, Bonner, wait up."

Damn!. It was Thor Berkle. Of all the guys I didn't want to see, he
was pretty near the top of the list. Not just for now. I really never
wanted to see Thor. He was a guy who didn't belong at McKinley. He
lived over on Hawthorne or Longfellow - one or the other, I'm not sure
which. Never been to his house. He was a rich kid.

Hawthorne and Longfellow were two streets that curved between
Compton Avenue and Russell, just east of Grand Avenue. Up near
Tower Grove Park. They were streets with mansions and huge green
lawns around them, where rich folks had lived a hundred years ago.
Still do, I guess. They were as out of place in this neighborhood as if
you'd dropped a spaceship or something down there. If there were any
other high school age kids who lived on those two blocks they went to
private schools. Thor was the only person anybody knew from that
area and he made sure everybody understood where he lived. That he
was a little better.

"So, Bonner, how'd you do on the SAT?" Berkle asked in that sophisticated sounding rich voice of his.

"I don't know, Thor. Guess we'll have to wait and see." What the hell kind of name is "Thor" for a kid, anyway? What kind of self-important jackass names their kid after the Thunder God?

"Yes," Thor smiled in that phony-ass sweet way of his, "We'll have to see who gets the scholarship, won't we?"

That one hit me kinda hard. The story had spread around McKinley for the past few years that somebody - some old alum or something - had put together a full-ride college scholarship for the kid who scored highest on the SAT. It was a subject of some importance to me, but up to that very minute I had no idea Thor had any interest in it at all.

"You're going for the scholarship?" I asked.

"Well, certainly. Father believes it would be quite a feather in one's cap, so to speak. Not that we need the funds, of course."

"Yeah, I suppose so," I mumbled.

His little taunt over, Berkle started walking away.

"Well, so long, Bonner," He grinned, "And may the better man win."

"Yeah," I said, grinning right back at the jerk, "If it's a man."

There were a lot of smart kids at McKinley. Most of the guys I hung out with fell into that category. I guess maybe I did, too. When it came to those standardized tests five of us did pretty good.. It was no secret. Everyone knew who we were, being in class together and all, and because the scores on the PSAT were pretty much common knowledge. I was one of the five. I'm not bragging. I didn't think it meant much of anything, because I knew a lot of kids who didn't do so hot in school but were really a helluva lot smarter than me. I was just good at taking tests.

Unfortunately, Thor was also among the five, along with Bob Lee and a girl, Agnieska Krimisz. Agnieska was some kind of foreigner, Polish, I think. She spoke with a funny kind of accent and she was very serious about her studies. In fact, Agnieska had absolutely no sense of humor. You couldn't kid around or joke with her at all. She'd just look at you funny. What she did have was one helluva gift for mathematics. I envied her. Math came as easily to her as most other subjects came to me.

I mean, I didn't envy her in a bad way. I guess it was more that I admired her math talent. Wished I had it, but I didn't and that was okay. Maybe everybody's good at something.

Thor, on the other hand, hated Agnieska. He couldn't stand to have anyone better than him at anything, and, at least in math, Agnieska was better than anybody at McKinley. That's why I had to throw my little comment in to him like that. Served the rich little prig right. If I didn't get the scholarship, I hoped it would go to Agnieska, or maybe to Lee. If not one of them, then maybe it would go to Smart Kid #5, Martin something. He was a black kid who had a photographic memory. Like he could read a page and then recite the whole thing back verbatim. If not one of those, maybe the scholarship could just get lost or something.

The truth was, I wasn't sure I even wanted the scholarship. I didn't know if college made sense for me. Seemed a long way away, even though it was just next year, and trying to plan your whole damn life was kinda scary. I mean, I didn't know what was going to happen later on this week, let alone next year or on after that.

I headed on towards the door, passing Coach Brown's office on the way. He was the basketball coach. He was standing just inside the door and stuck his head out as I went by.

"You're gonna play next year, right, Bonner?"

"Sure, Coach, I'll be there."

"Okay, I'm counting on you. Try to work out a little over the summer if you can."

"Yeah, I'll try."

It wasn't like I was this big basketball stud or anything. Wasn't like that was going to take me anywhere. Mostly, it was just that I was a little over six feet, which back then was pretty tall for a high school kid, and I was still growing. I was pretty fast, too, for my size. Could hit a decent jumper if there weren't too many guys in my face. I liked playing the game and all, long as it didn't get too serious. But I knew I was never going to be really good at basketball and I didn't much give a damn. There were a boatload of kids a whole lot better than me right down the street at the playground. McKinley was a football school, anyway. The only gym we had to practice basketball in was in the basement and the court had like four building columns smack in the middle. Maybe that was why our team did okay, though. Those columns were like the other team's guys - you had to dribble around them, keep from running into them. And if you passed the ball to a column, man, you got razzed for half an hour.

"Take care, now," Coach said and disappeared back inside his office.

I stopped along the way and talked with a few more kids in the hall, then finally made it out the door and headed down towards work.

I noticed Tony's car parked about half a block down. It was easy to spot - a black '55 Chevy convertible, always polished to a blinding gloss. Never a speck of dirt on it. Cruiser skirts and spinners and a big V-8 under the hood that growled like a mountain lion. But what really made it stand out was that Tony had gotten a special canvas touneau cover made for the car with a big cartoon fox painted on it. Tony had the coolest car I'd ever seen. I think he had the coolest car anybody had ever seen.

He was sitting behind the wheel laughing and talking with not one, but three girls in those tight little skirts they used to wear that showed off their butts so nice, especially if they happened to be bending over a car.

Tony looked up as I walked by and I gave him the old cocked-gun salute, where you make like your hand is a pistol.

"Hey, Bonner," he called out, "Need a lift?"

"Nah," I said, "Looks like you're pretty busy. Maybe catch you later?"

"Yeah. What time you get off?"

"Around nine."

"Maybe I'll come by then," he said and went back to his harem.

Tony Brulio was his name and he was every bit as cool as his car. Everybody knew Tony, or at least knew who he was and wanted to know him. I felt lucky that I was actually pretty good friends with the guy, mostly because he was one of Bryan's buddies from way back. I mean, to know Tony was one thing, but to be friends with him, well, that made you cool by association.

Tony was Italian, a WOP, my Old Man would have said, and he'd dropped out of school some time back and gotten a great job in construction. Now he always seemed to have plenty of cash, which he didn't mind spreading around, and lots of time on his hands. Nobody knew exactly what he did, but the story was he worked with the Calcatorri's at their contracting company down on Seventh Street. Story was they were connected to the mafia. The Post-Dispatch always had some article about the Calcatorri family, most often about somebody who'd screwed with them showing up dead in the trunk of a car or blown to bits. Car explosions were real big in St. Louis around that time. Why just stab or shoot somebody when you can blow their ass to Kingdom Come?

I don't really know for sure about the Calcatorri's mob connections though, because although I spent a fair amount of time with Tony, he never talked about it and I never asked. Seemed like he was just a nice guy, a good guy to know. If I didn't get into college, I thought I might be able to find some kind of construction work through Tony. I didn't know if that would turn out, but it was at least a possibility.

I walked on down Russell Boulevard past Tony and the three butts, giving him a kind of casual wave without looking back, like trying to say, hey, I'm cool too, man.

I didn't mind walking to work. It was a nice walk. Big old trees shaded the sidewalk most of the way, at least down as far as Twelfth Street, and I didn't have to hurry or anything, because the walk only took about half and hour and I had a whole hour before I had to be at work.

At Twelfth I cut over towards Geyer. Used to be, you could walk all the way to Lafayette Avenue, but now I had to take a little detour and go down Geyer instead, because they were already starting to do some digging where the new highway was gonna go under Twelfth Street.

It was kinda fun to watch the hole they were digging get deeper and deeper. Funny, though, your sense of scale gets all screwy or something. Seemed like that hole was way too deep for any kind of street underpass I could imagine. It was like they were digging to China. They worked on it for months and months, digging first with steamshovels and bulldozers and then with those big diesel graders and scrapers, making it deeper and wider. When I walked by, I knew what it must feel like to be a mountain climber, only in reverse, because seeing that huge hole like that made me want to climb down in it. I wanted to climb all the way down to the bottom, just to see what was down there, even if it was only dirt and mud, just like was all around me. It was all fenced off and everything, but I always figured some day I'd go over after the workers went home, sneak through the fence, climb down and see what was going on.

Another reason I went this way was to avoid Jimmy Zollner's gang down by Pontiac Park. Jimmy and his guys always hung out by the

Tastee Freeze across from the park on Ninth Street. They were always there, any time day or night. It wasn't like they were such badasses or anything. I mean they weren't a really tough gang like the Aces or like that. I guess they were between the Aces and our Eleventh Street gangs. They thought they were tough, but they didn't have the cool jackets and, basically, they weren't cool. They just hung out on the sidewalk and dicked around and gave you crap if you happened to be a guy walking by there by yourself. I wasn't afraid of those guys but it was just easier to avoid the hassle by going around. That was something I'd learned from Bryan: why fight if you don't have to?

I walked down Geyer to Ninth, safely a block north of Jimmy Zollner's hang out. There was a little grocery store on the corner of Ninth and Geyer that belonged to the Valverde family. Angelica was out in front of the store sweeping the sidewalk, and I stopped to talk with her a while. She was in some of my classes.

"Hey, that was pretty cool what you did to Mr. Jenkins yesterday," she said.

"What?"

"You know, with Edgar Allen Poe and all."

I'd already kind of half forgotten about that. Jenkins was the English teacher and he and I had gotten into an argument about Poe in front of the whole class. I don't remember how the thing got started, but I'd said something about when Poe lived in England. Jenkins sneered that Poe had never left America. That pissed me off enough that I'd grabbed up my book, scanned through it for the part I knew was there, and then read out loud the paragraph talking about Poe going to school in Scotland and England, the Manor House School at Stoke Newington and all. I knew that because it was the setting for "William Wilson." Jenkins didn't say a word, but the kids all started clapping and laughing his face got real red. Served him right. You're gonna teach Poe, you oughta know a little something about the guy.

"You really showed old Jenkins up," Angelica said.

At McKinley, it wasn't cool to be too smart, except in special situations, like if you could embarrass the hell out of a teacher, especially a jerk like Jenkins.

"Well, I just used to read a lot of Poe stuff."

"What, you mean like outside of school? For fun?"

"Yeah, Angelica, he wrote some cool stuff. Scary stuff - *'The Pit and the Pendulum,' 'The Tell-Tale Heart'* - they even made movies out of some of his stories. Vincent Price, I think."

"Edgar Allen Poe wrote movies?"

I was about to explain a little more when Mr. Valverde came to the front door. I didn't see him very often, but he seemed like a pretty neat guy. He was a little short Mexican guy and every time I saw him he was smiling. I think he thought that Angelica and I liked each other or something.

"Tomas," he called out to me, "Come inside. I got something I wanna show you."

He held open the screen door and I walked inside the little store. He led me down one aisle to the back, pulled a small bottle off a shelf.

"Here," he said, "I want you try some of this."

The bottle was all kinds of bright colors and the label was all in Spanish. I wasn't sure about this

"Well, thanks," I said, "But I don't think so."

"Come on," he urged, "It won't hurt you. You'll like it."

Angelica had followed us inside and was just standing there with a curious expression on her face.

Mr. Valverde took the top off the little bottle and offered it to me.

"Put the tip of your finger to the bottle, shake it a little bit and then touch your finger to your tongue."

I figured whatever this stuff was, that much of it couldn't hurt me too much, so I did what Mr. Valverde told me to do.

It was a mistake. BIG mistake! This was the hottest stuff I'd ever had in my mouth. Felt like I'd caught fire, like maybe I'd gotten inside of one of Poe's stories and Mr. Valverde had made me drink some potion making me spontaneously combust. The ONLY thing I could think about was getting that junk out of me, getting some water to cool it off.

Meanwhile, of course, Mr. Valverde was just pointing at me and laughing his ass off. His entertainment for the day, maybe for the week.

He saw me running for the drinking fountain.

"No, no," he said, laughing, "You don't want water, Tomas. Water make it worse. Here, try some salt."

He grabbed a saltshaker from the counter and offered it to me. I'd already been stung once by this guy, so I wasn't sure what to believe. I glanced back at Angelica, who, bless her, was not laughing at this joke her Dad had obviously pulled before. She nodded okay, so I tried the salt, pouring a little in my hand and licking it like he showed me.

It took a while, but I was at last able to talk again.

"What was that stuff?"

"Es habanero," Mr. Valverde answered, still recovering from his own laughter.

"Habanero?"

"Si, yes. You like it?" Then he started laughing all over again.

By then Angelica was starting to get a little pissed at her old man.

"Daddy!" she said, "It's not so funny." She grabbed my arm and led me out of the store. "It's some kind of Mexican sauce," she explained, "About the hottest we have. He loves pulling that on people. I'm sorry."

By then I was starting to be myself again. "Ah, it's okay," I said, "I guess it was pretty funny."

"Yes," she said, touching my arm, "But he shouldn't do that to people. I'm sorry."

She didn't need to apologize so much. Heck, I was already thinking about who I could pull this gag on.

"Well," I said, "I gotta be goin. See you around."

"See ya," she called after me, "See ya at school tomorrow, okay?"

I headed on over Ninth Street to Soulard Market, then down Lafayette. There was a playground that ran alongside the Lafayette Avenue side of the market. I saw Jeffrey sitting on a low rock wall by the sidewalk across the street with a couple of guys I didn't know. I was hoping I could make it past there without him noticing me. No such luck.

"Hey, Bonner," he waved at me.

"Hey," I yelled back without stopping, "Gotta get to work."

"Wait up, I'll walk witcha."

Damn! He crossed the street and punched me on the shoulder, semi-friendly like. We walked down Lafayette together towards the library.

"So, how's it goin? How was school?" he asked, making "school" sound like preschool or something.

"'S'alright. Whatdyou been up to?"

"Me, I been workin on our little problem. Talkin to some friends."

"Yeah?"

"Yeah," he said, "Case we need a little help with Freddie and them."

"What kind of help, Jeffrey?"

"Just muscle, Tom, just muscle. Nothin dangerous or nothin. Nothin you'd hafta worry about. But there is more of them than us, you know."

"Yeah, I know. So who's your friends?"

"Just some guys I know," Jeffrey said and winked.

I didn't like that wink and I didn't like the looks of those guys, but I had to admit we were a little outnumbered compared to Freddie's bunch. After what had happened last night, I figured maybe I ought to stay cool with Jeffrey.

"You wanna grab a dog or something?" I asked.

"Thought you were goin to work."

"Yeah, but I still got a few minutes."

We headed over towards the market. Soulard Market was like this historical big deal. It had been operating since, I don't know, seventeen hundred something, still going strong. It was mostly a farmers market type of thing, with two covered walkways running between Ninth Street and Seventh. The walkways were open on both sides and farmers would back their trucks up to them and load fruits and vegetables out into stands along each side. Folks from the neighborhood would stroll through and get fresh produce from a bunch of different vendors. On Saturday mornings, especially, the market was jammed with people doing their shopping for the week. My Old Man never missed a Saturday. When I was a kid, he'd make me walk down there with him all the time. He still wanted me to, but I'd gotten better at finding excuses.

The middle section of the market was a two story brick building modeled after some kinda Italian temple or something. Inside was the market office and a few stands that stayed open all week. One of them was a hot dog and sausage stand and that's where Jeffrey and I headed.

"What kinda dog you like?" I asked.

"I dunno, let's see what they got." Jeffrey turned towards the man behind the counter. "Whatdya got good today?"

"You got eyes, right?" the guy growled, pointing at the display that separated him and us, "What's it look like we got?"

The guys who manned the booths didn't take a lot of guff off people. I mean they were usually okay, and with a guy like my Old Man they'd joke around and stuff, but they weren't going to put up with crap, especially from a kid.

Jeffrey, naturally, snapped right back at the guy. "What's it look like? It all looks like crap to me," he said, giving the display of hot dogs

47

and various types of sausages spinning slowly and sweating on those little chrome tubes a once-over. Before the counter guy could jump on him any more, he added, "Gimme one a them bratwursts there."

I asked for a bratwurst, too. The guy forked them off the rollers, laid each one in a bun, wrapped them in white butcher paper and handed them across the counter.

"Six bits," he said, still giving Jeffrey the cold eye.

Jeffrey made no move to pay, busying himself instead with slathering mustard and ketchup all over his brat. I fished the money out of my pocket and paid the guy. We headed for the door, walking along enjoying the sandwiches.

"Geez, Jeffrey," I said, "How come you gotta give everybody a hard time?"

"Me?" he said, "Me? Hell, that old guy was the one hassling me."

"Think so?"

He looked at me like I was nuts. "Hell yes, I think so. I know so. People are always trying to mess with you."

"Why do you think that is, Jeffrey?" I asked.

He thought for only a minute. "Who knows?" he said, "Who cares? Maybe they know my old man was a Golden Gloves Champ. The important thing is you don't let 'em get away with it. You gotta give it right back to 'em only twice as hard. If not, then they peg you for some kinda wussy."

I was trying to figure out what Jeffrey's Dad being a Golden Gloves Champ could possibly have to do with people wanting to mess with him, but he interrupted my train of thought.

"Yeah," he said, "My old man's a jerk, but he showed me how to take care of myself. Taught me what it's all about, how people's always tryin to make a ass of ya."

"Yeah," I said, looking for some point of agreement, "I guess some people are like that."

"Damn straight they are," Jeffrey gestured emphatically with his bratwurst.

I took one final gulp of my sandwich. "Well, I guess I better get on."

"I'm headin that way, too," Jeff said, "I'll walk you over."

Would I never be rid of this guy? We walked together back over to Lafayette and down towards the library. Next to the library was a barbershop, and right before that was a jewelry store, Gettelmen's. I always liked to stop and look in the window at the rings and bracelets and necklaces and stuff. I wasn't going to let Jeffrey interfere with that.

I don't know, maybe it sounds fruit or something for a guy to like to look in a jewelry store window. Sounds more like something a girl would want to do - look at wedding rings or nice diamond earings or stuff like that. I mean, I probably wouldn't have gone out of my way to look in a window like this, but since I had to go right past it every day on the way to work, it just got to be something I liked. I think the store mainly did watch repair and stuff like that, because there weren't too many folks in the neighborhood who had the dough to be buying jewelry.

They kept the windows sparkling clean though, and had the stuff laid out real neat, with satin and felt and flowers and stuff, so it always looked nice. They changed the display every few months or so to keep up with the seasons, but there was one ring that was always there.

Actually, it was two rings - I guess a wedding ring and engagement ring set. The rings were white gold, the only ones in the window that were like that, and the main one had a pretty good size diamond in the middle, with these green stones that I guess were emeralds or something alongside the diamond. The engagement ring had smaller stones. They came in this neat little wooden box, and there was always one of those spotlights shining right on the rings, so they shimmered and glowed, even in the middle of a sunny day.

Before I figured out it was a wedding ring deal, I used to dream about being able to buy that set and give it to my Mom. Before I knew they were wedding rings. I just thought they were pretty and my Mom didn't have much stuff that was pretty like that. I don't think she had any jewelry. If she did, she didn't wear it - except for her gold wedding band, of course. Other than that there were no earings, no necklaces, no bracelets - nothing. I don't know, maybe she did have some of that kind of stuff, but she might have thought it was uppity or showing off or something to wear it around, because that's the way she was. I thought that maybe if I gave her something nice, though, she might wear it.

Today though since I knew it was a wedding ring, I was thinking about how it would be to buy it and give it to Elaine. I mean, I really wasn't thinking about marrying the girl, or anything. Hell, I hardly knew her. It was just like a fantasy, I guess. It was such a pretty ring and she was such a pretty girl, seemed like she ought to have a ring like that to wear. I imagined giving it to her - how excited she'd be and all, unwrapping the box and then finding the ring inside, and then I'd slip it on her finger and we'd kiss.

Okay, I know it's stupid. I didn't want to marry the girl. She was nice and I liked her and I wanted to make her happy, that's all. You're allowed to have fantasies, right? And they don't have to make sense, do they?

I guess I must have slowed up a little and been looking in the window when Jeffrey and I walked in front of the store and maybe he caught a look in my eye or something.

"Nice stuff, huh?" he said.

"Uh, yeah, I guess."

"Expensive, though."

"Probably."

"Yeah, when they don't put the prices on, you know it's gotta be real expensive."

I wanted to move on. I mean, this was my fantasy, but Jeffrey kept jabbering. "Be real nice to be able to give your girlfriend a ring like one of these, huh?"

Uh-oh. Was he reading my mind, or was this kind of thing every guy's fantasy, even a guy like Jeffrey?

"Yeah," I said, "If you had a girlfriend."

"So, which one you like?" he asked.

Well, I didn't see any reason to lie about it, so I pointed out my ring set.

"Oh, yeah," Jeffrey said, "Those are cool. Probably the most expensive ones in the window, too."

I hadn't even thought about what any of this stuff might cost. Whatever it was, it would have been way too much for me - too much for my old man either, for that matter.

"Yeah, they might be," I said quietly.

Then Jeffrey looked over at me with this real wicked grin on his face. "You want 'em?" he said slyly.

"Huh?"

"No, I mean, do you want 'em? Cuz we could get 'em."

"Jeffrey, what the hell are you talking about?"

"It wouldn't take much," he went on, "We could bust right in that front door, get in and get out with as much as we could carry. We could do it."

I really couldn't believe what I was hearing. "Jeffrey, you're nuts."

"Why?" he said, "Why am I nuts? Cuz I want us to have somethin nice? Cuz I want you to have somethin nice? I mean why should the old kike who runs this joint have all the nice stuff and we got bupkus?"

"Listen," I said, "For one thing, there's probably alarms all over this joint, and me, I don't especially wanna go to jail."

Jeff thought about that a minute. "Yeah, I guess there might be alarms, huh?"

"Well, if not, Gettelmen's would probably be the only jewelry store in St. Louis that didn't have one."

"Yeah," Jeffrey mumbled, "Yeah. Well, hey, I was just kiddin anyway. I mean I ain't no robber or nuthin."

"Naw," I said, "I know that, Jeffrey."

Jeffrey was like in some kinda trance or something. "Sure would be nice to grab some a them diamonds, though, wouldn't it?"

I didn't say anything and finally he kind of snapped out of it and grinned at me. "Well, listen, I gotta go. Maybe see ya later on or somethin?"

"Yeah, see ya later, Jeffrey."

He headed back up Lafayette towards Ninth and I went on the other way, past the barber shop and started climbing the big flight of marble steps leading up to the front entrance of the library. Halfway up I turned and looked back up the street. Jeffrey had turned, too, and was looking back my way. He saw me looking at him, grinned and gave me a little wave.

I was pretty sure he hadn't been looking back at me, though. He was looking back at that jewelry store.

FIVE

"Life is like playing a violin solo in public, and learning the instrument as you go along."

Samuel Butler

I'd been working at the Soulard Branch Public Library for almost three years. How I got that job is kinda funny. Wasn't looking for a job at the time, but a library visit was part of the Old Man's Saturday morning routine since forever. He'd roust me out of bed early Saturday mornings with a way too hearty "Rise and Shine," or maybe "The world's on fire - wake up and piss!" We'd have to walk down to the market and after shopping we'd go over to the library.

I didn't like the market part. The Old Man had to walk through the whole place twice. Once just to check prices, then we'd go through again to actually buy stuff. Too, he had to stop and talk with damn near everybody he saw. It seemed like it took hours to make it through the market. It was worse if watermelons were in season. He had to teach me how to pick a good melon.

"Here," the Old Man would growl at me, grabbing a watermelon from one of the stands, "Listen to this." He'd thump on the melon with his knuckles.

"Hear that?" he'd say, "No good, see?" Then he'd stick it back on the pile, pull out another one and thump it. He might go through four or five like that until he found one he liked.

"Now that's a good one, huh?" he'd say, holding the chosen watermelon close to his ear with one hand and thumping it with the other. He'd give the guy behind the counter a look like he'd just turned the tables on him - avoided all the rotten melons they were trying to foist off and found the very one the guy had been hiding away for himself or his special customers. Then he'd look at me to see if I'd learned anything.

"Yeah, Pop, that's a good one," I'd have to say. You kidding? Hell, they all sounded exactly the same to me. They sounded like watermelons.

When we finally finished shopping, we'd take the grocery bags full of stuff and head over to the library. I guess we weren't the only ones with this routine, because the little foyer area where we left our bags usually had a bunch of other folks stuff, too. You could leave your groceries right there and nobody would swipe anything, at least I never saw anybody. I guess maybe library people are just honest like that or something.

I didn't mind the library at all. It was real easy to get lost in there and there were some really cool books. World War II books about this seventeen year old kid who gets to be a fighter pilot: *Dave Dawson at Dunkirk* and others in the series by R. Sidney Bowen.

I know it sounds dumb now, but I liked those books. Then I graduated what they used to call "Space Books." I read every single book in the juvenile section in that category before I was ten, and then the Old Man let me use his card to check out books from the adult section. Got some math books and taught myself a little algebra. Why? I don't know. Just something to do.

Anyway, one day during one of our Saturday visits the head librarian, Miss Walker, asked if I wanted to work at the library. She was stamping our cards to show we'd returned our books from the week before and she looked over at me and said, "Thomas, we're going to need someone to help out over the summer and I wondered if perhaps you might be interested."

I'd looked at the Old Man and his face was just frozen. Looked like he was in some kind of rapture or something. First, I guess, that someone thought his son might actually be able to do something worthwhile, and second, because a job offer out of the blue like that was as close to a miracle as he'd ever come across.

I would have liked to have thought the deal over a bit, reconciled the time demands with my social calendar and all, but it was pretty obvious only one answer was possible. Worked there ever since. Wasn't too bad of a job, really.

So after saying goodbye to Jeffrey, I walked in past the main desk and checked in with Miss Walker. I liked working for her. She was always real calm and in charge of things. One of the other librarians was not so nice. It was like she was ambitious or something - always scurrying around and fussing with stuff. I don't know what librarians' ambitions are - maybe get a promotion to the big downtown library or something - but this lady was sure after something and not happy being stuck down at old Soulard. But Miss Walker was her boss and a nice lady. Yeah, she was a lady.

"Hi," I waved to her, "Where do you want me to start today?"

"Good afternoon, Thomas," she replied, looking up from her desk, "Perhaps you could begin with the shelving."

That was the way I normally started on school day afternoons. As books were checked in, they were stacked on a library cart of polished walnut with smooth rubber tires. I had to sort the books, then wheel the cart around re-shelf them, straightening the shelves as I went along.

Soulard library was pretty much just one large room with bookshelves lining the walls, and some free-standing chest-high units around the room. Over the wall-mounted shelves were tall, slender windows that tilted open from the top for ventilation. No air conditioning at Soulard Library. There were three small alcoves partitioned off from the main room. Each of the alcoves had a small stained glass window, the only windows in the library at normal window height. The stained glass made the alcoves look like chapels, and that was the way I always thought of them. Two were on either side of the main entrance and the third was on the back wall.

One of the entrance side chapels had been my father's domain for as long as I could remember. It held the library's collection of Western and Mystery novels. The Old Man had started years ago with the Westerns, and when he'd read his way through every Louis Lamar and Zane Grey, he switched to Perry Mason. He was about three-quarters of the way through the mysteries and had become quite a connoisseur of the genre. It got to where it was no fun to watch a mystery movie or tv show with him, because he could usually figure out the plot within a few minutes. And he had to tell you, of course.

The second chapel, the one on the back wall, held mostly philosophy books. I called it the Philosopher's Chapel and I was kinda fascinated by the books in this section. I'd checked out and tried to read some of them. I couldn't figure Neitsche out at all, but I kept going back to Immanuel Kant's *The Critique of Pure Reason*. Mostly, I think, because the title sounded so cool. The only one of these I actually made it through from cover to cover was Thorstein Bunde Veblen's *Theory of the Leisure Class*. It pissed me off. Leisure class? There's a leisure class? How come I got left out?

Then, too, the Old Man discouraged too much philosophizing. He used to warn me, "If you keep thinking about stuff like that you'll go nuts."

The third chapel I called The Poets Chapel. It had more than just poetry books, though. It was the other one next to the front entrance and was the beginning of the non-fiction section. Under the Dewey Decimal System this meant it contained books about language - dictionaries, thesauruses and the like, plus drama and poetry. In some ways I liked that chapel the best of any place in the library. I had a little friend who liked it, too.

I'd saved The Poets Chapel for last during my shelving rounds as I always did. Only three books from that section needed to be shelved, but I spent a good amount of time straightening up the shelves. Straightening shelves and searching for something.

Finally, on the second shelf from the bottom, near the little window, I saw the scrap of paper I was sure I'd find in there somewhere. It was tucked against the black metal bookend. I glanced around to make sure no-one was watching, then pulled it out. Recognized the handwriting.

It was written with a blue ballpoint pen in the cursive script I'd come to know. Over the past couple of months, once a week or so when I'd go into The Poets Chapel, I'd find a note. I hadn't thought too much about it at first, but after a while, I started thinking the notes were addressed to me. I started looking forward to finding them. From the handwriting it was clear they were written by a girl, and I thought I knew who.

This note was more direct than usual.

"Drink to me only with thine eyes,
And I will pledge with mine;
Or leave a kiss but in the cup
And I'll not look for wine..."

Whoops, I thought to myself, Ben Johnson. Kinda serious, here. We'd better lighten this up some. I thought for a while, trying to figure out exactly how to respond to this note. I'd started writing back after the first few notes, once I'd figured out it was really someone, some girl, writing these things and I guess maybe wanting me to find them. I had an idea who it was, but I didn't want to encourage things too much until I knew for sure. I remembered part of a W. B. Yeats thing, pulled down a volume of his work and, checking that there was still nobody paying any attention to me, scribbled out on the back of a 3x5 card:

"Never give all the heart, for love
Will hardly seem worth thinking of
To passionate women if it seem
Certain, and they never dream
That it fades out from kiss to kiss;
For everything that's lovely is
But a brief, dreamy, kind delight."

That was more like the kind of stuff we'd been writing to each other. Stuff that made you think. Maybe a little romantic, but not too heavy on that end. Way too soon for that kind of stuff.

I slipped the card back into the space where I'd found her note, looked around one more time to make sure I hadn't been noticed, then wheeled my cart quietly back to the main desk, a little glow warming me. A funny little excitement making me see things a little sharper and making everything a lot brighter in the dusky old library.

"All done, Miss Walker," I said, scarcely concealing a smile, "What now?"

"Well," she answered, "I suppose the children will be coming in soon, so you might begin checking in."

I didn't care too much about that part of the job. It was working behind the counter, taking books in as people brought them back, stamping their library cards and then fishing the book card out of the little wooden trays and placing it back in the book pocket so it would be ready for the next person to check out.

Mostly what I didn't like about checking in was the condition the books were in when some people returned them. My folks had always taught me that a book was a special thing, to be treated with respect. More so if it was a book that was just loaned to you. I guess a lot of people didn't see it that way, or their Mom and Dad never taught them, because sometimes books would come back looking like somebody'd played football with them or something. The binding would be all loose and screwed up and the cover flopping off, or there would be ketchup or mustard stains all over, or the book would just be really dirty.

It was the worst in the summer. There was one family of three or four little chubby kids that I just hated to wait on. The kids were always sweaty and it was like they'd carried their books in their armpits or something. I mean they would be just soaked and like real greasy to touch. You wanted to wring them out or scrub them, deodorize them or something before you put them back on the shelf for regular people to look at. But I don't know, those chubby little kids were always real happy - smiling these big smiles at me as they were handing over their dripping volumes - so it was hard to be mad at them or anything. I just wished they could have been a little drier.

I was standing behind the counter checking books in when Diane walked through the door with her little red-haired girlfriend, Lovey. Lovey was about the same age as Diane and the two of them hung out together after school, although why Lovey wanted anything to do with Diane was a mystery to me. The two of them were completely different. Diane was always pulling stuff like she'd done at the clubhouse, trying to be a smartass and stuff, and thinking she was cute.

Lovey was as quiet as Diane was boisterous, and she always seemed to be a half-step behind Diane and like in her shadow, except when Diane was putting her up to something, which she did a lot.

The two of them came up to the counter where I was working and Lovey handed me a couple of books she was returning, looking up at me just for a second with this shy little smile, then glancing down at the counter in front of her.

"Well go on," Diane urged, "Say something to him."

Lovey didn't say anything, just looked down harder at the counter and got a little red around the ears. I felt kinda sorry for her. That damn Diane would tease the crap out of anybody.

"Hi, Lovey," I said, "like the books?"

She looked up at me and I noticed for the first time that she had these really pretty soft brown eyes. She really was a nice looking girl. I mean, for a kid.

"Oh, yes," she said quietly, "I liked them very much."

"Oh, yes," Diane mimicked, "And I like you very much, Tom."

"Shut up, Diane," I snapped, "Nobody's talking to you."

It was too late, though. Poor Lovey was mortified. She spun around and retreated to the far side of the library. Diane followed, no doubt to give her more crap. That goddamn Diane needed a spanking more than anything else.

I glanced down at the books Lovey had returned. One of them was *Treasure Island* and the other was some kind of mythology thing, King Arthur or something. Diane hadn't returned any books. In fact, I'd never seen Diane ever check out a book. For that matter, I'd never seen her even open a book. She'd only started coming in to the library a few months back, and then only with Lovey.

I decided I was going to go out of my way to be nice to Lovey. I mean I didn't know if she maybe really did have a little crush on me or if Diane was just ragging on her, but she seemed like a nice kid and I figured maybe I could balance off the scales a little, take the edge off Diane's bullcrap. Of course, I'd have to be careful. I mean, she was just a kid, and I didn't want her thinking I really liked her or that we could be boyfriend and girlfriend or anything like that. But I knew how it felt to like someone that way and be kind of embarrassed about the way you felt.

There weren't any customers at the counter right then, so I went over and searched out a book about Sir Lancelot that I'd read a few years before. I walked over to where Diane and Lovey were sitting.

"Lovey," I said, "If you liked that King Arthur thing, this one kind of picks up where that left off. You might enjoy it, too."

"Oh," she said, "Do you like the knights of the round table, too?"

"Well, I haven't read any of that for a while, but I used to be really into it. Sir Galahad and the Holy Grail and all that stuff."

"Yes, it's really neat." She took the book and gave me this big smile. "Thank you, Tom, I'll read this tonite."

Surprisingly, Diane didn't say a word, but I could hear the two of them whispering as I walked back to the counter and went back to checking in books.

Besides working the check-in counter, the other thing I didn't like about the library was the bums. Soulard had two resident bums, Jim and The Snotnose Man. I mean there were other bums who might stop in once in a while, but Jim and Snotnose were regulars. They knew Soulard's schedule and, especially during the winter, they'd show up not long after the library opened and stay until closing. They usually cut down their hours some over the summer, but they were still around at closing most nights.

They kind of dressed alike. I guess maybe it was the standard bum look - crap-colored clothes, baggy britches and always a coat or jacket, no matter how hot it was. They both walked the same way too, sort of hesitant, with their eyes always looking down. They both smelled pretty bad, but they were two different sorts of bums.

Jim was quick and traveled light. I never saw him carrying anything with him. The Snotnose Man, though, was a slow-moving kind of man who never went anywhere without his two grocery sacks right with him. They were the old-style sacks with twine handles and they were overflowing with god-knows-what. Probably everything the old guy owned. He walked with a sack dangling from each hand, weighing his shoulders down in a permanent stoop. He brought his sacks into the library with him, carefully stowed them under the table where he sat, and trudged out with them when the library closed.

Jim and Snotnose spent a lot of hours just about every day within a few feet of each other, but they always sat at separate tables and they never spoke. Not to each other, not to anyone.

Jim actually read while he was at the library. He'd sidle along the shelves, pick out something that caught his interest, go back to his table and sit and read for hours. Knowing how the shelves were arranged, over time I came to know that his preference was strictly non-fiction. He spent a whole lot of time in the Philosopher's Chapel and even some in the Poet's Chapel.

Jim might doze off in his chair from time to time, but he was a light sleeper and if anyone passed by him, he'd jerk awake, clear his throat and go back to reading whatever book was in front of him. Seemed like it embarrassed him to be caught napping.

Snotnose, on the other hand, made little pretense at scholarship. He'd fetch himself one of the daily newspapers attached to one of those varnished wooden poles, open it in front of him and then promptly fall deeply asleep. He'd snooze for several hours at a stretch. I saw it happen many times. His head would nod forward, he'd start snoring and before long the mucus would start oozing out of his nostrils.

I don't want to be gross or anything, but this wasn't just a thin trickle of clear fluid. The Snotnose Man earned his nickname from a really disgusting mass of thick, yellow crap that came snaking out of his nose while he slept. I couldn't figure out how a guy could sleep, or even breathe, for crissake, with that junk blocking up his nose. I do know that he never had to worry about anybody wanting to share his table or asking if he was finished with the newspaper.

I didn't spend all my time watching these bums or anything, but when you're there five or six days a week and they are too, you notice stuff. Seemed to me that there was like this hierarchy or something among bums. Jim, for instance, was a fairly high-functioning bum who took pretty decent care of himself. I mean, for a bum. Somebody - I can't remember who - told me that he'd been a soldier in World War I and had been exposed to mustard gas and had maybe gotten shell-shocked, too, and maybe that was the reason he was a bum. Nobody knew anything about Snotnose and I don't think anybody gave a damn.

I sure as hell didn't. The only thing I cared much about as far as those two bums was concerned was staying the hell away from them as much as possible. It wasn't just the way they looked or smelled, either. There was something else, too, something that made me hate even going near them to shelve books. There was something that kind of embarrassed me about just being around them. I was afraid one of them might say something, or somehow that something might kind of rub off on me, or that people would see me near them and figure somehow that I was some kind of bum, too. I know that sounds pretty dopey, but I didn't say I thought that way, just that I felt that way.

Funny, too, but there was something familiar about Jim. Like I knew him from someplace else or something. I couldn't put my finger on it, and I wasn't sure I wanted to, but it worried me a little. It was kind of a creepy feeling, and I didn't like it at all.

And you know, the way I felt about those two guys, I think Jim felt the same about Snotnose. Like I said, the two of them never talked, and I got this impression that Jim thought old Snotnose was a lower class type of bum or something, and that he felt as bad about being associated with him as I felt about both of them.

I don't know, maybe I just had too much time to watch these bozo's and make up crap about them. Maybe, like my Old Man said, I read too much of that philosophy crap and it was starting to make me nuts.

Anyway, the evening wore on and pretty soon it was nine o'clock and time to start closing up the place. Diane and Lovey had left long ago and I'd been too busy to notice. The library was pretty quiet. The only people left were Miss Walker, me, and Jim and Snotnose. I blinked the light switch in the usual closing signal and the two bums slowly got up and ambled towards the door, Snotnose lugging his shopping bags. I walked behind them to lock up while Miss Walker went downstairs to her office.

After locking the main doors, I went downstairs and gave the key to Miss Walker, who hung it in its place on a hook just inside her office door. She already had her purse and stuff and was ready to leave. We walked together out the small side door.

"Goodnight, Thomas," she said, locking the door and testing it to make sure it was solidly closed, "We'll see you tomorrow."

"Yes, Ma'am," I said, "Goodnight."

We climbed the concrete stairs together up to ground level, then she headed back towards the small parking area behind the library that was reserved for librarians, and I headed out towards Lafayette Avenue and the long walk home.

When I got out to the street I saw Tony sitting in his convertible. I'd forgotten he said he might come by after work. I gave him a little wave and started heading towards the car, but then I noticed something weird happening on the main stairs to the library.

The Snotnose Man was like stuck or something on the next to the last step. He was standing there trying to get down, but for some reason he couldn't make it. He had his grocery sacks and was swinging them back and forth like he was trying to build up momentum to get him down that next step, but it just wasn't working. There wasn't anything I could see keeping him from taking that last step, but his mind I guess, saw some obstacle or barrier or something in front of him.

As I got closer I could hear him grunting, straining to get going. I could see the pained, almost desperate look on his face, and I could see old Snotnose was fighting some kind of demon only he knew.

I guess it was the first time I knew there was a lot more wrong with this old guy than just being a bum. So, what the hell do you do? I mean, should I go over and give him a shove or something? But then the old fart might fall down or something and I'd be in deep do-do. I could have called the police or something, but what the hell would I say - "There's this old bum stuck on a stair?" They'd think I was the one who was nuts.

Maybe the best thing would be just to walk away like I hadn't even seen this goofy crap.

I stood there for what seemed like a long time trying to figure out what I ought to do. Then I saw Jim come across the street and over to the stairway. He looked over at me for a second, then went up and took Snotnose gruffly by the sleeve.

"Come on, for crissake," I heard Jim mutter, tugging at the other bum's jacket, "Let's go."

It must have been enough to break the spell. The Snotnose Man stumbled forward and made it down the last step to the street. I stood there and watched as the two of them shuffled down Lafayette to Seventh, then headed off in opposite directions. Jim patted the Snotnose Man on the shoulder as they parted.

Something about watching that really hit me. I mean, had old Snotnose got stuck like that before? How the hell did Jim know what to do? Why was he still hanging around anyway? What the hell were these two bums to each other after all?

Then I really went off and started wondering about where these two old bastards went after they left the library, who fed them and where they slept. I started wondering about what Jim was looking for in the Philosopher's Chapel, and I wondered if a word or a touch from someone who cared might once have made a difference - might have kept both of these crazy old bums from getting stuck there at the library.

Then Tony honked his horn.

"Hey, Bonner, let's get the hell out of here."

I shook myself out of this stupid mood I'd gotten into, standing there in the dark. I slid into the shotgun seat and closed the door behind me. "Yeah, man, let's go."

"What the hell was that all about, with them two bums?" Tony asked.

"I dunno," I said, "They're just a couple of old bums who hang out at the library."

Tony looked over at me, then dropped the Chevy into first, revved her up and popped the clutch. "Outta here," he laughed as the car screamed away from the curb.

The St. Louis night air was heavy and all misty-hazy around the light poles as we headed away from the library. The wind felt good. It felt good to be with a friend like Tony and going out to have some fun and not having to worry about stuff. Not even about two old bums that I didn't know why I gave a damn about anyway.

"Where to?" Tony yelled, hitting second gear and leaving another strip of rubber behind us.

"Who cares?" I yelled back. We both laughed and headed out into the night, leaving the library and the bums and just a whole bunch of crap behind us.

SIX

"To live is so startling it leaves little time for anything else."
Emily Dickinson

"Y'hungry or anything?" Tony asked as we headed west on Russell.

"Yeah, maybe just a burger or something." I was fiddling with the radio, trying to find some decent music. Usually, I'd be looking for WIL, a Top Forty station with some DJ's I liked, especially Jack Carney and Dick Clayton. Tony was too cool for something like that though so I tuned in KATZ, a black station from the East Side. They broadcast blues and jazz from the Blue Note Lounge over across the river.

"So, howzit goin, man?" Tony asked.

"Aw, you know. The usual crap."

"Yeah. You about finished with school, or what?"

"Well, almost," I said, "I mean for this year. I still got another year to go, though."

"You gonna go back?"

"I don't know for sure," I said, "Probably, but it kinda depends."

Tony took the shortcut through Tower Grove Park, expertly navigating the traffic circles and avoiding the spot where the cop always sat watching for speeders or homo's hanging out around the park johns.

"Well, if you wanna go to work," Tony said, "You know, make some real money, just lemme know."

"You think you could find something for me?"

He looked over, smiled and winked. "Sure," he said, "The boss is always lookin for a good guy."

We'd had this conversation before. Tony was always trying to talk me into following him into "the trades," meaning carpenters, electricians and like that. I had to say it had sure turned out good for him. I mean he had this great car and didn't seem to have to work all that hard. Tony was kind of a dark skinned guy, but he also had like this perpetual tan that I figured must have come from working outside all the time. And Tony knew how to dress. Had the clothes. What more could a guy ask for? I decided to push the talk just a little further this time.

"Tony," I said, "lemme ask you - you serious about this?"

The smile left his face. "I'm serious if you're serious," he said, turning right out of the park onto Kingshighway.

"Well, like what kinda stuff would I have to do?"

He thought about it a minute as we headed west again on Columbia Avenue, through the heart of The Hill. "You probably start as like a day laborer or something like that. You know, carry stuff around, go fetch for a carpenter or bricklayer or something."

"Geez, you mean like carry a hod?"

Tony laughed. "What you do with your 'hod' is up to you, man."

"Aw, you know what I mean."

"Yeah," he said, getting serious again, "Well, really, hod carrier is a step up from where you'd start, but even as day laborer you'd be getting union scale, which ain't bad."

"Like what would it be?"

"It's around $4.50 or so."

I was making seventy-five cents an hour at the library.

"Course, then you do good," Tony went on, "Keep your eyes open and your yap shut and follow directions, it won't be too long you could be making a lot better than that."

"You think so?"

"Sure," he said, "I talk to my boss and he lets some people know and pretty soon maybe you get a chance at some special assignments."

"Special assignments?"

"Yeah. You know, a chance to show what you got. You know what's goin on, Bonner. I think you're up for it."

We'd peeled off Columbia onto Hampton Avenue and Tony pulled into the Steak-n-Shake drive-in just south of Oakland Avenue.

"Is that the way you got started, Tony?" I asked.

"Pretty much," he said, "Of course, knowing Moe Calcatorri didn't hurt any."

"No," I said, "I guess not."

"Right, and you know me."

The car hop ran up, popped her chewing gum and flashed Tony a big smile. "Whatcha havin', Tony?" she asked. Everybody knew Tony. This was a really cute little carhop, too. They made them wear these tight black pants. Showed off her butt really nice. Steak-n-Shake hired guy car-hops, too, but ninety-five percent were girls. A couple summers ago Steve and I had looked into trying to go to work there, but the deal was they only paid a buck a nite plus tips. They said you could make pretty good on the tips, but it just kind pissed me off that the company was getting by so cheap and I didn't think I could smile and kiss ass enough to make crap off tips. Anyway, like I said, most of the carhops were girls.

We ordered a couple of steakburgers, fries and shakes, then sat back and admired the carhop's butt as she scurried off.

"Not bad, huh?" Tony said.

"Cute little pooper."

"Name's Melody. She goes to Southwest."

Southwest High School was a few miles south on Kingshighway. It was the newest high school in the city - the only new school, actually. It served the St. Louis Hills area and I guess maybe Dago Hill, too. Mostly it was rich kids who went there. The only time I ever saw Southwest kids was like this, cruisin Steak-n-Shake with Tony or maybe at a football or basketball game.

"Hey," Tony said, "You wanna meet her, wanna go out with her?"

He was always pulling crap like that on me. "Naw, man," I said, "I can find my own women."

"Aw, hell," Tony said, "I know. It's just if you wanted to meet her or something I could set you up."

I didn't know how many girls Tony knew or how many girlfriends he had, but it had to be a bunch. "Thanks," I said, "But really, no, man."

"Well, it's up to you, but she is pretty cute, huh?"

"Yeah," I said, "She's real cute, Tony."

After a while, the little cutie brought our order and hooked a little metal tray up to the driver's side door. Tony shot the bull with her and I could see that if she wasn't working she'd probably have been happy to hop in the car with us. Finally, another car pulled in a couple of spaces down and she had to pull herself away to go take their order.

Tony passed over my stuff. "So," he asked, "You who're you goin out with these days?"

"Nobody special."

"No?" he said, "But there is somebody special, right?"

I could feel myself starting to get a little red. I didn't say anything.

"Come on," Tony teased, "You got a girl, doncha?"

"Yeah, well, kinda."

"Ha!" Tony said, "I thought so. Who is she?"

I'd let myself get trapped and now there was no easy way out. "Well," I said, "There's this Elaine girl."

"Yeah, and..."

"Well," I said, "Nothing, really. I mean, we've just kinda talked a little."

"And you're carrying a hod for her?" Tony laughed.

"Aw, Geez, Tony," I said getting really red, "It's not like that."

"But you have gone out with her, right?"

"Well," I hesitated, "Not really."

"What the hell are you waiting for, man? I mean, you know enough to know if she digs you, right?"

"Sure," I said, "I think so. It's just..."

"Just what?"

"Well, she's a couple years younger."

Tony shook his head in mock disgust. "So what?"

"Well, I mean, younger."

Tony looked over and put his hand on my shoulder. "Listen, Bonner," he said, "If she digs you and you dig her, you're sure not doing her any favors lettin a coupla years get in the way."

"Yeah," I said, "I guess you're right."

"Tony is always right," he said, "Just like Tony is...?"

I gave him the expected reply, "Always cool."

We finished up our burgers and fries and were just sitting working on the last of the shakes, listening to Ike and Tina Turner on the radio and talking about what to do next when I saw Freddie and a couple of his gang pull up across the way in the beat up Ford they always ran around in.

"Oh, crap," I mumbled to myself and kinda slid down in my seat.

"What?" Tony said, looking over at me.

"Nothin."

Tony looked puzzled for a minute, then followed my gaze over to Freddie's car. "What?" he said, kinda laughing, "Them guys?"

I didn't say anything.

"Those guys givin you a hard time or somethin?"

"Nah," I said, "At least not yet. They hang out across the street from me."

"Yeah," he said, "I know. Bunch of jerk-offs."

"Right."

"No," Tony went on, "I mean it. I've seen those dicks. They jack around and stuff, but they're goin nowhere."

"Yeah, I know, Tony."

"I mean if you're gonna go around the corner, you oughta know why the hell you're doin it."

"Yeah," I said again.

"And you gotta do it the right way. Guys like them, they don't know diddley squat. Don't get in with them, man."

"I'm not getting in with them."

"Those dicks get smart with you, you let me know, okay?"

"Tony," I said, "I can take care of myself."

"Yeah," Tony said kinda looking off into space, "Yeah, I know you can. Still...."

"Listen," I said, "Let's get the hell outta here, huh?"

Tony brightened up. "Yeah, whatdya wanna do?"

"Run over to the Peppermint?"

"Good call," Tony said. He honked and the cutie ran over and grabbed the tray off Tony's door. He paid her and told her he'd see her around, then we pulled out onto Hampton Avenue.

"How much I owe you?" I asked.

"Don't worry about it," Tony answered, "Gotcha covered."

We dropped down off Hampton onto the Express Highway, shot out to Skinker and headed north past Washington U. toward the Peppermint Lounge. I knew there were places Tony would probably rather go. Usually when we were cruisin, we'd wind up at the Black Horse, a little jazz joint over in Gaslight, but the last time we'd been in that place, some goddam fruit had come onto me - patted my knee. Gave me kind of a weird feeling and I wasn't sure I wanted to go back there for a while. Besides, I was in a rock and roll mood, and Peppermint was for sure the place for that.

We pulled into the parking lot behind the bar, packed as usual. Peppermint was always busy. It was one of those places that didn't watch their customers' ages too closely. Technically, you had to be twenty-one to drink in Missouri, eighteen across the river in Illinois, but if you knew where to go, you just had to look like you were cool.

Tony parked and we got out and headed for the back door of the Peppermint Lounge. He'd left the top down and hadn't bothered to lock the car. If that had been my car, I'd have made sure it was closed up and double-locked, if possible. Tony never gave a damn about stuff like that, though, and nobody ever bothered his car. Nobody ever touched his car. Everybody knew whose car it was and I guess everybody knew not to mess with Tony.

There was a buck cover. Tony paid the door bouncer for both of us and we stepped inside. Once you made it through the door you got hit with the Peppermint all at once. The smoke hit you and the dark and the red lights and the strobes and, I guess, most of all, the heavy, chest-thumping beat of Screamin Joe Beal and his band.

Screamin Joe was this ugly black guy. His whole band, including the two go-go girls were black, but all the Peppermint customers were white kids. I never thought about whether or not black customers could even get into the place, but I never saw any. Screamin Joe really couldn't sing, I don't think, but he sure as hell could scream. You probably couldn't hear him if he did sing, anyway, the music was so loud - guitars and drums and brass - and screamin.

It was a great place, a place you could get lost in. A place full of kids who wanted to kinda get lost a little bit - dance and make out and not have to think about school or tomorrow too much. Drink and get sick in the parking lot and feel bad for a day and then come back a few days or a week later and do it all over again.

Tony and I pushed through the crowd to the bar and naturally, Tony knew the bartender.

"Whatdya want?" Tony asked me.

Usually I kinda stuck to Budweiser, but, being with Tony, I tried to think of something maybe just a little cooler.

"Singapore Sling," I said.

"You heard him," Tony told the bartender, "Bourbon and water for me."

Tony and I turned around while we waited for our drinks and watched the kids on the dance floor. You couldn't really dance out there, it was too crowded. You just kinda stood next to somebody and moved with the beat. I mean, in the whole history of rock and roll, The Dog and The Horse have to be the simplest dances there ever were, but you couldn't really even do that on that dance floor. Strictly speaking, you really didn't even have a partner. You just got out there and were part of the group, everybody moving together.

Or you could just stand and watch, like Tony and me.

The bartender brought our drinks and about a minute later some blonde chick came over and draped herself around Tony like she wanted to do it right there by the bar. She was saying something right into his ear and kinda nibbling on it at the same time and after a while the two of them moved away from the bar and disappeared into the crowd.

I was enjoying myself just standing there and sipping on my Singapore Sling, feeling the music and watching the crowd. I really didn't know what the hell a Singapore Sling was, but it wasn't bad. You couldn't taste the alcohol too much. I didn't really drink all that much, but you had to do something to be cool, and so I worked on the drink a little at a time until I'd finished the whole thing. By then I was starting to feel pretty good, so I found the bartender and ordered another.

He set it in front of me with a smile.

"How much?" I asked.

"No charge," he answered, "You a frienda Mr. Brulio's."

Geez, I thought, how's Tony do this?

After a while I got kinda tired of just standing there, so I headed over to the other side of the place, where there was a long, curvy, sofa-like thing that ran along the whole rear wall, cocktail tables setting out in front of it. The sofa was pretty much occupied, but I managed to find a vacant spot not too far from the dance floor and sat down.

I don't think I picked the spot for that reason, or even noticed at first, but after a bit I saw that I was sitting next to this girl. I don't know, maybe I did sit there because of her. I mean, sometimes you do things sorta unconsciously like that, and, to be honest, that second drink was kinda hitting me.

Anyway, she was a pretty decent looking girl and she was sitting next to another girl, so I figured maybe there was no boyfriend here. I was being cool, though, and not paying any attention to her.

Some guy sat down next to the other girl and to fit him in, they both had to squeeze down towards me, which meant that the one girl and I were actually touching. Hip to hip.

I was still working on my Singapore Sling and the girl had some kind of drink on the table in front of her that she was sipping, too. We weren't looking at each other, but we were both kinda rocking to the beat of the music, our hips touching like that.

I don't know how long that went on. Seemed like a long time, and I was starting to get pretty worked up. I was looking at her out of the corner of my eye, trying not to really look at her.

After a while I noticed her hand was kinda just resting on her leg and I took a big chance and kinda brushed my hand up against hers. She didn't scream or slap me or anything, so I let my hand rest there for a while, touching hers.

Like me, she was still just watching the band and the dancers and so I took another big chance and reached over and took her hand in mine. She didn't do anything, but kinda squeezed my hand back. We still weren't looking at each other or anything, but now we were holding hands.

We sat there like that for a long time. Then I slid my hand away from hers and carefully reached my arm around her shoulder. This seemed to be going pretty well, but I was still making my moves real slow-like, so as not to scare her. Or myself, I guess.

She didn't object when I put my arm around her, so I reached over with my other hand, and grasped the hand I'd been holding before.

She kinda slid up against me and nestled into me.

I was getting really excited, by then. I could smell her hair and feel it brushing against my cheek and I was just goddam flabbergasted that the girl was going along with this deal.

Finally, she turned to face me. She looked at me with this kinda unfocussed look and kinda stroked my cheek. The girl wanted to be kissed!

I don't know how you know that kind of thing, but I knew.

Seems like a guy's dream, too, doesn't it? Got this girl, don't even know her name or anything and you're gonna be kissing her. No strings attached. What a deal.

But I'm looking at her, we're up real close face to face and I'm thinking, I can't do it. I mean she was cute and all; that wasn't it. I wanted to kiss her. It would've been easy to go along with the invitation, but instead I'm thinking, she wouldn't be kissing me, Tom Bonner, she'd just be kissing some guy that happened to sit next to her. You could pop me out of that seat and plug in some other guy and it makes no difference.

She took her free hand and ran it up along the back of my neck, pulling me closer.

It was getting kinda hard to breathe.

Instead of kissing her, though, I just kinda put my face beside hers. You know, like cheek to cheek. Maybe it was a cop-out. Maybe I was chicken. To do more just didn't feel right, though. So, it was just kind of a hug that went on for what seemed like a real long but short time. I mean it seemed like a long time but then it was over and it seemed like maybe it hadn't happened at all.

What happened was the Peppermint was closing down. The band quit and the lights went up and it was time to go. Maybe it had been ten minutes this girl and I had been semi-making out or maybe it had been half an hour. I don't know.

This other girl and guy she was with were getting ready to go. All this time we'd been doing this stuff, we still hadn't said a single word to each other. I never figured it would be me to do it, but finally I had to break the silence.

"So," I said, knowing Tony would for sure go along with it, "Can I drive you home?"

"Well, no," she answered sweetly, "I came with them and I gotta go home with 'em, too."

I couldn't quite figure out the logic, but I wasn't going to argue. Somehow, it made as much sense as what we'd been doing for the last who knows how long. I don't know, maybe she was mad because I wouldn't kiss her.

"Well, okay," I said, "Maybe see ya again sometime."

"Yeah," she said, "Maybe." Then she got up and gathered her purse and stuff together. She bent over and gave me a little kiss on the cheek, then turned and walked out with her friends.

Whew! Man, I couldn't believe it. I was just sitting there like in shock or something. I mean this had been some heavy stuff and then she'd just walked off. Not an adios or so long or go screw yourself. It left me feeling funny and kind of alone and empty, like. My head was kinda spinning from the alcohol and and stuff too.

I stood up and headed out the back door, the cool, fresh air outside feeling really good. There was a lot of commotion, with a whole bunch of cars trying to get out of the parking lot at the same time. I leaned against the wall and tried to put myself back together a little while I waited for Tony to show.

All of a sudden, he was there next to me. I didn't know if he'd just come out the door or whether he'd been out in the parking lot the whole time.

"Hey," he said, "You doin okay?"

"Yeah," I said, "Sure."

"Well, you ready to go?"

"Yeah," I said, "But not home. Not yet."

We walked over and got in the Chevy. Tony fired her up and started pulling out of the parking lot. He was going pretty slow because it was just gravel paving and he didn't want to screw up the finish on his baby.

"So," Tony said, "You wanna go do something?"

"Yeah, let's go."

Tony looked over at me with this real serious look. "No, no," he said, waving his finger in the air in front of me, "What I'm sayin, Tom, is do you want to go do some thing - maybe go do some place?"

It didn't take a genius to figure out what he was talking about. I was a little scared to answer, and still feeling kinda messed up in the head from the booze and the make-out session. I mean, I didn't want to get in any trouble, but on the other hand, I sure as hell didn't want Tony thinking I was chicken, or not cool.

"Whatdya got in mind?" I asked, hoping to gain a little time and throw the thing back in his lap.

"Ah," he grinned back at me, "We'll figure something out. That is, unless you got a special project in mind."

My first thought was that of course I don't have anything in mind. I mean, I'd never done anything like what I thought he was suggesting - yeah, some minor stuff here and there, but I didn't think that was what he was thinking about. Then, like out of the blue, a picture of that jewelry store window popped into my head. I probably should have just kept my mouth shut, but instead I found myself telling Tony about the stuff in that window, and especially that one wedding ring set.

Tony listened real carefully, nodding when I said there would probably be some kind of alarm system protecting the place. After I'd described the whole place I told him about the conversation with Jeffrey about the store.

"You did the right thing," he said at last, "Going after a store like that takes a lot of planning or you just wind up in the slammer with the rest of the clowns and nothing to show for your time."

"Yeah," I said, "That's the way I figured it, too."

Tony didn't say anything for a while. We just cruised along with the radio playing real low. He was heading back towards the neighborhood. Finally he looked over at me and smiled.

"Listen, Bonner," he said, "I'm gonna tell ya something and I want you to hear it and to file it away for good, okay?"

"Sure, Tony, what is it?"

"Tom," he said, "Knocking over places, even jewelry stores, is not the way you make a buck if you're smart. There's better ways."

"But what about what you said before?"

He laughed. "Aw, we're just gonna have a little fun tonite, that's all. Zero risk. This don't have nothing to do with business."

I was kinda relieved, though I still didn't know what he had in mind. I wished I hadn't said anything about the jewelry store and I hoped he didn't think I was too big a jerk.

Before long we were heading down Cherokee street, past the shopping district between Compton and Jefferson, its little stores all closed and shuttered for the night, and then down towards Broadway. It was real quiet at that time of night, practically nobody out. We passed the low concrete block building that housed Cherokee Confections Company and Tony whipped around the corner, down the side street for half a block, then cut into the alley, checking around to make sure nobody was watching.

We drove slowly up the alley, just past the back of Cherokee Confections. Tony pulled into a dark little parking area and killed the engine. We sat there a minute while Tony looked around and listened to make sure no-one was around.

When he was sure we were the only ones there, he quietly opened the car door. "Come on," he said.

We crept together down the alley to the fence behind the Confections company. Tony found a place where the fence was loose and pulled it away from the post, motioning for me to crawl through. Inside the fence, he took the lead again, heading to the side of the building with me right behind.

The building had basement windows right at ground level, covered by some kind of wire grates. We passed by three of the windows and at the fourth Tony stopped and started wiggling the grate and pulling on it.

"Damn," he said, "They fixed the stupid thing again." He pulled a pocketknife out of his pocket and started gouging at the wood frame where the grate was attached. In a short time he freed one bracket and then another and swung the grate away from the window. Moving quickly, he slipped his knife blade between the upper and lower parts of the window, throwing the lock.

"Time to go shopping," he said, opening the window and dropping down inside the Confections company basement. I followed him in.

It was dark down there, but not completely pitch black. There was some kind of dull glow coming from somewhere and you could make out it was just one big room, with all sorts of boxes and cans and stuff stacked all over the place. Tony started strolling down the aisles between the stacks of supplies, stopping here and there to try and read some of the labels.

"So, what you in the mood for tonite, Bonner?"

I was walking down the aisle behind him, but it was really too dim to see the labels very well. "I don't know," I whispered, "Let's just grab something and go."

"No rush, man," Tony said, "I been here before. It's like taking Confections - Cherokee Confections - from a baby."

We roamed around inside there for maybe ten minutes. There was a whole bunch of stuff down there. I finally figured out the light was coming from a window in a door that led to a stairway up to the main floor. You could read the labels on the stuff that wasn't too far from that door.

I found some stacks of these big blue tin drums, maybe a foot and a half around and two and a half feet tall. They were a little too far from the door to read, so I dragged one of them closer. Rold Gold Pretzels.

"Tony," I said in a loud whisper, "Here's some pretzels. Let's grab one of these." The same time as the words were coming out of my mouth, I saw a shadow on the stairway and heard somebody coming down.

Tony must have heard it too. He motioned me back into the stacks, then put his finger in front of his lips. We both got back into the aisle just as the door opened and this big old guy stepped through. My heart was beating like crazy. I thought for sure we were going to jail. I got this picture in my mind of my folks having to come down to Third District to bail me out.

The old guy lumbered into the room and over to the far wall. I could see him pretty well from where I was standing with my back pressed up against a row of boxes, but it was dark enough I guess he couldn't see me. Really, he wasn't looking around that much. The way he walked was a little like the bums at the library. I saw him take some kind of key that was hanging from his belt on a chain and stick it in a little box on the wall. He stood there for just a few seconds with the key in the box, then removed it and walked slowly back to the door, barely glancing around on the way. He closed the door behind himself and I could hear his heavy footsteps as he climbed the stairs. I didn't realize I'd been holding my breath until he was gone and I could start breathing again.

Tony came up behind me. "Well," he said cheerfully, "That was fun, but we really should be going."

"Who was that guy?" I asked.

"They musta put on a night watchman, I guess."

I wanted to just get the hell out of that basement right then, but Tony insisted on taking something along with us as our pay for the evening. I told him again about the pretzels.

"Yeah," he said, "That's cool. Let's grab three or four and head out."

"Three or four? How 'bout one? What are we gonna do with three or four barrels of pretzels?"

"Don't worry," he said, "They won't go to waste."

I climbed up and out the window we'd come in through and Tony passed four of the blue barrels up to me, then climbed out himself. He carefully closed the window and returned the grate to its original position. Then we each grabbed two barrels and skulked back to the car. Tony pried open one barrel and pulled out a couple of bags of pretzels. Then he closed the barrel again and we dropped all four of them in the trunk.

By the time we made it down Cherokee to Seventh and started heading up towards home I was starting to feel pretty good - mostly, I guess, relieved about not having gotten caught, but also it had been a pretty good adventure. It had been fun and we'd pulled it off, Me and Tony.

We were roaring across Seventh Street with the radio going and both kinda laughing. "Hey," Tony said, tossing a pretzel bag at me, "You're a good man, Bonner. Here's your cut."

We were at Seventh and Sidney, just a block before where Tony would have turned up to take me home, when we saw the fiery glow in the night sky.

SEVEN

"My witness is the empty sky."

Jack Kerouac

You could see a kind of orange glow just over the steeple of St. Peter & Paul, north of where we were. That steeple was really tall, so it had to be a big fire.

"Geez," I said, "It must be up around the market."

"Let's go see," Tony said.

I was already late and the Old Man was going to be pissed, but I figured what the hell, after what I'd already been through it wouldn't be right to pass up another adventure. Besides, Tony had already downshifted to second and dropped a nice strip of rubber heading on up Seventh past my turnoff.

It only took a couple of minutes to hit Lafayette Avenue and we heard sirens as we drove. We could see the flames from the corner. It wasn't the market on fire, it was something just beyond the library that was burning. We'd beat the fire trucks to the scene. They were only then racing up Lafayette from the fire station down below Broadway. A couple of police cars were already there, and a few onlookers had gathered.

"Let's get a little closer, Tony," I said.

"You go on," he said, "I don't want the car too close to the cops with the stuff in the trunk."

I'd already forgotten about the stash back there. I wasn't too good at this crime business. Had a lot to learn, I guess.

"I'm gonna walk up the street, then," I said.

"Yeah, you go on. I'll catch you later."

I hopped out of the car and Tony eased it on across the street, finding a dark spot behind the market to park.

The cops already had barricades up blocking the street and sidewalk in front of the library, so I crossed over and joined the growing crowd in the park. It looked like maybe it was the building next to the library that was on fire, but a fire truck pulled up and blocked the view so we couldn't see for sure. The firemen started snaking hoses across the street in front of us, hooking up to a fireplug.

"What's goin' on?" I asked a bleary-eyed man with a huge pot belly sticking out from under a torn skivvy shirt.

"Gee, kid, I dunno," he wheezed, "It's either Gettelman's Jewelry Store or dat flat out back."

"How long's it been goin?"

"I dunno - just got here, but I don't think too long."

Just then a lick of flame burst through the roof and traced an arc in the night sky. You still couldn't tell if it was coming from the back of Gettelman's or the four family flat right behind it.

More police and fire trucks were screaming in, and folks were running from all around, gathering in the park to watch the show. Fires were always a great source of entertainment. If this had been during the day, or earlier in the evening, there would probably have been somebody there selling snowcones or maybe the hot tamale man would have showed up.

The firemen had hooked up the hoses and run them down the alley between the library and the Gettelman building. By then Gettelman's windows were shattering from the heat and flames were leaping out all over. Maybe it was both Gettelmans and the flat on fire. I watched as two firemen braced themselves, holding onto the hose nozzle and getting set to spray the building from the alley. When the guy twisted the nozzle, though, instead of the huge stream of water you'd expect there was just this droopy little flow.

One of the nozzle guys yelled back to the truck to check the hydrant and another fireman ran over and tried to crank the big wrench they'd left on the nipple on top of the plug. It didn't move much and he yelled back to the guys in the alley, "It's full open!"

There was barely enough water coming out of the hose to make it to the window, and for sure not enough to put out this fire. Three or four firemen at the truck, including one I figured to be the chief or captain or whatever, were yelling all at once and waving their arms around. The Chief shoved one of the other guys towards the second fire truck, which had parked up the street a bit, and he climbed in the cab and drove it a little way further.

There was another plug up there and they ran a hose over to it, hooked it up and cranked on the nipple. Then they grabbed the nozzle end and ran back down to the alley. It was the same story, though - just a dribble of water, like you might get out of a garden hose. In fact, when they turned that one on, the water coming out of the first hose dropped off some and those firemen started cussing at the other guys.

I edged up closer to the truck where the Chief was still yelling at the two firemen closest to him and pounding on the side of the truck. He reached went around and reached inside the cab, grabbed some kind of telephone-like deal and started squawking into it. I couldn't make out much of what he was saying, but I did hear him say something about "...those goddam redevelopment projects" and I definitely heard him screech three or four times in a row, "You gotta shut off the goddam main down there. Redirect the water here. Now!"

Meanwhile, the jewelry store building was shooting fire all over the place. Flames were leaping out every window and nasty black smoke was pouring out of the place up into the sky. It was the first time I noticed there was a big old full moon out, and I only noticed because the smoke was blowing in front of it every once in a while, blotting it out.

I noticed another thing, too, and it really worried me. The brick wall of the library right across the alley was starting to look kinda yellowish-red. I didn't know if it was just the light from the flames or if the heat was starting to get to it. It didn't look good.

By this time, there was a really big crowd watching the fire. Everybody from blocks around must have heard the sirens and maybe seen the flames, too. Some of the AC gangs were there. It was hard to miss those shiny jackets in the glow from the fire. I saw a bunch of guys over at one side of the park with the Aces AC emblem. One of them was so goddam big I figured it had to be The Beef Butcher.

Of all the tough guys of all the gangs on the South Side, Beef Butcher was the toughest. And the meanest. Not too many people had actually met or even seen Beef Butcher, but he had such a rep just mentioning his name was enough to scare the crap out of most guys.

All that I knew about Beef was that he was a Mexican. That, and the story everybody had heard, that it had once taken seven cops to bring him in. I mean, there were tough guys like Bryan and Freddie, but then there was a guy like the Beef Butcher, who probably could have taken both of them with one hand. The Beef was the Aces' tough guy, and because he was by far the scariest SOB on the South Side, the Aces were *The* gang and *The* cool guys.

It had to be Beef Butcher I was seeing. He was facing away from me and all I could see was his back, but he was about five feet tall and five feet broad. He didn't have a neck at all, just this massive head that sat right on top of his bulky shoulders.

I mean, maybe you think Beef Butcher is a kind of goofy name or something. If you'd lived around there at that time, though, you wouldn't think that. All you'd think is I hope I never run up against that guy. That name was almost like magic. Black magic. Big brothers would scare little kids, not with the boogie man, but by saying "Beef Butcher gonna gitcha." He was the kind of guy that if you saw him coming down the street, you'd cross over just in case something about the way you walked or looked might piss him off.

But that night, Beef, if that's who it was, was just hanging around with his buddies watching the fire like the rest of us. Nobody, except guys with Aces AC jackets, though, were getting anywhere near that end of the park. I know I was keeping my distance.

I don't know what the heck happened to Tony. I hadn't seen him since I got out of the car and I figured he'd sat in his car and watched until he got bored and headed on home. I was looking around to see if I could spot him when I saw Bryan instead. He was standing right next to one of the barricades on the street behind the nearest fire truck. I was really happy to see him, and headed over that way.

"Hey," he said as I came up. I was coming up from behind him and I don't know how he saw me or knew I was there, but Bryan was always doing that sort of thing, so it didn't surprise me too much.

"Some show, huh?" I said.

"Yeah," he said, "It's a show alright. Where you been?"

"Aw, I been here for a while."

"No," he said, "I mean before. I was lookin for ya."

"Oh, I was just out. Cruisin' with Tony."

Bryan turned to look at me. "Get in any trouble?" he asked.

"Nothin I couldn't handle," I bragged.

"Yeah, well, be careful with that guy. You could get in real deep real fast, you know?"

"I thought he was your friend," I said.

Bryan thought for a minute. "Yeah," he said, "We were friends. Once"

Old Gettelman's place was burning pretty good and it looked like it was going to burn to the ground. The firemen had shut off one of the two hoses, trying to concentrate what little water pressure there was. Whatever main the Chief had been trying to get closed must have done some good, too, because every once in a while the hose would act like you'd expect it too for a little while. The water would come rushing out like it was a real fire hose for a minute or so, then sputter and go back to a trickle.

The firemen were starting to get worried about the library, too, because every once in a while they'd turn the spray on the library wall or up on its roof.

Bryan and I were standing there and he was lighting up a cigarette when Jeffrey came running up with this really crazy look in his eyes.

"Hey, Jeffrey," I said, "What's goin on?"

"Oh God," he said with his voice all shakey, "Have you guys seen Diane?"

"Diane? No, why? She supposed to be down here?" I asked kind of nonchalant-like and frankly glad that if she was around, I hadn't seen her.

"Oh, Jesus," he croaked, almost crying and pointing towards the building behind Gettelman's, "She's spending the night back there - with Lovey."

"Crap!" Bryan said and headed around the truck to where the Chief was, motioning me to follow.

The Fire Chief was still waving his arms around, trying to direct his crew and yelling at another guy in the truck who was working the telephone thing, talking to downtown or the water department or somebody trying to get the water problem fixed. He saw us coming his way and tried to wave us off.

"Get outta here," he yelled at us. Then he grabbed one of the firemen standing next to him and pushed him in our direction. "Get these goddam kids the hell outta here!"

The fireman put his arms out like he was going to shepherd us back away from the Chief, but he didn't know Bryan. Quick as a wink Bryan took hold of the guy's arm, twisted it behind him and pushed him aside.

"Just a minute, Sir," Bryan said, getting right up in the Chief's face, "We need to find out about the folks in that house back there."

I think Bryan kinda shook the Fire Chief up a little, jolted him out of the business of trying to put the fire out, at least long enough to recognize we were there. Bryan had a way of getting people's attention that way.

"There's nobody in that building," the Chief said quickly, "Everybody was evacuated."

"You sure you got everybody out?" Bryan demanded.

The Chief furrowed his brows like Bryan had insulted him or something. "Of course we got everyone," he snapped, "Who the hell are you, anyway?"

Bryan ignored his question. "What about the two girls? You get them, too?"

"What two girls? Whatdya talkin about? There's no girls in there."

Bryan put his hand up over The Chief's face, shoved him hard back against the fire truck, then spun and ran for the alley. The Chief stumbled back hard against the truck, bounced off and fell to the ground. Pulling himself back up on one elbow he yelled out, "Stop him! Stop him! Somebody grab that crazy kid!"

For a minute it was like I was kinda paralyzed there and it seemed like everything was happening in slow motion, The Chief yelling at the top of his lungs and waving his fist after Bryan, and Bryan whipping around the corner and up the alley. What I did next wasn't because I thought about it or anything, but more like a reflex or something. I ran up the alley after Bryan.

A bunch of the firemen were converging on the spot Bryan had just been, but they were watching him disappear up the alley and not looking for another damn fool like me behind them, so I just crashed through, scattering the whole mess of them and scooted on up the alley.

The alley was a goddam disaster. Water everywhere, slippery as hell and full of debris from Gettelman's, some of it still burning. Glass and debris everywhere. Right behind Gettelman's there was a small yard and then the flat. Wooden stairs up to a porch. It was one of those two story wood porches with one set of stairs leading to the two first floor apartments and then a flight of stairs going up to the second floor porch and the apartments up there. The place was on fire.

Just as I got around the corner of Gettelman's, I saw Bryan running up the stairs and in the door of the nearest first floor apartment. I stopped and just stood there, scared silly because the whole goddam porch was on fire and there was smoke coming out of the flat all over the place, including the door Bryan had just run through. I didn't know what the hell to do. I was breathing hard from the running and all of a sudden my stomach wasn't feeling too good, either.

I could hear the firemen running up the alley and before I could think too much about it, I headed up the burning stairway, onto the porch and across to the other first floor apartment. The door was open and smoke was coming out, but not as bad as the one Bryan had gone in. I took a deep breath and plunged inside.

It was like being in . . . I don't know what it was like being in. There was too much smoke. I could barely see, and I was afraid to breathe. I was in the kitchen. There was a table in the middle of the room and I felt my way around it. I could see as far as the walls and there was nobody in the room, so I headed into the hallway. There was a bathroom sorta like in my house, and I looked in there and found no-one. I went on to the next room and then the next, feeling my way down the walls. With my last breath, I yelled out, "Anybody here?"

No answer. I found the front door and slammed against it with all my might, shoving it open and crashing outside. I fell down a couple of stone steps and rolled onto the front lawn, my breaths coming in huge heaves that I could feel all the way down into my lungs. My head was pounding and for a minute I was like blind or something.

When I came around and could see again, the first thing I saw was Bryan kneeling next to me and holding my head up.

"You okay?" he asked.

"Yeah. Yeah, I think so."

"Find anything?"

"Nothing."

"No," he said, shaking his head, "Me neither."

I was surprised at how dark this side of the building was. There were no fire trucks and no firemen running around and the light from the fire was kinda blocked out by the building, which made like a silhouette against the sky. It was kinda pretty, almost.

"Listen," Bryan said, "You stay here, now. I'm gonna try upstairs."

"Like hell I'm stayin here," I said, crawling up to one knee, "If you're goin back, I'm goin back."

"Goddam it, Bonner," he said, cocking his arm, "You stay here or I'll belt you one."

85

"No," I yelled at him, "It's too much for one guy. Let's go in together."

Flames were starting to jump into the sky from the top of the flat. Bryan looked at the building, then back at me. "Stay here," he said, "Your Mom and Dad'll shoot me if you croak."

He hopped up and ran around back. I got unsteadily to my feet and followed him. By the time we got onto the back porch it was really burning and hunks of stuff were falling off into the yard. The stairs looked bad.

"Okay then" Bryan said, "Let's head on up."

I nodded and he ran up the stairs, taking them two at a time. I went after him. The second floor was in a lot worse shape than down below. The windows were all busted, fire licking out, curling up at the top..

"Now listen," Bryan said, looking hard into my eyes, "I'm goin in and if you wanna help the best thing you can do is just wait here. If I don't come out pretty soon, then you come in after me, okay?"

He didn't wait for an answer, but kicked the door in and pushed his way inside, his arm up in front of his face to shield him from the flames. I stood out on the porch and counted.

He was in there a long time. A real long time. There was so much smoke it was hard to breathe even out there on the porch, and it was getting awful damn hot, too. The banister was on fire and chunks of it were falling off into the yard. I counted to a hundred, then to two hundred. Come on, I was thinking, come on out of there, Bryan. I decided I was going to give it to three fifty and then I was going in after him. When I got to three hundred I was counting and praying at the same time. God, let him come out now! I went through some Our Father's and a couple of Hail Mary's. I was wishing I knew more prayers or that this whole thing was just a nightmare or something, when Bryan came charging back out the door, carrying a limp body.

Bryan's face was all black and his arms were red and blistered. His blue jeans were charred and smoking and he was coughing so hard I could see it was hard for him to breathe.

"Take her," he wheezed, "Take her on down."

He passed her from his arms to mine and it was like I didn't feel her weight at all. It was Diane and I felt so sorry for all the nasty stuff I'd said about her and thought about her that I was afraid maybe I was going to cry or something, because I didn't know if she was dead or alive, but then at the same time I knew I didn't have time to wuss out. I had to get her down the stairs and out where she could get help. Bryan had turned her over to me and it was my job to make sure she got out okay.

I held her up close to my chest and headed over to the stairway. The stairs didn't look like they could take us. They were burning up. The banisters were gone and the steps were on fire. How the hell can you walk down something like that? But I had to. I had to get Diane out of there and out to the street. I made it down one step, then two and three. It was one step at a time and I didn't know how far we'd make it. I was trying to walk real light. I didn't want to breathe because taking a breath might be enough to make the stairs fall down.

I looked back to find Bryan. "Wait 'til I get all the way down before you start," I yelled up at him, "Then come down fast!"

Bryan smiled and waved to show he understood. Then he said, "Adios, Tom," and ran back through the door into the burning apartment.

"No, Bryan! Don't!" I yelled, but it was too late. He'd already disappeared. I didn't have time to think about it much though, because right away I had to concentrate on getting down the stairs with Diane. The bottom of the stairway and the whole first floor porch were completely ablaze. There was no way I was going to make it through that alive. I looked all around trying to figure out another way down, another place to go.

Out in the yard, the Chief and four or five firemen were trying to help, trying to spray water up at me and on the stairs. The water just wasn't coming, though, and the fire kept getting worse. It was reaching up for me. The heat was too much. I couldn't stay where I was any longer. Only one thing I could think to do.

It was too far to jump down to the yard, but that was the only way. I pulled Diane up to my chest as tight as I could and tried not to think about what was going to happen. Then, with every bit of strength I had left, I leaped off the stairs, out into space and into the yard below.

It's funny when you're in something like that, because everything seems to go real slow. I mean I'll always remember what it felt like falling through the air, because it seemed like I was floating there for about ten minutes. I could see the scared look on the faces of the firemen and I could see separate little drops of water from their hose and I could feel Diane up against me and the wind blowing my hair and my clothes as I fell, and that acrid burnt wood smell from the house was filling up my nose.

We hit the ground and tumbled forward. Diane was getting pulled away from me, but I held on to her and fell over her and up again as we rolled. I was holding my arms taut so I wouldn't fall too hard on her, and a sharp jab of pain went up through my shoulders and into my neck when my elbows hit the ground.

We rolled over and over I don't know how many times and then the firemen were all around us and grabbing Diane and some reflex thing or something kicked in and I wouldn't let her go until I kind of came to and realized what was happening. I let them take her from my arms.

I was in and out of it for a while. I saw Diane stretched out on the grass with a couple of the firemen doing artificial respiration on her and then the Chief was standing over me yelling, "You stupid little jerk! Who the hell do you think you are, some kinda goddam hero?"

I didn't know if Diane was dead or alive and I tried to go over there, but I couldn't stand. I started crawling over to her, but my breathing wasn't working good and then it was like some kind of lens closing or something and everything went black.

When I came to again, I looked around and Diane was gone. One of the firemen was on his knees beside me holding some kind of mask over my face. I pushed it away and yelled out for Diane.

"Easy," the fireman said, "Your little girlfriend is okay. They've taken her up to City."

I was happy and then right away I was pissed off. "She's not my girlfriend, you asshole," I said.

The fireman laughed and yelled over to some of the others, "This one's gonna be okay, too."

I pulled myself up to a sitting position. The four family flat didn't even look like a house anymore. It looked like a huge bonfire, with flames shooting way up in the air, and crackling and sparks everywhere. Behind me, Gettelmen's was completely gone. There were just a few smoldering black sticks poking up in the air where that building had been just a little while back.

My legs felt real wobbly, but after a couple of tries I managed to get to my feet. "Bryan, where's Bryan?" I asked.

The fireman just gave me this blank look.

"Goddam it," I yelled at him, "Where the hell is Bryan?"

He just shook his head and looked sad. "Oh, you miserable bastard," I yelled and started running back towards the flat. I couldn't run very good and I was stumbling and veering off from one side to the other and then the fireman or somebody tackled me and I fell hard to the ground.

"Get 'em out of there," I yelled, "You gotta get 'em out of there!" I was still trying to get up and to run at the same time and the fireman was holding onto me, like hugging me to him and I couldn't get away and all I could think about was Bryan and Lovey were burning up in there and we had to get to them.

"Lemme go, damn you," I yelled, "I gotta get 'em outta there!"

"It's too late," the fireman said, "It's too late, kid."

And it was too late. Anybody could see that. There was no way anybody could be in that building and still be alive. The building was collapsing in on itself, sending huge showers of sparks and flames up into the sky, and all I could do was sit there with that fireman holding on to me and watch it come to an end.

"No, no," was all I could say, and I guess I was kinda crying or something. "Oh, no," I said, "Oh, God, no." I could feel the tears running down my face, and I didn't even care.

A lot of things go through your mind at a time like that. Really, I'm not sure if they're going through your mind or some other part of you. I mean you're thinking and you're feeling at the same time and that gets you all mixed up, for sure, but the other thing you're doing is you're seeing. You're seeing the way things were and the way they are and the way they're gonna be. You see the friends you've lost and the empty place that's ahead where they used to be. It makes you want to cry and cry and keep crying because it's never gonna be the same ever again.

Nothing else matters at a time like that. It doesn't mean crap about school or girlfriends or basketball or anything. You're just there and all around you is this awful thing that happened and you see through all the bull they try to give you about how you should try to get ahead and better yourself and make a boatload of money and none of it means a dam thing because you're just there all by yourself at the end and crying and maybe if you're lucky you've got some kinda goddam fireman or somebody to hold onto and even though he doesn't know you and you don't know him it doesn't make any difference because nothing makes any difference but you're glad there's somebody there, whoever the hell it might be.

I don't know how long I sat there and cried that night and I don't know who I was crying for more, Bryan or that poor little Lovey girl, who hadn't even barely started living and now she was gone. I wished I hadn't seen her earlier that evening. I wished I'd never known her and

I wished I'd known her better than I did. I wished I'd seen what kind of woman she'd have grown up to be. And Bryan. Oh, man. I couldn't even think about him not being around. He was part of me, for crissake. Without Bryan, there was no Tommy, was there?

Finally they put me on a stretcher and carried me out to the street and there were lights and people and noise and it was all just too much and I got really tired and kinda fell asleep or something.

EIGHT

"Life is a series of incidents that seem important at the time."
Michael Cormany

I guess you'd think that something like that, like all the stuff that happened the night of the fire, would change your life completely - like you'd wake up the next day and be a totally different person. But when I woke up I was still Tom Bonner. At least I think so. I don't really much remember the next day very well. It was more like a couple of days later when I really woke up.

After they dragged me out of the yard that night, they put me in an ambulance and hauled me off to City Hospital, ran a bunch of tests and stuff and said I was lucky. Just some smoke inhalation and a few second degree burns. My folks were there at the hospital right away and the doctors gave them some ointment to put on the burns and told them they had to keep me quiet for a few days. Then they gave me a shot that knocked me out, which I didn't even mind because I was still a little nuts thinking about Bryan and Lovey. My Mom was bawling and when the shot took hold I started feeling just real nice and mellow and then I drifted away.

When I finally came to, I was back in my own sofabed in the front room of my folk's place and the sun was pouring through the window. The first thing I thought was that I was probably late for school. My Mom came in and the look on her face brought everything back to me and one or the other of us starting crying and then she was sitting on the bed next to me holding onto me and we both cried for a pretty long time.

It's funny, but after a while you get tired of crying. I mean, things are still sad and all, but you just can't cry anymore. You run out of tears. And then, too, some things are just so goddam sad that you have to stop thinking about them, have to put them away somewhere, lock some big door behind them and hope they don't ever get out.

I asked my Mom about school and she laughed and said it was okay, I didn't have to go that day. She said I'd only missed two days and she was taking time off work, too, and that I should stay home until I felt like I was ready to go back.

At first that sounded pretty cool, but as the day went on she kept asking me if I was okay and then if I was sure I was okay and then half the time she was telling me how brave I'd been and the other half saying how dumb it was and making me promise I'd never do anything like that again. What was cool was that I got to eat whatever I wanted and at first I was super hungry and kept asking for stuff and my Mom would make it and bring it in for me on a little tray and I got to eat right there in bed and listen to the radio.

But as neat as that sounds, you don't stay hungry forever and hanging around the house gets kind of boring after a while. Besides, when there's nothing much to do, all that stuff in your head that you're trying to keep away starts banging on that door and wanting out. You can be in the middle of chowing down on a really good cheeseburger with the bun all greasy the way you like and first thing there's this goddam tear running down your face and the cheeseburger doesn't even taste very good anymore and you just want to walk away and stand facing a wall somewhere and make it all back the way it was before but you know you can't.

So, yeah, I was still Tom Bonner but it was a different Tom Bonner. Something was torn open. Ripped. Shredded. I'm not sure exactly what. Whatever it is that makes the world make sense. I mean last week it made sense. A coupla mornings ago it made sense. Confusing, sure, but you felt like you *could* figure it out. It was like math. You learn the rules, you practice and you solve the problem. Now, though, the whole idea of ever being able to understand anything seemed like a big lie. A lie they've been feeding you for years.

After a day like that I couldn't take any more laying around thinking. The next morning I set the alarm and headed off to school. Picked up Mick just like usual. As we walked, I told him a little about what had happened, but not too much. It's funny, but when something like that happens you kinda think everybody already knows about it. Like it was so big and so important that everybody would have heard, and when you find out they they don't know the whole story about what happened, you really don't feel much like telling them.

I couldn't hide it completely because my face was still red and I had the burns on my arms with that gooey ointment all over, but I just said there was a fire down by the library and let it go at that. Mick started to ask some more about it, but then he could see I wasn't in the mood, and so he dropped it. I think it takes a pretty good friend to know stuff about you like that, when you don't want to talk and stuff.

It was a good day to get back to school because we had chemistry class that day. I bet not too many kids think chemistry is much of a fun subject, but me and my friends really liked it at McKinley, because it was so goofy.

The guy who taught the class, old Jake Eller, really didn't have a chemistry degree. Instead, his degree was in animal husbandry. I guess maybe that was as close as any of the McKinley teachers had to something in science, so the principal figured he ought to be able to teach chemistry. Jake lived way the hell out in the country someplace and it took him like an hour and a half to drive in to school each day, so he was always tired and would sometimes fall asleep in class, especially if he was showing a movie and the room was real dark.

The chemistry classroom was mostly a lab, and then it had these old-fashioned desks bolted onto this bleacher type of thing with rows of desks, each a little higher than the one in front.

I knew I was in luck when I walked into class that morning, because Jake already had the projector set up. I went to the back of the room, found the box of rubber test tube stoppers and stuffed a handful into my pocket. Other kids coming in and seeing the projector went through the same routine. After everyone had filed in and taken their seats, Jake announced we'd be seeing a movie first and then running some kind of experiment on the stuff we'd learned in the movie. He said we'd have a test next week. Then he fired up the projector, flipped off the lights and sat down at his big desk in front of the bleachers.

We were all real quiet and acted like we were real interested in the movie, but at the same time we all kind of had one eye on Old Jake. Sure enough, it took about five minutes and his head was starting to pitch forward. Pretty soon he was sound asleep.

Steve was sitting behind me. He leaned forward and whispered, "Let's get the test."

I nodded and he and I slowly stood up and eased over to the side of the bleachers, watching the whole time to make sure Jake's eyes were still closed and that he was really asleep.

There was a long lab table next to Jake's desk and in front of the bleachers and Jake always set his briefcase up there. We crept around Jake and over to the briefcase. We'd done this before and had the routine pretty well down. I stood between Jake and the briefcase, so he wouldn't be able to see it in case he woke up. Steve carefully opened the briefcase and rifled through it to find the answer sheet for the upcoming test.

Jake always used these standardized multiple-choice tests, so it was easy once Steve found the answer sheet, to jot down the answers on a sheet of paper.

Steve wrote quickly. "Okay, got it," he whispered when he was done and we both skulked back up to our seats. Naturally, everybody in the class had been watching us and as soon as we had our illicit little treasure they were all clambering for copies.

"Okay, okay," Steve said, "Everybody gets a copy. Just give me a minute, here."

"Yeah, but listen," I warned, "No more of those hundred percenters like last time, you guys. I mean miss a few, okay, or you're gonna blow this thing."

It was always the kids who were not very bright to begin with, who probably wouldn't pass these tests except for having the answers, who also weren't bright enough to realize old Jake might get just a little suspicious when they started all of a sudden aceing every goddam test. Then, too, there are kids who can't even get it right when they have the answers. On the last test, one of the guys wound up flunking anyway because he was like one space out of alignment all the way down the answer sheet. If old Jake had moved the answer sheet down one question, that kid would have gotten a hundred.

Once the answers were all passed out, we started having fun with Jake. Setting next to him on the desk was this metal electron chart he used to illustrate chemical bonds. It was circular, about a foot and a half in diameter with circles painted on it to show electron orbits. The circles made it look like a target.

The rubber stoppers came out of everyone's pockets at just about the same time and a hail of them rained in at the electron chart. Not all of them hit, of course, but enough did to provide a nice "bong-bong-bongety-bong" effect. Jake's snoring broke off and his head, which by then was laying flat on the desk, starting rolling around some.

The trick was to whale your stoppers in to provide a sort of alarm clock for old Jake, but not get caught doing it. Sometimes Jake woke up quickly, but other days it was like he was in a coma or something. You had to be in tune with the guy's sleeping habits.

This was one of his slow mornings and he still seemed kind of groggy as he raised his head off the desk, so a few braver kids zipped in one or two more stoppers just for good measure.

Jake was coming around now. "Aw," he growled, "You guys."

That was one thing that was pretty cool about Jake. He never got real pissed off at stuff. He just had this sort of aw-shucks attitude and took things in stride. It was like he knew he was somewhat of a doofus and kids were going to tease the hell out of him. What could you expect when you fell asleep in class? I could imagine him going into the teachers lounge, saying, "Well, guess what they did to me today."

You could only push him so far, though. We screwed around with the guy but we knew when to cool it. I guess that meant in some weird way we had a certain amount of respect for Jake. I mean we knew it wasn't easy trying to teach chemistry to a bunch of jerks like us.

Jake got up and stumbled over to turn on the lights. "Okay," he said, "I hope you all learned something from that movie, 'cuz now we're gonna do the experiment."

He recapped a little of how to proceed with the experiment, and then we all went over to our lab stations.

It's funny, but although not too many kids were real interested in chemistry, you can't say they weren't interested in anything. Bruce, for example, had gotten real interested in this old Bunsen Burner he'd found in a drawer back in the storage closet. Where the usual Bunsen Burner was this pencil-thin thing maybe six inches long, the one Bruce found was about three times as big around and at least eight inches long. It was real rusty and crummy looking when he found it, but he snuck the thing out of school, took it home and cleaned it up, lubricated it and all, polished the brass to a bright shine, and brought it proudly back to class. You know with a Bunsen Burner how you can adjust the flame by twisting the barrel? Well, Bruce had fixed his up so he could spin the barrel and the flame would go shooting out about a foot. He was real proud of this and liked to demonstrate it by aiming it at some unsuspecting kid sitting on a lab stool trying to actually work on an experiment. Whenever you heard the thud of a kid hitting the floor it was a pretty good bet Bruce had just demonstrated his flame thrower.

I don't recall exactly what the experiment was that we were supposed to do that day but it involved the use of bromine water. If Jake had actually used bromine water in the experiment, everything might have been okay, but he tried to save a few bucks by buying some regular old household bleach instead. He figured anything bromine water could do, chlorine water ought to be able to do just as well. Same halogen family.

He was probably right, too. The only thing was that by the time most of the kids got around to looking for that big white plastic bleach container, what was inside wasn't chlorine water. A couple of the guys had taken the bottle to the back store room, emptied out the bleach and, finding a whole new use for a thistle tube, filled it up with a nice sample of male teenage urine.

The word spread slowly at first, but before long most of the class knew what had happened and decided they might just skip that part of the experiment. It always seems like there's one or two kids, though, who get kinda left out. In this class there were two: Gerry, a guy who carried his Bible around with him to class, and Irene, a nice enough red-headed girl, just a little on the ditzy side.

Me and most of the guys had already finished up our work and were sitting back in our seats in the bleachers goofing off. Irene was having a helluva time getting that experiment to work. We could see her working at her lab station from where we were sitting. She looked real puzzled that whatever the hell was supposed to precipitate out of the bromine water mixture just wasn't precipitating.

"Shake the test-tube," one of the guys encouragingly called out to her. Irene looked up and smiled, then put her thumb over the end of the test-tube full of piss and shook it as hard as she could. Naturally, we were all laughing our asses off.

Finally, in desperation, Irene went over to Jake at the lab bench in front of the bleachers. "I just can't get this to work right," she complained, handing the test-tube to Jake.

"I tell ya, ya gotta shake it," the same kid yelled, "Shake it hard."

Sure enough, Jake put his thumb over the tube and shook it up. Nothing happened in the test-tube, but the class was in stitches.

Jake held the test-tube up to the light and squinted, looking real close at the yellowish fluid inside. Then he took his thumb off the end, held the test tube up to his nose and took a big whiff. The dopey expression on his face and the way he wrinkled up his nose would have been reward enough for this little escapade, but besides that, Jake uttered a classic Jake line that will live forever in the minds of everyone who was sitting in class that day.

Wrinkled-up nose and all, Jake looked down at the little red-headed ditz next to him and said, "Irene honey, I don't think that's chlorine in there."

Well, like you'd imagine, the whole class went totally nuts. I mean kids were actually falling out of their desks and rolling around on the floor. Even some of the girls were laughing so hard their faces were getting red and tears were coming down.

And me, I was laughing right along with them. I mean it was one of the funniest things that had happened at school in a long time. Even Irene was laughing a little, even though she didn't have a clue what was funny, and Jake had this goofy grin on his face, too.

Then something kicked me in the chest and took the laughing right out of me. Two things, really. First, I was thinking about how funny all this was and how I was going to tell the gang about it that night and it hit me that I wasn't going to be able to tell Bryan, because there wasn't any Bryan anymore. And then, at the same time that was hitting me I was looking at poor old Irene standing up there kinda bewildered by it all and she seemed so lost and all that for some reason she started reminding me of Lovey. I mean, she didn't look anything like Lovey, except the hair, of course, and Lovey was for sure no ditz like Irene, but whatever it was, I was seeing Lovey up there with everybody laughing at her and all of a sudden none of this seemed very goddam funny anymore.

So then I wasn't laughing anymore and I wasn't feeling so good. My stomach started hurting pretty bad and I thought I might have to get up and leave the room, but then the PA system came on and announced that class would be dismissed ten minutes early and when the bell rang everybody was to proceed to the auditorium for a special session. I didn't even wait for the bell, but got up and left without saying anything to anybody.

Outside in the hallway I leaned up against the wall and closed my eyes and waited for my stomach to start feeling better and my head to quit spinning around. There wasn't anybody out there and the quiet was nice and the air seemed like maybe it was a little cooler. I guess it was only a few minutes I stood there like that and then the bell rang and everybody came charging out of the classrooms up and down the hall.

I lurched up from the wall and headed down towards the aud. Elaine came out of one of the rooms along the way and she saw me and waved and smiled. "Hi," she said, "Going to the aud?"

I was working kinda hard trying to get myself back together and act normal. "Yep," was the best I could do.

"Well," she said, giving me one of those right-in-the-eye looks, "Why don't we sit together?"

"Uh, okay," I mumbled brilliantly.

We walked together down to the aud and I guess she must have noticed something was a little weird about me.

"Tom, you okay?" she asked, "You look a little pale or something."

"Nah, nah, I'm fine," I said, mustering a weak little smile I know had to look phony as hell.

"Well, I hope so," she said. Then our arms kind of brushed together as we were walking and she reached over and took my hand. Her hand was so small and delicate and it felt nice and warm in mine and I didn't even think about being embarrassed or anything as we walked down the hall to the aud like that.

When we got inside the auditorium I told Elaine I wanted to sit next to the aisle. I said it was in case this got too boring and I might have to sneak out, but really it was because I didn't know if I might start getting sick again and really have to leave.

The principal herself was up on the stage. Old Mildred Hilliard, the big boss at McKinley. Not Conklin this time. It had to be some kind of pretty big deal for Hilliard to be up there.

She waited until everybody was got in and found seats and then she raised her arms to quiet everybody down. "Alright," she said, "Settle down, now, people."

The strange thing was that everybody did. Settle down, that is. I mean, Hilliard was just this tiny little old woman - couldn't have been more than five feet three, a scrawny hundred pounds at most - but she had this way about her that made you listen. She never even had to shout or bluster around like Conklin, you just knew she was the boss. For one thing, I guess, she was Doctor Hilliard. We didn't have too many PhD's at McKinley. As far as I knew, she was the only one. Maybe that was why they made her principal. Whatever it was, when she was talking, everybody was pretty quiet and polite.

"We are here this morning for a very special purpose," she began, "Something I think unprecedented during my tenure at William McKinley High School."

That was one thing I kind of didn't like about her. She was always talking about William McKinley, like trying to make the school sound more impressive that way or something, like John Burroughs maybe. It wasn't William McKinley, it was just plain old McKinley.

"Only once in a very great while," she went on, "Does someone, one of our students, so distinguish himself that it brings great pride upon our school and upon each of us who attend or teach or work here. Such an event occurred a few days ago and it is my privilege to share it with you at this time."

Elaine and I were sitting there still holding hands and she was kind of snuggled up next to me. Usually I'd have been sitting with my buddies and we'd be joking around about whatever was going on up on the stage, but I didn't miss that at all this time.

"Some of you may already know about the fire that consumed several buildings not far from here," Hilliard said, and a little alarm went off inside my head.

"But what you may not know is that the heroism of a McKinley student resulted in the saving of at least one life that night."

"Oh, no," I thought and looked around to see if maybe I could make it out the auditorium door without getting caught.

But Hilliard was still speaking. "At this time," she said, "I'd like to ask Tom Bonner to join me on stage."

I just sat there. Everybody was turning around looking at me and I could feel my face getting real red. Elaine was squeezing my hand and looking up at me, too. "Go on, Tom," she urged, "Go on up there."

I didn't want to go up there. I wanted to run and keep going out the front door of the school and just keep running as far as I could. This was not good.

Mick was sitting a few rows in front of us and he came up the aisle and sort of pulled me out of my seat. He put his arm around me, like, and started helping me down towards the stage.

"Mick," I said, "I don't wanna go up there."

"Tom, you gotta, man."

"I am not getting up on that goddam stage."

"Okay, okay," Mick said, "Let's just go up in front then."

He pulled me up to where I was standing right in front of Hilliard, but down on the floor instead of up on stage. He motioned to Hilliard and she bent over and he said something to her and then went and sat down in a vacant seat in the front row not far from me.

"Young ladies and gentlemen," Hilliard said, gesturing towards me, "Your fellow student, Mr. Thomas Bonner, ignoring the peril to his own life, earlier this week plunged into a burning building and brought out a young girl who otherwise would almost certainly have perished in that blaze."

I think she said a bunch of other stuff, too, but I was getting real uncomfortable up there and I kind of blanked out on a lot of what she was saying. I just wanted to go sit down.

"To commemorate Mr. Bonner's heroic actions," Hilliard went on, "I am hereby proclaiming today Thomas Bonner Day at McKinley High School." The whole thing was getting so strange it was like it wasn't really happening. I was standing there kind of zeroing in on the fact that she hadn't even said William McKinley when everybody started clapping and hooting and stuff. It was real embarrassing. Then it got worse.

The noise quieted down and Hilliard continued. "One more thing," she said, "It seems Mr. Bonner has arranged a little treat for us, as well."

I couldn't figure out what the hell she was talking about with that one. I looked around behind me at her and out of the corner of my eye I spotted Tony standing over next to the curtain at the corner of the stage.

"One of Mr. Bonner's friends contacted me early this morning. It seems Mr. Bonner's uncle is employed by a pretzel manufacturer and Mr. Bonner has enticed him to contribute a sample of his products to the students at William McKinley. Mr. Brulio, if you will."

Hilliard turned in Tony's direction and he stepped out from behind the curtain with a sly grin on his face, carrying one of those goddam big blue pretzel barrels under each arm. He brought them out to the front of the stage, set them down and popped the tops off. "Come and get 'em, everybody," he shouted and started tossing bags of pretzels out into the crowd.

Well, you know what? It's possible for things to get just too goddam weird. I mean this was just too much. It was bad enough having to stand up there in front of everybody while Hilliard talks about you being a hero and stuff, when really you weren't a hero at all, and the real hero wasn't even here, but then she goes along with handing out a bunch of pretzels you swiped just a few nights before.

At first I thought maybe I was going to have to kill Tony for what he did, bringing in those pretzels, but then I thought about it a little more and I figured it was probably pretty good what he did because it was just so goddam goofy and all and you couldn't really think about what was going on there without grinning to yourself.

The kids in the aud were going nuts, of course, shouting and grabbing for the bags Tony was throwing out. I don't think Hilliard knew he was going to throw the bags, because she was up there next to him looking kind of stern and disproving. Me, I took advantage of the diversion, ducked down and started heading up the aisle for the doors. Mick saw what I was doing, hopped up and caught up with me on the way out.

That dick, Thor Berkle, was standing in our way about halfway up the aisle. He grabbed me by the arm. He had this big phony smile all over his face, but he whispered in my ear, "I don't think you're such a goddam hero, Bonner, and I don't think you're getting that scholarship, either."

I should have probably punched the jerk, but instead I just shoved him aside and kept going. Elaine joined Mick and I and the three of us walked out of the aud together. Elaine was all excited and everything and jabbering away, but all I could think about was trying to find a place to get away from all this and find some peace and quiet and not have everybody looking at me. There was just way too much to think about.

I looked down the hall and who do I see heading right for us but Old Man Conklin with some other guy in a suit and two cops. Conklin looked even more serious than usual and the other guys were pretty grim looking as well.

I didn't know where to go or what to do, so we just stood there. They came up to us and the guy in the suit flashed a badge. "Thomas Bonner," he said, "You're under arrest."

Oh, man, what a day. "What," I said, "For some lousy goddam pretzels, for crissake?"

The cops grabbed me, pulled my arms roughly behind me and snapped the cuffs on. "This isn't about pretzels, Bonner," the guy in the suit said with a sneer, "You're under arrest for arson and murder. Let's go."

101

NINE

Ethel Mertz: "He'll ask me and I'll confess."
Lucy Ricardo: "Why?"
Ethel Mertz: "Because while he's asking me he'll have his fingers
around my throat."
The Lucy-Desi Comedy Hour

he Third District Police station was an ugly, squat building at Twelfth and Lynch just a few blocks from where I lived. The station was brick, newer than most of the buildings in the area and it was a different kind of brick, a fancy brick. Most of the neighborhood houses had red or brownish brick but for some reason the police station was a pukey yellow-green brick. It didn't have many windows and the few it did have were small and square. Overall, it looked like pictures I'd seen of World War II pillboxes. Maybe that was what they wanted it to look like, ugly and threatening.

On the Twelfth Street side of the station there was a stairway leading up to double doors. In the summer the main doors were kept open and wooden screen doors provided ventilation. No air conditioning.

Since it was so close to home, I'd been by the Third District hundreds of times. I'd walked past it, ridden my bike past it, driven past it. I guess I'd also gotten in a little trouble from time to time. But until the day that detective - Pearse was his name - and the two cops hauled my ass in, I'd never actually been through those screen doors. I'd never seen the inside of Third District.

It was a busy place. I imagine a few years back it was probably a plum job for a cop to get assigned to Third District. You know, not a lot going on. The neighborhood changed though, and so did life at Third.

They hustled me past the main desk and through a corridor lined with glass panels. You could see inside the rooms and offices. There must have been a hundred cops working all through there, talking on their phones or to people sitting beside their desks or else scribbling away on a note pad or typing away clackety-clack on some old black typewriter. It was pretty interesting, really. Probably would have been a lot more if I hadn't been so goddam scared.

I mean I was acting pretty cool and tough and all, but this was a lot worse than anything I'd ever been in before.

Pearse shoved me through a door into this little room with nothing but a table and chair inside.

"Get your ass in that chair," he snarled.

I sat. He came around, unlocked the cuffs and took them off. Then he slapped a pen and a yellow lined pad down on the table. "Start writing," he said.

I didn't know what he was talking about. "Writing what?" I asked.

"Your confession, asshole," he said real disgusted like. Then he walked out of the room, slamming the door behind him.

Confession? What the hell? I hadn't done anything - well, except that Cherokee Confections thing, of course - but this sure wasn't about that. I sat there and rubbed my wrists where the cuffs had them all red and raw. Those damn things hurt!

The room was maybe ten by ten and the walls were some kind of concrete block with a shiny glaze on them. Pretty much the same color as the brick outside the station. There was a big mirror on one wall and I'd seen enough TV to know that was probably one of those one-way jobs where they could watch and see what I was doing. Other than that, the table and chairs, and the florescent light on the ceiling, there was nothing in the room. Not a picture on the wall, not a lamp, not an ashtray.

I guess I'd been sitting there for maybe ten minutes when Pearse came back in. He glanced at the pad and saw there was nothing on it. I was afraid to even doodle on the darn thing.

"Alright," he said, "I guess you're gonna make me do this the hard way."

"Listen, I don't know what any of this is about," I said, "What do you think I did?"

104

"Shut up, you jerk. You know goddam good and well what you did and so do I. Before I'm through, everybody else in St. Louis is gonna know, too."

By then I was starting to get a little pissed off. "Well," I said, "Could you at least maybe give me a hint?"

Pearse pulled back his right hand like he was going to belt me one, but then he thought better of it. "That's it, Bonner," he said, "You keep up the cute act and see what happens. You think you can burn a place out and get people killed and just laugh it off?"

"Wait a minute," I said, "you talkin about the fire down by the library?"

"You talkin about the fire down by the library?" he mocked, "Yeah - I'm talking about the fire you set that burned two buildings to the ground, put Gettelman's out of business, damn near torched the library and croaked at least two people. Yeah, that's what I'm talking about."

I couldn't believe that was what they were accusing me of. "You gotta be nuts," I said, "I didn't have anything to do with that!"

"You sayin' you wasn't there?"

Uh-oh. Was this guy trying to trap me, or what? "Sure I was there. I helped pull Diane Deems out."

"Yeah," Pearse said, "That was pretty clever. The question, though, is who'd you leave still inside?"

I didn't know how to answer that. He must have known who was inside those buildings a lot better than me. What the hell kind of game was he playing? Did he think I wanted Bryan and Lovey to die?

"Listen," I said, changing the tack a little, "By the time I got there the fire was already goin."

"And that proves what? We know the fire was set and you're smart enough to figure out how to make a little tick-tick device go off when you're far away, right?"

"But why me? Why would I do something like that?"

Pearse got right up in my face. "Why me? Why me?" he mocked, "Bonner, we've got you on this one. We know you talked about knocking over Gettelman's, and we've got you linked to that little chippy you wound up fryin."

"Me? I never said I was going to rob anything."

"You're so full of crap. We've got you planning the deal, saying you'd need a way around the alarm system."

It was Jeffrey. He must have told them about our conversation that day. Changed it all around to make it sound like I was the one who wanted to rob the joint. Why the hell would he do that though, unless maybe the cops just scared the crap out of him and he fingered me to take the heat off himself. But what was that other thing Pearse had said?

"What's this about a chippy?" I asked.

"Your little girlfriend, Lovey Felder? Yeah, we know all about you and her."

"What the hell are you talking about?" I shouted, "She's not my girlfriend."

"Well, not anymore," Pearse snickered, "And frankly, I think she was a little young for you. Of course now she's toast."

"Listen, Pearse, she's just a kid who came in the library."

"Yeah," he said, "A kid you used to pass notes to and flirt with, right? Then you burned her ass up."

"Pass notes...?"

"She had one of them on her when we found her. She was holding on to this book and we found your note inside, like she was using it for a bookmark or something."

"What was the book, Pearse?" I asked, dreading the answer.

"I don't know, some kind of queer knights-in-shining-armor thing."

"Oh, no," I said, "It wasn't Sir Lancelot was it?"

"Yeah. Yeah, I think that was it. Some foreign sounding name like that."

"And what was the note?"

"Like you don't know, right? Like you weren't writing poems to the little gal, swapping 'em back and forth for the last coupla months."

Damn, it had been Lovey who'd been leaving the notes for me there in the Poet's Chapel? I'd always figured it was Elaine, sneaking down and leaving the notes when I wasn't around and picking up my replies.

"I swear, I didn't know it was her. I wasn't writing to her," I said.

"Bull," Pearse yelled, "Even that little Diane jailbait told us about you and Lovey writing back and forth."

"But I didn't know it was her. I thought it was someone else, Pearse, I swear."

"Don't give me that crap, Bonner," he scowled, "We've got your ass on this. Anyways, I don't blame you too much. Looked like she mighta been kinda cute. I mean, for - what was she, twelve or so?"

"For God's sake, Pearse," I pleaded, "Even if it was like you say, why they hell would I try to kill her?"

"Well," he admitted, "We ain't figured that out yet. Maybe you were nailing her trim little ass and she was gonna tell her old man or something. Or maybe she just got caught in the mess when you torched the jewelry store. You know, you could make it easier on everybody if you just told us about it."

I was getting really tired of this. "Aw, goddam it, Pearse, there is nothing to tell. I didn't do it. I didn't do anything."

"Okay, tough guy," he said, "You think you're a big man, you don't hafta talk. Maybe we find out how tough you are." He kicked back his chair and walked out.

My head was spinning. How could they think I did this? It made no sense. I mean, first, if I was going to rob Gettelman's I sure as hell wouldn't try to do it by burning the place down. Putting myself in Pearse's shoes, though, and knowing what Jeffrey'd told him about the jewelry store - his version of what we talked about - I had to admit that it wasn't completely stupid of him to see me as a suspect. A suspect. I was a suspect in arson and homicide. You read about suspects in the paper and it's like they're already guilty. They're already criminals. Just being in that room inside Third District, having Pearse go at me like that made me feel like a goddam criminal. It was weird. I was innocent, but having them think I did it made me feel guilty. Guilty and dirty.

The door opened and two burly cops came in with their sleeves rolled up. They grabbed me and yanked me up out of the chair. "Let's go, tough guy," one of them said, "It's play time."

They hustled me down a narrow corridor and down a flight of stairs to the basement. They were moving so fast I lost my footing and they dragged me the last few steps, across the concrete floor and into a boiler room in the far corner of the basement. They had a hunk of rope and they tied my hands together and then looped the rope over a pipe up near the ceiling. They pulled the rope tight, yanking my arms up over my head.

"Ow," I yelled, "Hey, you don't want to do this. Believe me, you've got the wrong guy."

"Shut the hell up," one of the guys yelled right in my ear, "There's just one thing we wanna hear outta you."

I heard some rattling around behind me and then I got this wallop right across the back of my knees. "Howdya like that, tough guy?" one of the guys said.

The rubber hose treatment. I'd heard about it. Now it was my turn.

They worked me over pretty good. Seemed to like the back of the knees a lot, but the small of the back was one of their favorites, too. Up and down the legs they went, up and down the back. Not too much on the ass. I guess that seemed too much like a kid's spanking or something to them.

A rubber hose makes a funny kind of sound when it hits you. It's like a "thwack," but kind of hollow-like. More like "thwonk." Hurts like hell.

At first I kept trying to twist my head around and tell these assholes that I didn't goddam do it and they couldn't beat me into saying I did something I didn't do, but they weren't listening. Just seemed to whale away harder every time I tried to say something, so I finally gave up, just hung there and took it as good as I could. That's how I started concentrating on the sound the hose made. You know, to take my mind off how much it hurt.

I think I blacked out for a little while, because I remember sort of coming to while they were untying me. They were both really sweating and in a funny way it made me feel proud that beating the crap out of me at least made them sweat and so I got something out of the deal, anyway. They slung me between them and half carried me back up the stairs. They took me to another part of the station and threw me in a cell. Then I fell asleep or passed out or something.

When I came around, there was no doubt I was in jail. I was in a cell in jail with bars all around me and I was sprawled on the concrete floor where those two bozo's had dumped me. It wasn't too bad on the floor, nice and cool, and so I just laid there waiting for my head to come back together.

I was alone in a cell, but there were guys in other cells in a row connected to mine and then another row across the way. Some of the cells just had one guy, and others two or three or four guys. Some of the guys were talking or playing cards or stuff. Others were just laying on a little bunk, sleeping or just doing nothing.

I was pulling myself to my feet, holding on to the bars in front of my cage and still feeling every thwonk of those hoses when there was this big commotion down the way. I pressed my face up against the bars to see what was happening. A bunch of guys were coming through the door at the end of what the cell block, and everybody was cussing and shouting and there was all this banging around and crap as they shoved some guy down my way.

As they got closer, I could see that it was a bunch of cops around this Hispanic guy. Two cops on each arm, plus a cop behind him pushing him along and a cop in front pulling him. Every one of the cops was taller than the guy they were working, but he was bigger around than any of them. No doubt in my mind who this was, but if there had been, the chant that went up and down the cellblock would have put it to rest.

"Beef!" they were chanting, "Beef! Beef! Beef!"

It was the goddam Beef Butcher. I was going to be in jail with The Beef Butcher.

But Beef didn't want to be in jail. Even with all those cops on him, he was giving them a run for their money. He'd push off this way and that, crash one of the cops into the bars on one side or the other. Then he'd pull an arm loose and start bashing on one of the cops, or he'd run a couple of steps forward, bring his arms together and crash cops into each other. All the while he's doing this grunting, like "Huh! Huh! Huh!" and my fellow inmates are chanting "Beef! Beef! Beef!"

It was pretty entertaining.

Finally they got to the empty cell right across from me. The lead cop kept ahold of Beef's collar with one hand and with the other unlocked the cell and swung the door open. Beef raised one leg and tried to kick him in the balls, but the cop was too quick and jumped back out of range.

The other cops started pushing Beef into the cell, but he reached his gigantic arms out and grabbed hold of the bars on either side of the door and they couldn't move him inside.

"Goddam it, Beef," one of the cops yelled, "You know you're goin in there, now give. uh! it. uh! up."

Beef wasn't going anywhere. Six cops pushing on him and he wasn't moving.

Finally the cop behind Beef kicked out as hard as he could at the back of the Beef's right knee. The knee gave and Beef lunged forward, relaxing his grip on the bars as he tried to steady himself and then they had him inside. The cops all shoved together and Beef went stumbling across and slammed into the far wall of the cell like some kind of injured bull. The cops backed out real quick and slammed the cell door.

"Why do you always have to make it so goddam hard?" One of the cops yelled at him through the bars.

Beef came charging back and slammed up against the bars so hard that for a minute I thought he was going to crash right through them. I guess the cops thought so, too, because they all backed away.

"I gotchu hard," The Beef answered in this hoarse half-whisper, grabbing at his crotch, "Right here."

"Yeah, yeah," the cop said, "We've heard it before. Why don't you just cool off awhile?"

"You come down Broadway some time," Beef said, "You get cool real quick."

I guess the cop couldn't think of anything else to say, so he just flipped Beef the bird as he and the other cops walked back up the corridor and out the door, straightening their uniforms as they went.

Beef Butcher went a little nuts. "You come back here, you leedle preek," he yelled, "An I show you sumptin." He was flinging himself around the cell, into the bars on every side and just making a hell of a racket. I don't know if it was more like a bull or a goddam gorilla like you'd see in a zoo. Except in a zoo you feel safe from the animals. Here I didn't feel safe at all.

Beef finally calmed down a little, but then he noticed me standing across the way looking at him. Definitely not so good. He looked right over at me. The guy's got this ridge brow that makes him look kind of Neanderthal, and he didn't look happy to see me.

"You," he spit, "What you name?"

I gulped and told Beef Butcher my name. He turned away and paced back to the far wall. Hit the wall with both arms like he was going to knock the whole place down. Seemed to me like if he'd been maybe just a little bit stronger he might have done it. Then he paced back to the front bars and fixed me in that animal stare again.

"Bonner." he said, "Bonner, yeah, I hearda you. You kill dat little girl?"

Oh crap. Even the Beef Butcher had heard the goddam story. Had heard of me. I didn't think it was a good thing for Beef to have heard of you like that.

"No," I said, "I didn't kill that girl."

"Yeah?" Beef growled, "Well, I tink you did kill dat little girl. Whatchu tink if I kick you ass?"

Well, I thought to myself, this is wonderful. If I ever manage to beat the rap on this deal, what I've got to look forward to is getting out of jail and getting killed by the Beef Butcher.

"You know dat little girl brudder he's a Ace?" Beef asked.

"No," I said softly, "I didn't know anything about her."

"Okay," he said, "Den we get outta here you know I find you and kick sheet outta you, right?"

I almost had to laugh. Maybe I did laugh. It was hard to think of any way things could get much worse. "Help yourself," I said, "But the cops already beat you to it."

"Dem cops, dey whip you?"

"Yeah," I said, "They did a pretty good job on me."

"You tink dat bad," he said, "wait til dey getchu in de Workhouse."

Beef Butcher paced back to the other side of his cell to think that over and at the same time the door at the end of our block clanged open. One of the cops came down and opened my cell. "Visitors," he said and lead me out.

He took me back and put me in a room that looked a lot like the one Pearse had first interrogated me in. In a couple of minutes, my Mom and Dad came in.

They were the last people I wanted to see. Just seeing the two of them made me feel like a kid again and the last way I needed to feel here was like a kid. Mom was already blubbering. She walked up and stood next to me and hugged me to her.

"Oh, Tom," she said, "You didn't do this. We know you didn't do this."

"No, Mom," I said, "I didn't do it."

"We're gonna try to get you outta here, son," my Old Man said, "But the best thing you can do for now is co-operate with the police."

"Yeah, Dad," I said, "Co-operate."

My Mom pulled back and looked at me real long. "Oh my God," she said, "They haven't beaten you?"

"No," I said, "No, Mom, nothing like that." When you were in this kind of a spot, you just kind of learn that snitching on a cop isn't a good idea.

"Well, you tell us if they're not treating you right," my Mom said.

"Yeah, Mom. Sure. I'm okay."

"Alright, son," my Dad said, "We're gonna try to find you a lawyer. I used to work in the courts, you know."

"Yeah, Pop, I know you'll find me a good one. I didn't do this, Pop."

It was funny, but I wasn't sure they quite believed me. Despite what they said. Despite everything. It was like what I thought before - when somebody accuses you of something, you're already half guilty. I think Mom and Dad wanted to believe me, wanted to believe that their son couldn't have done this thing but Geez, he was accused and all.

I wanted to make them believe me, but there was nothing I could say. It was my own Mom and Dad but then here's their kid, accused of setting a big fire and killing people. Couldn't blame them much if they didn't believe me. It was getting to where I almost didn't believe myself.

Pearse came in and ushered my Mom and Dad out of the room. Mom was really bawling by then. "We're gonna get you outta this," my Dad said as he left, "Just don't worry, son."

I was there by myself in the room after they left feeling more alone than I'd ever been in my whole life.

Pearse came back in. "You had enough time to think this over?" he asked.

"I've thought about it," I said.

"And....?"

"And I didn't goddam do it!"

"Alright, kid," he said, "Back to the lockup then." He pulled me up and led me out of the room and back to my cell.

I don't know what time it was then, but it was probably pretty late at night. Everybody was quiet, even Beef Butcher. I sat there on the bunk in my cell and I thought about how crappy it was that my Mom and Dad had to come down to Third District to find their son and what a big jam I was in. Thinking about my Mom bawling like that almost made me bawl, too, but I couldn't. Couldn't do that here. I had to be tough. Had to be cool. Always cool.

I laid back on my bunk and looked at the ceiling. How the hell had I gotten myself into a mess like this? Was I just too much of a smart-ass? What if I hadn't gone out with Tony that evening?

Wait a minute, I thought, I was with Tony. So I couldn't have started the fire, right? No, they already had that angle covered with the idea I'd set off some kind of timer or something.

Then I started thinking about Tony. I'd told him about the jewelry store. Could he have been involved in this somehow?

Nah, Tony wouldn't hang me out to dry like this. It was just something that happened. A fire got started and the cops put two and

112

two together and got five. It made me understand how the Old Man felt about the death penalty.

"Justice isn't perfect," the Old Man always used to say, usually over some article in the Post, "Until it is, gummint got no right killing people."

I fell asleep for a while. I was dreaming about the night of the fire. In the dream Lovey came floating up to me. "Why did you burn me up?" she asked in this ghost voice, "Why? Why?"

Then I saw the library and Jim and Snotnose and Ms. Walker and they were all pointing at me and saying, "Why, Tom, why did you kill her?" All around there was fire licking at me, wanting to get to me and on the other side of the fire was The Beef Butcher, telling me come on over and he'd break my damn neck. He grinned and showed me how he could just jerk my head to one side and that would be it.

I woke up sweating all over. I jammed my eyes closed again as hard as I could and prayed that I was really back at home in my hide-a-bed, that I'd just dreamed or imagined all the crap that had happened and that everything was really okay and back the way it had always been. But when I let my eyes open up I was still there in the same cell in the same place in the same jam and I just wanted to go back to sleep and dream about another place and another Tom Bonner. I wanted to be another Tom Bonner.

It was real dark by then. Everybody was sleeping except me. I got up and stood by the bars. "God," I prayed, "Please get me out of this and I'll be straight from here on, I swear. And please let my Mom get some sleep tonite."

Then the door at the end of the aisle clanged open and a cop came down and stopped in front of me. "Okay, Bonner," he said, "Another visitor."

When he took me out this time instead of taking me to that little room they took me up to the front desk. Standing there in this cool white turtle neck was Tony.

"Hey, Bonner" he said with the usual Tony smile as he saw me coming, "How ya doin? Ready to get out of this crap-hole?"

I didn't say anything. I couldn't say anything. Tony was signing some papers on the big main desk in front of him and talking to the desk guy like he'd known him all his life.

The cop let go of me and I think I would have fallen on my ass except Tony grabbed hold of me and held me up. He put his arm around me and acted like I was standing OK on my own and so the two of us walked out the front screen doors of the Third District, out into the cool night air.

I think I kind of slumped a little when we got outside. Tony sort of half-carried me to his car and dumped me inside. The top was down, as usual, the Cartoon fox emblem showing on the tonneau.

"Got yourself in a pile of crap, huh?" Tony asked.

"Yeah, just a little pile," I said, trying to maintain some cool, "How'd you get me out?"

"Well," he said, "I always told you that you could go to work for us. Now I guess maybe you are."

I looked over at him. "What was the bail?" I asked, "How much do I owe you."

"Fergettaboutit," he said, "Just part of the deal."

"How much?" I demanded.

Tony dropped the Chevy into gear and laid rubber right in front of the Third District. "Ten thou," he said.

Ten thousand dollars, I thought, more than my Old Man made in two years. How the hell could I ever repay this?

Still, I was out of that hell-hole of a jail and Tony was the guy who seemed to know what he was doing, more than my Old Man. And here we were, heading out again with the wind blowing in my face all cool and nice and Tony wasn't asking any questions about the fire or what I'd done or anything.

It felt pretty good.

"Tony," I said, "Where'd you come up with the dough?"

He just kind of laughed. "Well," he said, "Let's just say you're working for the Calcatorri's now."

TEN

"Everyone behaves badly given the proper chance."
Ernest Hemingway, <u>The Sun Also Rises</u>

A few days later I stopped by the clubhouse. I was back in school and mostly everyone was trying to act like nothing had happened, except something had happened and everybody knew it and so it was all real phony and stupid, but I couldn't think of anything to do about it. It was hard to concentrate in class and I could tell some of the kids were whispering about me behind my back and the whole place just seemed a lot colder than it had been just a couple of weeks earlier. Wasn't much I could do about any of that, though.

I'd been avoiding the clubhouse because just thinking about going there reminded me of Bryan and how he wouldn't be there, but one day I was feeding Boozer and I looked over and saw Ronnie going down the stairs to the club. He noticed me and gave me a grin and waved for me to come on. Without thinking about it too much I just followed him downstairs and into the cool basement.

"Hey, Tom, how's it goin?" he said with this look that let me know he kinda really wanted to know and wasn't just saying it to say something.

"Aw, okay, I guess," I said, "I mean, you know."

"Rough, huh?"

"A little."

The rest of the gang was down there, too, except Cathy.

"Hey, guys," I said, and they hey'd back. Diane came over and put her arms around me and gave me a hug without ever saying anything or even looking at me. Then she turned around real quick and went back and hopped into one of the drain tub easy chairs and stared at anything but me.

I hadn't talked to Jeffrey since everything had happened and I didn't much know what to say at first but then he came over and he was just the same old Jeffrey except maybe a little more nervous or something.

"Tom," he said, "I gotta explain to you about them cops."

"Jeffrey, you don't have to explain anything."

"Didn't say I had to," he snapped, "I just thought you oughta know I didn't rat on you or anything."

I wondered how he was going to explain it away, but really, I didn't feel much like putting up with his line of bull. I just looked at him real hard. "Naw, man, you wouldn't do anything like that" I said, without showing whether I was being sarcastic or that he was such a great guy.

"Well," he said, "They came around asking all sorts of questions about you. Wanted to know if you'd ever been in trouble and stuff. 'Course I told 'em no. They asked if there'd been any suspicious fires around here and I said nope. They wanted to know how you spent your time and what kinda stuff you liked and all and I guess that diamond thing down at Gettelmans slipped out."

"You told 'em about that?"

"Yeah, well, I didn't think there was anything wrong with that. I mean who wouldn't like diamonds? I didn't tell 'em you busted into the joint or anything."

"Jeffrey, I didn't bust into the place."

"No, I know. I mean that's what I told 'em."

I was getting tired of this. "Yeah, well, it doesn't make any difference anyway," I said.

"Well, listen," he kinda of stammered, "Anyways, I wanted to tell you . . . .to say thanks for pulling Diane outta there like that."

It dawned on me that he didn't know, that maybe nobody knew, what really happened that night.

"Jeffrey," I said, "It wasn't me that pulled her out, man."

His brow wrinkled up. "No? Well, who then?"

"It was Bryan. Bryan pulled her out and dumped her in my arms. He's the one saved her. I just carried her down the stairs."

Jeffrey and Diane spoke at the same time. "Bryan?"

"Yeah," I said, "Then he went back for Lovey. I took Diane down and that was it."

Ronnie said, "Well, Tom, if you carried her down, seems to me like you saved Diane every bit as much as Bryan, anyways."

It didn't seem that way to me, but I didn't want to go over all the stuff that happened again, so I just kinda changed the subject. "I guess I was still out cold when they had Bryan's funeral," I said, "You guys went, right?"

The three of them looked at each other and then at me. Ronnie was the first one to break the silence. "Tom," he said, "There wasn't any funeral. They never found his body and it takes, I don't know, a few months or something before they can even declare him dead. For now they're just saying he's missing."

"They never found Bryan?"

"No," Ronnie went on, "After you got out some kinda gas line exploded. They found Lovey's body, but maybe Bryan just got blown to bits or something. Not enough left to find."

I didn't know what to think about that. I mean, it sounded pretty bad, but if you're dead I guess it doesn't make too much difference to you if they find what's left of you and stick you in the ground or if you just get blasted up into the sky. I figured Bryan's Mom and Grandma must be pretty upset and I was gonna ask if any of the gang had been to see them, but then I didn't because I was the only one who knew them. The only one, I guess, who knew Bryan even had a Mom and a Grandma to be worried about him and sad about what happened. I figured maybe I'd better go by and see Grandma, anyway. I wasn't sure where to find Bryan's Mom anymore. I hadn't seen her for a long time and I knew she'd moved from Menard Street but I didn't know where.

We were all pretty quiet for a while, thinking about what it would be like to be blown up like that, and then Ronnie let this huge fart. Jeffrey said it sounded like he was getting blown up, too and everybody laughed because we needed to get over being so damn sad and stuff. I thought it might have been the best fart anybody ever let.

After we got the laughing out and calmed down again, Ronnie said, "Well, what do we do now, hook up with Freddie and them?"

"What?" I said, "What do you mean?"

Ronnie rubbed his forehead and looked down at the ground. "Well, there's not enough of us for a gang anymore, is there? I mean without Bryan."

I hadn't thought about it until then, but he was right. About there not being enough of us, that is. The idea of hooking up with Freddie hit me pretty cold, though. It hit Jeffrey even colder.

"Freddie can blow me," he spit.

"Listen, I'm not too keen on the guy either," Ronnie said, "But without Bryan...."

"What?" Jeffrey said, "You think I can't take Freddie? You think I was ever gonna let Bryan take care of me like I was some kinda wuss or something? Maybe you guys are afraid of Freddie, but I sure as hell ain't."

It was one of the stupidest things I'd ever heard. I mean Jeffrey probably did know a little about boxing and stuff from his old man, but all you had to do was take a good look at him and Freddie and you could see Jeffrey had about as much chance of taking Freddie as a one-legged man in an ass-kicking contest.

"Knock it off, you guys," I said, "Nobody around here is goin' with Freddie. We just gotta find some more guys for our side, that's all."

Jeffrey chimed in, "Yeah, we'll just get some more guys."

Ronnie just let it go at that and we all just kinda goofed around for a while. It seemed real strange without Bryan around and then I realized somebody else was missing, too.

"Hey, where's Cathy?" I asked.

"She's all messed up, man," Jeffrey answered, "Went a little nuts when she found out about Bryan. My old man sent her down home 'til she gets herself straightened out."

Down home. Man, that phrase reeked of hoosier. Hoosiers were always talking about going "down home." Usually that meant someplace in Southeast Missouri or even down in Arkansas. It pissed me off that Jeffrey was talking like a goddam hoosier. I didn't say anything, though, because then it hit me I was thinking more about the way the guy was talking than about what he'd said. I could see Cathy being really shook up about Bryan. The truth is all of us were shook up. We just showed it in different ways is all. Who cares how you say things?

"Well," I said, "I hope she's okay." I looked over at Diane. She was still just sitting in the drain tub not saying or doing much of anything. Seemed like she was the one who ought to really be shook up, but she was a tough kid. She could take it.

"So, Tom," Ronnie said, "How you gonna get outta this mess?"

I didn't know the answer to that question, but I told him what I did know. "Well, Tony's people are helping me some. They went my bail and might be gonna help with a lawyer and Tony said they were doing some checking around to see who mighta torched the place."

"Who do ya think?" Ronnie asked, "Got any idea's?"

"Naw, man, I don't know. My Old Man says maybe old Gettelman filed a Jewish Bankruptcy, or maybe it was just a bunch of them hoosiers or something."

"Jewish bankruptcy?" Jeffrey said quizzically.

"Yeah, the Old Man says sometimes when a business isn't doin so good the owner'll hire somebody to burn the place down and then just collect on the insurance."

"Oh, yeah," Jeffrey said, "Goddam Jews."

"And hoosiers," Ronnie said with this sly little grin. winking at me.

"Yeah," Jeffrey said kinda absent-mindedly, "Them too." Then he brightened up. "Hey, Tom, that Thor guy at school was asking a whole bunch of questions about you the day of the fire."

"What do you mean?" I asked.

"Well, I dunno," Jeffrey said, "I was up at school that day and he was asking, like if you had a job and what kinda stuff you did, where you hung out and stuff."

"What did you tell him?"

"Aw, man, not much. I mean I told him you worked at the library, but I don't know the guy that well and it's none of his business, right?"

"Right."

"I just figured you oughta know, cuz maybe he was pissed at you or something and maybe he was the one tried to set you up with the fire and all."

"Well, I don't know," I said, "It sounds like kind of a long shot, but thanks for tellin me about it."

Man, that would be perfect. I mean of all the jerks around I'd like to be able to pin this thing on, none would make me happier than that prick, Thor. And if he really was as much of a prick as I thought, maybe he would see framing me as a way of cutting me out of the scholarship. I'm guessing they don't give too many college scholarships to guys who are in the slammer. Still, how would Thor know about the jewelry store? Unless it was just a lucky guess.

"You didn't say anything to Thor about Gettelmans, did you? I asked.

119

"What would I say?" Jeffrey answered, "But you know his old man is part owner in that place?"

"What? How'd you find that out?"

"He was bragging about it. When I told him about you working down at the library, he said 'Oh, yeah, my father owns a piece of a jewelry store near there.'"

I couldn't figure out whether that made it more or less likely that Thor might have been involved. I mean I couldn't see a guy burning down a place his old man owns, but then with Thor and people like that you just couldn't be sure of much of anything.

Then I had another real scary thought. If it really was Thor, then I was probably going to jail anyway. I mean his family was so goddam rich they probably knew all the lawyers and judges in St. Louis and even if they knew he was the one who did it, they sure as hell wouldn't let him be convicted. They wouldn't screw up the family name that way. They'd need a scapegoat, and Tom Bonner fit the bill pretty well. Hell, maybe they already knew he did it and that's why they came after me.

I didn't figure even Tony's friends, even the Calcatorri's could mess with the Berkle family and their ties. If it was Thor, I was screwed and that was that. I'd better start hoping it wasn't Thor.

"Well," I said, "Can you guys think of anyone else who might've done the job on Gettelman's?"

"Hell," Ronnie said, "Could've been just about anybody - I mean Jimmy Zollner's bunch hangs out not far from there, and what about them bums?"

"Who - Jim and Snotnose?" I said.

"Yeah," Ronnie said, "Those two bums who're always there at the library. Who knows what guys like that would do? Hell, if it was wintertime, they might start a fire just to keep warm."

"It's not winter, Ronnie," Jeffrey interjected.

"Aw, crap, Jeffrey," Ronnie said, "I know it's not winter. I'm just saying a bum might do anything. It wouldn't even have to make any sense."

I thought about that for a while. Those two bums were so, like, passive that I didn't think they would be able to do something so aggressive. But then maybe old man Gettelman had pissed one of them off sometime, like told them to get the hell away from in front of his store or something, and they decided to get even. If it was one of those guys, it would have to be Jim. Old Snotnose was too far gone to figure something like that out. But on the other hand Snotnose could start a fire accidentally or maybe part of him being so screwed up was being a firebug or something.

The more I thought the more possible explanations came to mind, and I didn't have any way to sort them out, figure out which one made the most sense. Hell, I wasn't a cop or a private eye or anything. What do you do when something like that happens to you? One thing is, you start suspecting everybody and you wonder if you really have any friends or if everybody is out to get you. You wonder what kind of lousy-ass world you live in.

The other thing is, you get to a point and you just can't think about it anymore at all. I mean it makes you feel so crappy and you just get so tired of trying to figure it out that your mind just wants to shut down on you. I was getting real tired of just sitting around in that basement, too.

"Listen," I said, "Let's get the hell outta here and go do something for a while."

"Yeah, okay," Ronnie said, "Whatdya wanna do?"

"I don't know. Anything. Let's just get outta here."

Jeffrey said they were working over on Dago and maybe we could go over and see what was going on. Nobody had a better idea, so the four of us headed on over.

Turned out there wasn't much happening. We walked down Victor Street and mostly there were just a bunch of flags and markers from surveyors and stuff. Down below Menard and almost to Tenth Street there were some houses that were going to be torn down for the Boy's Club. Two of the houses were already vacant and the windows were all busted out and stuff, but in between was one house that somebody was still living in.

"How do they do that?" Diane asked, "Make people move out of their houses?"

"I guess they buy the houses," Ronnie said.

"Well, what if you don't want to sell your house?"

"I dunno," Ronnie said, "Maybe they can condemn it or something, like they did with all the people down below Broadway."

"Yeah," I said, "Or they could just build around you. Maybe that's what's happening to this guy."

"I wouldn't let them make me move," Diane said.

The front door on one of the vacant houses was wide open and we went in. It was a real mess inside. Kids had gotten in and messed it up good. The walls were busted up and there were big places where you could see the lathing under the plaster and other places where even the lathing was busted up. There was glass all over the floor from kids throwing rocks through the windows, so you had to be careful how you stepped. In the bathrooms, it looked like somebody'd taken a sledgehammer to the crappers. We didn't go in, though, because it stunk so bad. Somebody was still using the place to take a dump in even though there wasn't a toilet bowl anymore.

The kitchen looked bad, too. The sink was hanging off the wall and there were some old metal cabinets that got torn down off the wall and were laying in the middle of the room, all beat up, the doors torn off. I thought it was a damn shame to waste stuff like that. I mean the cabinets looked like they'd been nicer than the ones in my Mom's kitchen. Now they weren't worth a damn to anyone.

The basement door was open and Jeffrey wanted to go down and see if there was any copper pipe left, but it smelled so damn bad just standing there in the door that the rest of us told him he could go down by himself but we were heading outside. He didn't say anything, but followed us out. Who knows what might've been down there? Down there in the dark.

There were boards and junk laying all over the back yard. Ronnie pointed out one window on the second floor that hadn't been broken out yet. He started pitching rocks at it and pretty soon the rest of us joined in. It didn't take long before the glass crashed in and then we were chunking at the little shards still standing until some old guy in the house next store came to his window and started yelling at us to get the hell outta there or he'd call the cops.

Naturally, we didn't pay much attention to the old fart except for yelling back at him that he could go screw himself, until he got real red in the face and it looked like he actually might call the cops. By then there wasn't much left for us to aim for anyway, so we yelled at him a little more and Jeffrey kinda halfway threw a rock up towards his window. Then we headed on out the back yard and up the hill onto Dago itself.

Being summertime, Dago was overgrown with all sorts of weeds and stuff, and it was like pushing your way through some kind of jungle. I mean, there were sunflowers that were taller than me, the flower part almost a foot in diameter.

"Hey, those are kinda neat," Diane said.

"What, the sunflowers?" I asked.

"Yeah, they're pretty. Where'd they come from - somebody plant 'em up here or something?"

"Nah, Diane, I don't think so," I said, "I think they're more like just a kinda weed."

"No," she insisted, "They're not weeds, they're flowers. Could you get me one of 'em?"

I grabbed hold of the next one we passed close to. The flower part was drooping down and hanging close to my face so I grabbed the stalk and bent it back and forth a couple of times and pulled 'til it came off. I didn't much care for it because the stalk had this fuzzy stuff on it that felt weird in my hands and when I broke it off this milky crap came out and got on my hand and felt all sticky.

Diane took the flower from me and looked at it real close and smiled and I realized it was the first time I'd seen her smile this whole day, so I guessed it was maybe worthwhile getting that milky stuff on my hands.

There were paths through the weed jungle and we pushed our way along one of them until we came to the clearing at the middle of Dago Hill. There was a big concrete pad in the clearing that collected rainwater and made a little pond a few inches deep. There were a couple of little kids playing in the water and we went over and asked what they were doing.

"We got these boats, see?" one of the kids said. He held up this little hunk of wood to show us and it was just like the paddleboats my Old Man used to make for me. A little hunk of plywood, maybe a quarter-inch thick, cut to an angle in front to look like the bow of a boat. A square was cut out of the back end and then that square was filed or sanded down and slipped right back where it came from, but hooked up with a rubber band to make a paddleboat.

The kid wound up the rubber band and then put the boat in the water and let go. It worked just like mine used to and paddled its way out into the middle of the pond. Then the kid waded out and fetched the boat, came back and went through the whole routine again.

Ronnie and Diane and I sat down on some stone steps at the edge of the concrete pad and watched the kids play. Each of them had a boat, had races to see which one would go farther. Had naval battles to see if you could get a boat to push the other one aside. After a while Jeffrey got bored and went off to explore the far side of Dago.

For me it was kind of fun just sitting there watching these little kids play in the pond. I mean, there were these huge weeds all around so you couldn't see out to the street and nobody out there could see you. It was like your own world in there, and all safe and part of being a kid. The sun was shining and felt warm and good and the sky was bright summer blue and none of us had to be anyplace or do anything, so we just sat there and watched the kids having fun with their boats.

We must have sat there like that for some time, because Diane was starting to get kind of drowsy or something. She leaned up against me and put her head on my shoulder. Things had really changed between us. Before, she would never have done something like that. Hell, if she'd tried I'd have pushed her away and made some sarcastic comment, or maybe she would have. But now neither of us cared. I mean, it wasn't like we were ever going to be boyfriend and girlfriend, but more like brother and sister. At least that's the way I felt, and I figured from the way she was acting she maybe felt the same. Anyway, I didn't mind her leaning up against me like that. I put my arm behind her to steady her a little and make sure she didn't fall over backwards and Ronnie didn't even say anything.

First thing you know, though, we saw the bushes getting jostled all around and Jeffrey came busting out into the clearing. "Hey, you guys," he yelled, "Come on, you gotta see this."

Diane kinda woke up and pulled herself upright and then we all got up and followed Jeffrey.

We were heading down this path that wound around towards the northeast corner of Dago and wondering what could be so exciting to get Jeffrey worked up like that, when he came to a halt right in front of us. When we caught up to him, we saw that the ground ahead dropped straight down into this big pit. It was almost to the Sidney Street side of Dago. In fact, we were on a little bit of a hill, and the way the ground dropped off, you could see the street, but the pit was far enough back that if you were out on the sidewalk you wouldn't know it was there.

We looked closer and saw that the pit was about twenty feet deep. Over at one side there was another hole that was all in shadow. You couldn't see into it.

Jeffrey turned back to us. "What the hell you think it is?" he asked.

Ronnie and I said "Sinkhole!" at the same time.

Jeffrey mulled it over for a bit. "You ever seen one up here before?" he asked.

"Yeah," Ronnie said, "They happen all the time up here, mostly at this corner. Usually they fill 'em in pretty quick, though."

"What causes 'em?" Diane asked.

"Well, there's supposed to be caves all under here," I volunteered, "There was a brewery here a long time ago and they used the caves to store beer and stuff. The ground over 'em just kinda collapses every once in a while, I guess."

"Yeah," Ronnie said, "I heard they run all the way down to the river from here."

"Let's go down and take a look," Jeffrey said, starting to climb down into the pit.

"Naw, man, you don't wanna do that," Ronnie said, "It's way too dangerous."

"Aw, don't be a wuss," Jeffrey mocked with a big grin.

"Jeffrey, Ronnie's right, man," I said, "That whole pit could give way. Look how loose the dirt is."

Jeffrey was already starting to slip in the loose soil. The dirt from above was piling in around his feet, like being in a big sand pile or something. He had to swing around to catch his balance and keep from sliding all the way down. He got kind of a scared look on his face and started trying to climb back up the slope.

He wasn't very far down, only a few feet, but the dirt was sliding down faster than he could climb up. He started slipping further down and was waving his arms around to keep from falling.

"Bonner, hold on to me," Ronnie yelled. He grabbed my hand, took one big step down the slope and grabbed hold of one of Jeffrey's arms with his other hand. I leaned back and tried to hold on to Ronnie and keep the two of them - or all three of us - from falling down into the pit. Diane grabbed me around the waist and held on, too.

We were just balanced there for a while, but finally we managed to pull Jeffrey up the hill just enough to where his feet hit some solid ground. On solid footing, he leaped up the rest of the way and all four of us went tumbling back into the weeds and bushes.

Diane was down at the bottom of the pile. "Hey, you lunks, get offa me," she yelled. We rolled off of her and all of a sudden the whole thing seemed kind of funny and we all started laughing.

"Deems," Ronnie said to Jeffrey, "We all knew you were going to hell someday, but for a while there it looked like you were going today."

Even Jeffrey had to laugh. "Yeah," he said, "Kinda felt like it, too."

We got up and brushed ourselves off and started back up the path. "Hey maybe we could get some ropes and flashlights and stuff and come back later on and really explore this thing," Jeffrey said.

We all said that might be a good idea, but I figured it was probably never going to happen. For one thing, with the construction getting started, they were going to find the sinkhole and probably fill it in for good this time. For another thing, all the stuff about the fire was starting to eat at me again and I knew I was going to be too goddam busy to come back over here and play around like that.

We dropped Ronnie off at his house and when we got to Jeffrey and Diane's place Jeffrey went right in, but Diane kinda hung outside for a minute.

I was getting ready to head on home when she said, "Tom, wait just a minute...please?"

"Yeah? What is it, Diane?"

She looked down at her shoes and didn't say anything for a while. Finally she said, "Well, I don't know, I just wanted to say something to you."

"Yeah?"

"Yeah. I guess just thanks."

"What, for the flower?"

"No," she said, "Not just the flower. For everything. For getting me down the stairs. For saving me."

"Listen," I said, "I told you - it wasn't me."

"Yes it was," she said, "Oh, I know it was Bryan, but it was you, too."

I just waved to her and started walking away. "Ah," I said, "Don't think about it."

"But I do think about it, Tom. A lot. And I know you woulda saved Lovey too if you coulda."

I kept walking.

"See ya, Diane."

"Yeah, see ya," she said and went inside.

126

ELEVEN

"We stand here surrounded by insurmountable opportunities."

Pogo

S unday was a day for playing. It was hard not to worry about the fix I was in but there wasn't much I could do about it. Hadn't heard anything from the lawyers yet. Might as well enjoy myself while I could.

First though I had to go to church with my Mom. I'd been trying to ease out of that Sunday routine, but since the fire the look I got if it even seemed like I was thinking about not going with her made me feel so guilty it was easier just to go and get it over with.

Assumption Catholic Church was just west of Ninth Street on Sidney. It had to be the poorest Church in the archdiocese. We didn't even have our own priest. Had to borrow a priest from St. Joe's or St. Agnes or one of them and of course they never sent anybody worth a damn. The Mass was in Latin, which was bad enough, but then we usually got this doofus old priest who should have retired decades ago. He mumbled his way through the service, seemed like he might fall asleep at any minute and you could never figure out what the heck was going on. At least I couldn't. It was just an hour of sitting and standing and kneeling, making a few signs of the cross and beating your breast a couple of times.

Actually, there was something appealing about that part. "Mea Culpa, Mea Culpa, Mea Maxima Culpa - through my fault, through my fault, through my most grievous fault." I sure had enough faults and it felt oddly good to admit it like that, especially now.

The other thing that was nice was that Assumption was a Polish Parish and sometimes the choir sang Polish hymns. They had such an odd sound to them, a wailing or keening or something. Beautiful. Heart rending.

The rest of it though just left me kind of cold. Maybe it would have been different if I'd gone to Catholic School and had to go through Catechisms and stuff like Norman, the kid who lived upstairs. Mom had done her best short of that to raise me a good Catholic and for a while it had looked like it might work. I got a Missal and kind of got into the Apostle's Creed and all that, but then I started thinking about some of the stuff we're supposed to believe and I couldn't help having some doubts. It wasn't just Catholicism, either.. I mean, the idea of Original Sin. What a load of crap St. Augustine foisted off on everybody.. A newborn baby already a sinner. It didn't make sense to me. Does to a lot of folks, I guess, and that's OK. Just not me.

Then, too, I'd read so much science fiction over the years and Greek and Roman mythology before that, that I couldn't help seeing how the whole Christian dogma just seemed like some kind of story. I mean it was a nice story and all, but still just a story somebody made up. I don't know, I guess I'm going to hell. I just can't bring myself to believe, to accept on faith.

Even Bryan had been a believer. I mean you wouldn't think it of a guy like that, but he was a big Bible reader. He didn't go to church much, but he used to go to revivals and even some of those Holy Roller places and he read the Bible and could quote from it. He wouldn't talk about it around most people, but sometimes when it was just the two of us, he'd say something and I could see this was pretty important to him.

There was this one time we were sitting down in the basement talking about weird stuff that had happened to us and I mentioned this strange thing that had happened to me a couple of times. It was really a funny kind of thing with my eyes, where I like saw these - well, the only way I could describe it was like liquid drops of fire. I mean it was like all around me fire was coming down like rain. It only lasted for a few seconds, but it had happened two or three times and it was a little strange, I thought. I never told anybody about that except Bryan.

He listened and thought about it a minute and then said simply, "Tom, you've been Dealt With." The way he said it was like "Dealt With" had capital letters. I didn't really know what that meant, but it seemed to be pretty important and to have something to do with God or something. Seemed to mean maybe I was something special, because for sure God wouldn't just *Deal With* everybody like that. I mean, I'd never heard anybody else talking about it raining fire around them.

But that had been a long time ago and whatever it really was, a momentary oxygen deprivation or a wayward migraine or whatever, had gone away. It hadn't come back and I didn't get Dealt With anymore. Besides, old Conklin's speech had said I wasn't anything special. Not me nor any of the kids at McKinley. Hey, an assistant principal oughta know, right?

So I sat in Church with my Mom on Sunday and kneeled and stood and sat with everybody else. I said a prayer for Bryan and another one for Lovey and I asked for a little help for myself. I listened to the old priest mumble to himself and I listened to the choir.

The hour went pretty slow, but then it was over with and I was free to go do whatever I wanted for the rest of the day.

What I wanted to do was shoot some baskets. I called Mick and Steve and a few other friends - Bob, Wally and The Schwantz. We agreed to meet at the playground at Sigel School just down from McKinley. Sigel was where some of the guys had gone to grade school. It had a decent outdoor basketball court and was in walking distance for all of us. I went by Mick's house and picked him up and by the time we got up to Sigel, Steve was already there. He'd picked one of the backboards where the rim actually had a net, one of those chain-type ones, and he was practicing his shots.

Mick and I joined him and started shooting around. Whoever got the rebound took the next shot. The ball was bouncing pretty high that day and making kind of a "boing" sound when it hit the asphalt pavement on the playground.

"Steve," I said, "I think your ball's a little overinflated."

"Yeah," Mick laughed, "And so's Steve."

"Up yours," Steve shot back at us, "You don't like my ball, bring your own."

Soon the rest of the guys showed up. It had been a while since any of us had played, so nobody was making shots. Didn't stop us from trying some fancy ones, though. Jumpers from all over, hooks, and the usual attempts at dunking. Mick and I were about the same height and although Steve was shorter, he had a pretty good spring, so we all had a chance at dunking. If you could do it, you were the king.

Steve was definitely not making it that day. He was coming up way short, and the thing about relying on spring is that if you don't make it early on, you get tired and lose that spring and you sure as hell aren't going to make it later on.

Mick was doing good. He was coming pretty close. He was heavier than me and I had to admire how he got himself up in the air like that. Whang! He got close enough to send the ball sideways into the rim and bouncing way out into the playground.

I chased it down, dribbled around to the left side of the court and then charged in on the basket. I was trying to concentrate on placing my steps so I got at the right spot ready to push off my left foot, the ball in my right hand. I jumped and brought the ball up over my head and towards the basket. Close, but - whang, again off it went just like Mick's.

Mick and I for sure had the advantage here because every time you try like we were, you're kind of stretching yourself out and sometimes if you do it enough, after a while you can make it.

Steve could see that he didn't have it that day and so he started making fun of me and Mick.

"Give it up," he yelled, "You bozo's can't do it."

Mick lumbered in and up towards the rim. He hit it off-rhythm and didn't even come close. The ball bounced off the rim and out into the yard, where Steve grabbed it up.

Steve had given up on the dunkeroo and was trying to show off hitting long range shots. "Watch this," he yelled, and tossed the ball up with a two-hands over the head shot from way beyond the head of the key.

The ball hit the rim, circled once and rolled off. I grabbed it up and went for one more try at the dunk. Again, I took it out left court and charged in to the right. Everything felt in sync and I went up at just the right point. Up. Up. It was like in slow motion. I could see the ball coming up towards the rim and edging over it and then down and...almost in. Whang! It caught the top edge of the rim and bounced out to right field again.

That was it. I just wasn't going to make it that day. Sometimes you can and sometimes you can't. Mick tried a few more and then gave up, too, and we decided to play Horse.

So we Horsed around for a while. We were all pretty evenly matched and I don't remember who won. It wasn't that important anyway. We just played until we got hot, sweaty and tired. Then we sat down under the basket to rest for a few minutes. Next we'd probably pick sides and play half-court until we were exhausted.

We were sitting there getting our breath and trying to cool down. "Mick," I said, "Man, you need to go out for the team."

"Nah," he said, "I couldn't. Too heavy. I'd never make it."

"Baloney," I said, "You're really good under the basket."

"Yeah, well, I dunno."

"No, really," I said, "I could talk to Coach."

Mick didn't say anything, but Steve said, "Well, I'm not sure Coach is gonna be listening to you that much, Tom."

I didn't know where that was coming from. "Whatdya mean?" I asked.

"Well," Steve said, "From what I heard, Coach is saying you might not be on the team next year."

"What?" Mick jumped in, "Why the hell wouldn't Bonner be on the team?"

"Think about it," Steve said, "All the stuff about that fire and everything. Coach doesn't need that kind of crap."

It hit me kind of hard. I hadn't thought about that kind of stuff. That people might not want me around because some of 'em thought I'd set that fire. Made me kind of sick to my stomach.

"Aw, that's baloney," Mick said.

"Hey," Steve said, "I'm not sayin it's true. All's I'm sayin is that's what I heard."

"Well, it's baloney anyway," Mick said emphatically.

I felt pretty lousy and then, to make me feel a little worse, I looked out towards Russell and who do I see but Ronnie and Jeffrey.

I don't know, it was kind of weird, seeing those guys when I was with these guys. I mean, they were just kind of separate in my mind. I had my school friends, like Mick and Steve and the guys, and then I had my home friends, like Ronnie and Jeffrey. Didn't seem like the two groups ought to ever come together. Maybe because I was a different person with each group.

But here they were. I saw them and they saw me. The twain was gonna meet. What the hell do you do? I couldn't just ignore those guys, could I?

They waved and I went up to the fence to talk to them.

"Hey, Tom," Ronnie said, "What's up?"

"Hey. Not much. Just playin some basketball."

"School friends?" Jeffrey asked, making it sound nasty somehow.

It pissed me off, the way he said it. Like I was trying to be high-falutin or something. Like he was saying I thought school friends were better than my other friends. Friends like them.

"Yeah," I said, without thinking it out much, "You wanna play?"

I didn't think they would. I mean I'd never played ball with these guys, didn't even know if they knew how to play or anything. Sure as hell, though, Jeffrey said, "Sure, we'll play with you guys."

They came into the playground and we all shot around a while. Jeffrey and Ronnie were pretty pathetic, really. I mean the ball was bouncing off the backboard and they just looked kinda goosey out there. I was a little embarrassed that Steve and Mick and them were seeing these guys, these other friends of mine, looking so dopey on the court.

No way out now, though, so I said, "Let's play."

"Okay, what's teams," Steve asked.

We divided up and played for maybe twenty minutes or so until Jeffrey called time. He was breathing real hard and you could see he was beat. Ronnie didn't look much better. It was a little embarrassing for them to call time like that. My school buddies and I would usually play for hours at a much faster pace than this. Shows what smoking does, I guess.

We sat down under the basket. Jeffrey and Ronnie were really panting. Part of it was, that they were wearing Levi's while the rest of us had shorts on. Had to be tough trying to run around in the summer heat like that with long pants on, especially jeans.

"Hey," Ronnie said, "You guys play up here a lot?"

"Yeah, well, once in a while," Mick answered.

"You always wear those sissy short pants?" Jeffrey threw in.

Nobody said anything. What a stupid damn thing for Jeffrey to say. I mean like NBA players wore jeans or something.

"What the hell are you talking about?" I said, looking over at Jeffrey.

He was too winded to come up with his usual smartass answer, so we all just sat there a while and didn't say anything. I didn't know how this was going to end. I wanted Jeffrey and Ronnie to just go away. They really didn't have any business here. This was school stuff. Basketball stuff.

Then things got a lot worse. We were sitting there and up Russell came this old Ford, windows down, real slow like. I saw Jay through the shotgun window and he saw me at the same time. They went on past and for a few minutes I thought we'd escaped a confrontation, but then they turned and came back down the other side of Russell. They pulled up next to the fence and got out.

There were five of them. Jay and Freddie and some of their asshole buddies. They sauntered into the playground and over to where we were sitting.

"Hey, Tom," Jay said, "Whatcha up to?"

"Not much," I said, looking up at him, "Just a little b-ball."

"B-ball, huh?" he said with a stupid grin, "Who's winnin?"

"Who cares?" I said, "Just a friendly game."

"Well," he said, "I bet we could take alla you pussies."

"What?"

"You heard me," Jay said, "We can whip your asses."

"I don't know about that," I said.

"Well come on then."

I had a real bad feeling about this. Freddie had this evil freaking grin on his face and it was like they'd set the whole thing up or something, but what could we do but play?

"Shoot for first?" I asked.

"Nah," Jay said, "You guys take it."

Mick took the ball out and passed in to Steve. He dribbled downcourt, then passed off to me and I immediately hit Mick, right under the basket. He put it up for an easy score.

One of their guys took it out and passed in to Jay. Jay impressed me a little that he even knew how to dribble. He went for the basket, tried a jumper and missed by a mile.

I took it out and passed in to Steve. He was acting a little smart-assed, seeing these guys didn't know that much about basketball, and he dribbled real fast past a couple of their guys and headed for the basket. He stopped a couple of feet short and hit a jumper instead of the lay-up I thought he was going for.

Their in. Jay brought it in himself and drove right for the basket. He tried a lay-up, but Mick was there and batted it easily away. Jay was fuming.

On our in, Steve took it out and passed to me. While I stood there looking for somebody to pass to or figuring out whether to take it in myself, I noticed a car parked over by the fence. There were two guys in suits sitting in the car. The guy riding shotgun looked a whole lot like Detective Pearse. Crap, I thought to myself, that guy's tailing me now.

"Come on, play ball," Jay shouted. I fed it in to Jeffrey and he tried to go to the basket but Freddie was in his way. As Jeffrey tried to dribble around him, Freddie lashed out. I saw it happen. Freddie swung his elbow up at Jeffrey's chin. Whop! I heard it connect and I saw Jeffrey go down.

This isn't the way you play basketball. I went running up to Freddie. "Hey," I said, "That's a foul."

"Oh yeah?" Freddie said with a sneer, "You want some of the same?"

I glanced over at the car by the fence and saw Pearse watching. He had a big grin on his cop face. "No," I said quietly, "Not just now, Freddie."

"Well," he said, "I guess if you ever want a piece of me you know where to find me."

Steve and Mick and the guys were wide-eyed. They'd never played basketball Freddie-style before. Ronnie was kneeling over Jeffrey to see if he was okay. It took a few minutes for Jeffrey to come around, and even then he was pretty groggy, his head kind of rolling around and all.

Jay was strutting around and gloating. "I guess we win, huh?" he laughed.

Ronnie and I got Jeffrey to a sitting position, then up to his feet. "What happened?" he asked. Neither Ronnie nor I answered.

"Hey," he repeated, "What happened?" Then it must have sort of dawned on him. "Did he hit me? He hit me, didn't he?"

Freddie and his guys had started wandering off, back to their car, laughing and cutting up the whole way.

"That rotten SOB hit me, didn't he?" Jeffrey was screaming by now and acting like he was going to go charging after Freddie. Ronnie and I were holding him up and holding him back at the same time.

"Yeah," Ronnie said, "Freddie nailed you with an elbow."

"I'll kill him," Jeffrey ranted, "I'm gonna kill the bastard."

"Take it easy, Jeffrey," I said, "You'll get your turn. Our time will come. This just isn't it."

The old Ford with Freddie's gang in it peeled away from the curb, pulled a u-turn right in the middle of Russell, and sped off east, tires squealing the whole way. Pearse acted like he didn't see it, never even took out after them, but just kept staring at me. I don't think there was ever a time I wanted to give somebody the finger so bad, but I stayed cool. I didn't have a whole lot of choice.

There was a little stream of blood coming out of Jeffrey's nose and he was still having a hard time standing, but still going on about how he was going to kick Freddie's ass. Ronnie looked over at me and mouthed the words, "Let's get him home."

I nodded. "Listen," I said to Mick and the guys, "We gotta get goin."

They were still a little dazed, I think. Steve said "Yeah, okay." Mick just stood there and didn't say anything. Neither did any of the rest of my school buddies. They seemed kinda stunned by how the basketball game had turned into something else entirely. Something they'd never seen before and probably hoped they wouldn't see again.

Ronnie and I started walking off, each holding on to Jeffrey with one arm to steady him. I looked back at Steve and Mick. "See ya next week," I said.

"Yeah," Mick answered weakly, "See ya."

I was wondering if I would see those guys the next week. I mean, first, because they'd seen the kind of guys I hung around with at home and I thought maybe they'd figure I was just a hood like the rest of them and wouldn't want anything more to do with me. They'd probably figure me for some kind of scuzz-bucket who'd just been hiding it all this time. That would be that.

Then too, things were just happening so fast and coming apart so fast that I didn't know what next week might bring. I might be back in jail or going to trial or who knows what? I'd always tried to keep school apart from everything else, but it looked like that just wasn't going to work anymore. Everything in my whole goddam life was turning to crap.

Ronnie and I got Jeffrey to his house and his Mom came to the door as we were trying to sneak him inside.

"What happened?" she screeched, "What happened to my Jeffrey?"

It embarrassed the hell out of him. "Aw Geez, Mom," he said, "It was a basketball game for chrissake."

"Jeffrey Deems," she said, "You do not speak like that. You do not take the Lord's name in vain. Now get in here and let me tend to you."

She pulled him through the door and the screen door slapped shut behind the two of them. Then she turned and looked back at Ronnie and me. "Thank you for fetching my son to me," she said, "I shall pray for your souls as well as his."

135

Ronnie and I looked at each other and grinned. He had the presence of mind as we turned to walk away to say, "Thank you, Mrs. Deems, and bless you."

The afternoon was only half over. Usually, I'd have been up at the playground until at least four or five, and would have come home exhausted. Because of the way the game ended, though, it was still just the middle of the afternoon and I sure didn't feel like going home just yet. Ronnie and I walked down the sidewalk a ways.

Finally he said, "Hey, you wanna come over to my place a while?"

"Sure," I said, "Why not?"

Ronnie lived just down the street from me. It occurred to me that like Mick, I'd never been in his house either. It wasn't because of anything weird like with Mick, though, it was just that there was never any reason for me to go in Ronnie's house. I mean we were pretty much always on the street together so I'd never had to go by to pick him up or anything.

We went around to the back yard and in his back door. I noticed something hanging on the side of the door frame that he touched as we went in and then he like kissed his hand where he'd touched the thing.

"What's that?" I asked.

"A mizzuza," he said, "You're supposed to touch it and say a prayer like every time you go in or out of the house."

"Huh," I said, "I never heard of that. That's not Catholic is it?"

"Nah," he said, "It's Jewish. It's a Jewish thing."

"Geez, Ronnie," I said, "I never knew you were..."

"A Jew?" he interrupted, "Yeah, we're Hebes." He didn't even look back at me when he said that. He was leading me down the hall, through a door and down into the basement of his house. He pulled the chain and turned on a light as we went down the stairs. I felt pretty dopey not knowing Ronnie was Jewish, him living that close and us being friends for so long and all. I was trying to think how many times I might have used a word like "kike" around him without even thinking about it. I mean, I didn't have any prejudice against Jews or anything, it was just a word my Old Man used all the time, and really, I don't think he was prejudiced against them either. Maybe it was a word his old man had used.

"Ronnie," I said, "If I ever said anything..."

"Ah, don't worry about it," he said, "It's my folks that're Jews anyway. I'm a B'hai."

"You're what?"

"B'hai," he said, "It's a middle eastern religion, only a hundred years old or so. It's real tolerant."

He walked across the basement turning on lights as we went. His basement had the same coal floor as most, but unlike mine, it seemed to be just one big open space, not divided up into compartments or anything. There was an old sofa against one wall and some other odds and ends kinda spread around the place, a few kind of odd pictures he'd put up on the walls. Under one of the lights there was a card table with a chess set all set up on it.

"You ever play?" Ronnie asked.

"Yeah," I said, "A little."

I'd taught myself the game a long time ago, and then taught my Old Man how to play. By the time I got to be thirteen or so, though, I was beating him all the time and he decided he liked checkers a lot more and wouldn't play chess with me anymore.

Ronnie had a bottle of some kind of stuff and the cap of the bottle had a little paint brush built into it and he went around to all the lightbulbs that were hanging down and painted the fluid from the bottle onto the bulbs.

"Ronnie," I said, "Whadya doin? What is that stuff?"

"Ah," he said, "Some kinda perfumey stuff. It kinda stinks down here. How 'bout a game?"

We sat down at the table to play. He had a set not much different than mine - a masonite board with plastic pieces. He picked up the two kings, hiding one in each hand and said, "Pick for white."

I guessed wrong and he started. King's pawn to King's Pawn three. He couldn't think I was that dumb, could he?

Turned out he did and he went on with the Fool's Mate routine. I thought that if he was going to try that, I might just as well piss him off with the old Scholar's Mate and brought my knights out.

It didn't take too long before both of us figured out the other guy wasn't going to fall for the easy stuff and we settled in to a pretty decent game of chess. It was pretty nice down in his basement. Dark and cool and nobody to bother you.

"So, this where you hang out?" I asked.

"Pretty much," he replied and took one of my rooks with his queen.

I retaliated by putting his King in jeopardy with one of my knights. "Check," I said.

He wisely castled to avoid the mate, but the advantage of the first check was mine.

"Well, what's this B'Hai stuff?" I asked, "I mean, do you go to church or what?"

He was advancing his pawns in phalanx, trying to pin me back to my side of the board. "Well, it's more like meetings where we talk about stuff," he said.

"What kinda stuff?" I asked, moving a knight out of danger.

"Stuff like why are we here and what should we be doing," he said, looking up at me, "You ever think about that?"

"Sure," I said, "I think about it a lot." I'd maneuvered around behind his pawns with a rook and was picking them off one at a time.

"And what do you think?" he asked.

"Huh?"

"I mean, why are we here? And where do we go when it's all over with. I mean look at Bryan, man. Where do you think he is now?"

"I dunno, Ronnie," I said, "I mean are you asking about the hereafter?"

"Well, yeah," he said, "I guess so." He had that queen in there again and took a knight. Five points for him.

"Well, here's what I think," I said real serious like, "It's sex. That's what I'm here after."

He looked up with this kind of hurt look on his face and then after a minute we both started laughing. "Yeah," he said, "I think that's what Bryan was after too."

"Yeah," I said, "And I bet wherever the hell he is, he's gettin his share."

"You think there's sex in heaven?" Ronnie said.

"Well if not, I'm not goin."

We laughed some more, but not at what was really funny which was that here were two guys bullshitting and making jokes about sex and neither one of us had "done it" in our whole lives. I mean at least I hadn't, and I figured Ronnie probably hadn't either, despite his sister being a whore and all.

It was a pretty close game. Ronnie was a lot tougher than I thought he'd be. Hell, I was surprised he even knew how to play. I was surprised at a lot of things about him and I really kind of wished I hadn't made that joke, because there was a lot of stuff I didn't understand and didn't have too many people to talk about with, but

138

then I figured there'd be other times for that. I hoped there'd be other times.

I took his queen with one of my knights and chased his king into a corner. I couldn't trap him, though, and the game ended a tie.

When I left Ronnie's place and walked across the street to my house, Pearse was parked half a block down, watching.

Watching. Always watching.

TWELVE

"One moment your life is a stone in you, and the next, a star."
Ranier Maria Rilke

I t was getting harder to go to school. Kids were avoiding me. Even friends. Steve wouldn't talk to me at all and even Mick seemed like he wasn't sure he wanted to walk with me anymore. It was like he was real uncomfortable being seen with me. I decided to let him off the hook. One morning while we were walking to school I told him I was going to start going a different way.

"You sure?" he asked, but I could see he was really relieved.

"Yeah," I said, "I mean I'll see ya once we get there and all."

"Right," he said, "OK."

I didn't blame him. Mick was a good guy. It was just hard hanging out with a guy everybody said was a jerk, a hood and maybe a killer, too. Had to be hard on Mick. I didn't blame him at all.

And really, it was easier for me. I mean I could just walk straight up Victor to McNair and then over. It was a lot faster, saved me a lot of steps and, well, it just saved me a lot of steps. It didn't bother me to have to walk into school by myself, to put up with the way kids looked at me. Screw 'em. I mean, what did they know? I was still me, and if they didn't like it, well, screw 'em. If they thought I was a hood, or that I'd burned a place down and killed some people, well, screw 'em.

There was a day when the results of the Big Test came out. The one we all figured the scholarships might be based on. Nobody at McKinley had ever won one of those. Nobody ever expected it would

141

happen at McKinley. Not the kids. Not the teachers. Probably not the head of the whole school system. McKinley wasn't that good. County schools were teaching calculus and stuff and McKinley was struggling with algebra. No way anybody at McKinley was ever going to score high enough to qualify for a scholarship.

The way the scores were given out was that you had to meet individually with the counselor, Miss Newman. She told you how you'd done and tried to point you in some kind of career direction. Each kid got about ten minutes worth of Newman counseling to decide how they were going to spend the rest of their lives. It didn't make much difference. Everybody already had that pretty much figured out anyway.

"Good morning, Thomas," Miss Newman said, ushering me into her little cubicle, "Please have a seat."

She was a tiny little woman, about a hundred years old and she looked like if you blew on her she'd shatter and crumble to dust.

"Well," she said, fumbling with some folders, "While I look up your scores, why don't you tell me your plans for the future?"

Where the hell have you been, I thought, my plans for the future are to try to keep my ass out of the slammer. Out loud I said, "Well, I'd thought about going to college."

"Hmmm," Miss Newman mulled, pulling up a folder, "Well, that may be difficult for you."

"Huh?"

"Well, your grades and scores aren't that good, you know."

"What? You sure you got the right guy?"

"Certainly," she said in kind of a snit, "Thomas Boudreaux, right?"

"Well, no ma'am, my name is Bonner."

"Oh, well, let's see then," she said, fumbling through more folders and selecting another one, "Oh. Oh yes, Mr. Bonner, you are definitely college material. Most definitely."

"So how'd I do?" I asked.

"Beg pardon?"

"On the test, how'd I do?"

"You did well," Miss Newman said, "Quite well, actually."

"Like?"

"Like 1480," she said.

"1480?"

"Yes, 1600 being a perfect score, of course," she said, kind of all a-flutter "Have you chosen a college yet?"

"Nah," I said, "Not yet Miss Newman. I thought I'd wait and go wherever Tom Boudreaux's goin." I got up and walked out of her little office.

It's funny, but it doesn't take long for stuff to get around, especially, I guess, competitive type stuff. Like PSAT and SAT scores were a competition among some of us, and even among the kids who weren't going to do so good, they wanted to know who was going to be the champion, or whatever.

Funny, too, but there always seems to be somebody who's the scorekeeper. A guy everybody goes to to find out how everybody did and who's winning. At McKinley, it was my friend The Schwantz. That wasn't really his name, of course, but because his name sounded close to that, once somebody figured out that "schwantz" was German for a certain part of the male anatomy, Bill became The Schwantz.

Anyway, when I left Newman's office I wandered down the hall and outside physics class Mick and The Schwantz were standing there, goofing around together. When they saw me come up, The Schwantz said, "So? How'd you do?"

Mostly I wouldn't have told people, but like I said, The Schwantz was kind of the scorekeeper, so I said, "1480."

He looked at Mick and then at me. "Well," he said, "You beat Agnieska and Bob. Haven't heard on Thor yet."

A month earlier it might have made me feel pretty good. I mean there was still Thor, but at least I was on top so far. Now, though, it didn't make too much difference. Didn't make me feel good. Didn't make me feel anything. I went on into the classroom and the day dragged on.

When school let out, I was getting my stuff out of my locker and Elaine came walking up.

"Tom," she said, "whatcha up to?"

"Nothin. What's goin on?"

"I dunno," she said, "Heard you're the Champ Test-taker."

"Yeah?" I said, "What about Thor and that Martin kid?"

"Nah, Thor came in under Bob and Agnieska. He's outta the picture and Martin dropped out of school a while ago."

"Huh," I said. This would have been important news not that long ago. There was even a rumor about some new scholarship, National Merit or something, based on either the PSAT or the SAT. Nobody seemed to know exactly how it worked and for me, it no longer seemed to matter much.

"Listen," Elaine said, "Whatdya doin after? I mean, ya wanna go for a walk or anything?"

"Sure," I said, "Yeah. A walk sounds good."

We went out together through the main entrance so we both had to give old McKinley's nose a rub for good luck as we went past. "Where you wanna go?" she asked.

"I dunno, let's just go."

We headed east on Russell and she grabbed my hand and we were walking together holding hands. It felt good that she liked me and all. I didn't know where we were going and she didn't know either but we were going there together and there was somebody who maybe believed in me and thought I was something besides a hood and a jerk and a guy who was going to jail.

Elaine was talking about stuff that happened in school and I guess I was answering and talking to her but none of it seemed like it was real or anything. We weren't even listening to a transistor radio like most kids would be doing on a walk. Finally, we'd walked all the way down to Ninth Street.

"Let's go over here," I said, and lead her south on Ninth Street to Lami.

At Ninth and Lami was the Polar Wave Ice House. It was a big building where they made ice, like for the old ice boxes and stuff before there were refrigerators.

On the Lami side of the building, there was this little chute where you could buy block ice. You put a quarter in the slot and a big old block of ice would come sliding down a wooden chute and into this box that was like made of zinc or something. The thing was that on a hot day you could stick your head in past the leather flap that covered up the box and it would feel all cool and icey and most of the time there would be chunks of ice down there between the wooden runners that the ice blocks rode down on. You could pop 'em in your mouth and they felt so good and so cold. Wasn't anyplace else like that.

So I showed that to Elaine and I showed her how to stick her head under the leather flap and I fished out some ice for her and for me and she acted like it was a big thing or something - something she'd never seen before. We took the ice and walked on down across Broadway and headed down towards the river.

It was a lot like a walk my Old Man and I had taken a hundred times. Down below Broadway. Down to the river. They were tearing things up down there, making way for the new factories and businesses, but you could still find your way through. Lotsa vacant houses, though. Empty business buildings, too. This was that Kosciusco Project my old man got so upset about. A thousand people kicked out of their houses. Small businesses forced to close up shop.

We zigged and zagged around a little and went past all the old stuff down there. Past Schneider Packing, where my friend Wally worked after school. Past Hager Hinge, where Bryan used to figure he'd end up working. There or Bemis Bag. How many of these places would be left, I wondered, when they got finished improving things?

When we got to the railroad tracks there was an automatic arm that went up and down if a train was coming and it made me think about how when my Old Man and me used to go down there it wasn't automatic. Instead, there was a guy who sat in a little wooden guard shack who pulled a lever or something to let the gate down or up. I wondered what the hell happened to that guy.

I told Elaine about it and she just said, "Well, Tom, things change."

"Yeah," I said, "But I don't know if I like it."

She didn't say anything, but just squeezed my hand.

The ground down there below Broadway, down close to the river, was real different. Like how it was in our basements, all coal-mixed and stuff. Except by the river it was reddish and mixed up with different stuff. From the old factories, I guess. There were rusty old metal shavings and stuff mixed in with the dirt and it made it all red and made it smell funny and be a way that was only around the river.

We walked on down past the factories, past the red funny-smelling dirt and got to the road that lead right along the river. I knew this part of the city like it was home. Me and the Old Man had walked down here a hundred times. I guess maybe that's something that's different about St. Louis, or at least about our neighborhood. You can walk down to the river and be away from everything and everybody. You can just *be*. California and Florida have beaches; we've got the river.

Elaine and I walked on past Lefton Iron Works. It was a scrap iron place where the dirt was even more red and had iron shavings and stuff all through it. You could watch the giant magnets on the end of a crane picking up hunks of metal junk and dumping it into the big old hopper cars on the rail line that ran along the river and you were in a different world from school or your Mom and Dad and all the stuff they were all trying to tell you. It made you want to stay there and watch and not be part of anything else.

"Tom," Elaine said, "Do you come down here a lot?"

"Not so much anymore," I said, "Used to."

We found a little spot off the road that looked out over the river and sat down together. Just up from us was the old railroad bridge and I remembered when I was a kid watching the guy jump off. For some reason, I decided to tell Elaine about it.

"We were just standing there together," I said, "My Old Man and me, and this guy jumps off. I saw him fall most of the way down but then the Old Man grabbed me and pulled me into him and wouldn't let me watch any more."

"How come?" Elaine asked.

"I dunno. I remember after, him telling Mom he was afraid I'd be scarred for life, seeing something like that."

"Sounds like he's a pretty good Dad," she said.

I guess I hadn't really thought about it that much 'til then. "Yeah," I said, "I guess he was. I mean is."

We sat there together for a while and didn't say much of anything. We were sitting close together, touching. It felt good. The sun was warm and the Mississippi was running there in front of us, all muddy and carrying a load of stuff down with it, big hunks of boards and tree trunks and all sorts of stuff. Just floating along, heading south, heading for the Gulf of Mexico, I guess.

I'd been down here lots of times, with the Old Man and with Bryan and sometimes by myself but there wasn't any time that felt better than this, bringing Elaine down here and sitting with her. Watching the river go by.

I mean, it wasn't really a pretty place or anything. It wasn't like there was a lawn or flowers or anything like that by the river. It was just a bunch of dirt and weeds and thistles and stuff and you could smell the river mud down close to the bank, but it wasn't so bad. At least you were away from things and you could think and talk and maybe make sense.

"So, Tom?" Elaine said.

I was kind of daydreaming or something and had to bring myself around. "Yeah?" I said.

"Watcha gonna do?"

"Huh? Whatdya mean?"

"Well," she said, "With all the stuff that's goin' on, and after it's over and all."

"I don't know, Elaine," I said, "I don't know what I'm gonna do."

"Well, I think you gotta get outta here," she said.

"You mean run away?"

"No," she said, "Definitely not run away. I mean you're gonna get through this thing that's happening now. I know you will. I'm talking about after that."

"I don't know if I can think that far ahead," I said.

"You gotta. This is gonna be over and done with and you're still gonna have a lotta decisions to make, Tom."

"Yeah, Elaine, I guess you're right," I said, "But right now it doesn't seem like I got many choices."

She looked up at me and took her hand and kind of caressed my face. "But you do have choices, Tom," she said, "And I hope you make the right ones."

She was looking into my eyes and she had this look in her eyes that was so soft and sweet that it made me feel all funny inside and I put my arm around her and pulled her close to me and pulled her face up to mine and her lips were close to mine. So close. I could smell her hair and then it just kinda happened. We were kissing. I felt her arms go around me and pull me close. I'd never felt anything like that before and it was way different from the other night at the Peppermint with that girl. It was like two completely different things and it made me feel almost kind of dizzy or something and I knew that there was something very special about Elaine. I knew that I wanted to be around her a lot and get to know her more and that I would never in my whole life, no matter what happened, ever forget that time. That time of our first kiss.

It was almost too intense. I had to get up and walk away. I went down the bank and picked up a rock and pitched it out at a plank that was floating by. Elaine came up behind me. "Can you make 'em skip?" she asked quietly.

"Sure, how many times?" I said, selecting two nice flat rocks and clacking them together to knock off any hunks of dirt that might spoil the streamlining. I tossed the first one out side-arm and low angled against the current - flup-flup-flup-flupflup - five skips, a modest first shot.

"Oooh," she said, "That was neat. Do another one."

The second rock was really smooth and round and hit the water with scarcely even a ripple, making a huge leap to the second impact, then skipping six more times before the skips were so quick and small you couldn't count them.

Elaine's face lit up and she clapped her hands. "Oh, show me how to do that," she said.

For a minute I thought she was bullshitting me. You know, the way girls do sometimes to make you feel like some kind of bigshot or something, even about something dopey like skipping rocks.

"Aw, come on," I said, "You can do it."

She picked up a rock and heaved it out and it went straight in like, well, a rock. She frowned. "Show me," she said.

I hesitated a minute and then thought that if she was bullshitting me she was doing a good enough job of it that at least I ought to pay her the respect of playing along.

"It's mostly about picking the right rock," I said, kicking around at the stones at our feet, "Look here."

We crouched down together and I sorted through the rocks and pointed out some that would make good skippers and others that wouldn't because they were too thick or irregular or too small or too big. She was looking at the rocks I was showing her, but also looking up into my eyes. It was a little disconcerting.

I gave her three or four stones I thought would work for her and then we stood up and I showed her how you hold the rock between your thumb and forefinger and aim low and toss it sidearm and give it a little spin as you let go. Her first try got one nice little skip.

"Yay," she said, "I did it. Now I'm gonna try for two."

She threw the rocks and asked me to find more for her. In a little while she was hitting three or four skips pretty regularly and it really seemed like she was having a good time.

"Can you fish down here?" she asked.

"Nah, I don't think so," I said, "I mean I guess you could, but there's so much crap in the water I'd be afraid to eat anything you pulled out."

"That's a shame," she said.

"Yeah. I mean I think maybe some of the folks over at the Hooverville might fish here, but that's about it."

"Hooverville?"

"Yeah, there's a Hooverville not too far south of here. I've been by the place once or twice with my Old Man."

"Tom," she said, "What is a Hooverville?"

It never dawned on me until then that somebody might not know what a Hooverville was. I mean it was a regular part of my folks' vocabulary. When times were tough, they'd joke about having to go down to Hooverville to live, and I was pretty sure most of the kids in my neighborhood at least knew about Hoovervilles, even if maybe they hadn't seen one. But then Elaine wasn't exactly from my neighborhood.

"It's like a little village for people who don't have homes. They're these little claptrap shacks put together out of whatever's layin around. They're folks who lost their jobs and stuff in the Depression. People call it different things – Hooverville, Chickentown, Happy-Land."

"Happy-Land?" she said and thought for a minute, "Can we go there?"

"No," I said, "Believe me, Elaine, you don't want to go down there."

"Why not? It sounds kinda neat."

"It's not neat. It's sad. And the people there, well, they're not like us."

"Hmmmm," she said, "Tom, do your folks talk about the Depression a lot?"

"Yeah. I mean not like every day or anything, but it's there."

"Mine, too," she said, "I guess it was a scary time, huh?"

"My Old Man's always talking about people jumping out office windows cuz they lost everything in the stock market, and how families lost their house and had to move in together, like with aunts and uncles and stuff."

"Funny they don't teach about stuff like that in school, isn't it?" she asked.

"Well," I said, "By the time they get done with Greeks and Romans and stuff that happened a thousand years ago, I guess there's no time left for stuff that happened to our moms and dads."

"I think history would make a lot more sense if they taught it the other way around," she said, "You know, starting with now and working backwards."

"Yeah, that makes sense, but I guess they've been teaching it the same way so long now that they don't know how to change."

"Isn't it funny?" she said, "I mean seems like once you're an adult you forget how to change, or get scared of it or something."

"Yeah," I said, "I hope I don't get that way."

She took my hand and looked up at me with those great liquid eyes of hers. "You won't," she said.

I couldn't look into those eyes very long without wanting to kiss her and do all sorts of stuff, so I turned away and tugged at her to follow. "Come on, lemme show you something."

I led her away from the riverbank, across to where the railroad tracks ran. Two locomotives were slowly pulling a short line of box cars our way. I picked up a couple of the white riprap rocks that lined the track bed and put them up on the rail nearest us.

"Got a penny?" I asked.

She fumbled in her little purse, pulled out a penny and handed it to me. I laid it on the rail a few feet from the rocks. There was a low concrete wall a short way from the tracks and I took Elaine over there and we sat down together. The locomotives pulled closer. They were the workhorse diesel jobs and they were drawing their load up a slight grade. You could feel the pounding of the huge diesel engines in your chest.

"Watch the rocks," I said.

The big steel leading wheel hit the first rock and the rock exploded in a puff of white smoke. A few seconds later the second rock met the same fate. It was a simple-minded kind of fun, I suppose, sort of a home-made fireworks display on a small scale, and Elaine seemed to like it.

After the train passed, I went over and retrieved the penny, handing it to Elaine. It was pancaked flat into a really thin, oblong shape. Elaine was delighted.

"Oh, neat," she said, "I'm gonna keep this and it will always be our - to remind us of today." Then she stood up close, looked up and put her arms around me and she was in my arms and we were kissing again.

We stood there and leaned against that concrete wall and kissed and held each other for a long time. Her hair was so soft and smelled so nice that I kept putting my face in it and nuzzling up against her neck and her ear. Her skin felt so smooth and fresh that just to have our cheeks touch like that, so light and just brushing each other, seemed like the nicest thing there could be. Seemed for a while like there wasn't anything else, just the two of us there by the railroad tracks, near the river on a sunny, warm afternoon.

After a while she pulled back and little and brushed the hair from her face, where I'd gotten it all mussed up. "Tom," she said, "Can I ask you something?"

"Sure. What?"

"Well, I don't want you to take this wrong, but..."

"What, Elaine?"

"Well, do you have any other girlfriends?"

"Huh?"

"I mean, are you going out with anybody or anything?"

"No," I said, "Of course not."

"Good," she said, "Cuz I wouldn't want you to be."

"Well, I'm not."

"Good. Can I ask you something else?"

"Go ahead."

"That girl at the library, was she your girlfriend?"

Oh man, that gave me a chill. I didn't think Elaine would even know about that. I mean I knew she knew about the fire and all, but I never figured she'd have heard about Lovey. It made me feel funny to even think about Lovey while I was here with Elaine. Just thinking the name "Lovey" made me feel sad. Broke up the mood with Elaine. I looked away.

"She was, wasn't she?" Elaine said.

"No, Elaine," I said almost in a whisper, "She was just a kid. Just a nice little kid."

We sat there for a while not saying anything and then Elaine just reached over and put her hand on my shoulder. "I'm sorry," she said, "I shouldn't have even asked about that, should I?"

"Come on," I said, straightening up and looking up the hill away from the river, "It's getting late. We better get going."

I started walking away and she fell in alongside me. It was steady uphill going and we didn't talk too much. I was thinking about her asking about Lovey and wondering if it was that she was jealous or curious or if she thought maybe I did it. Maybe I had something to do with Lovey and maybe I set the fire and killed her. The funny thing is that it didn't even make me mad that she might think that. It just made me sad and kinda tired or something.

It's a long climb going west away from the riverfront and it's real steep from the river up to Twelfth Street. After that it levels off a little, but it's still a hill. Elaine was keeping up with me and not complaining, but I could see it wasn't easy going for her and it made me feel kind of stupid for bringing her down there. I wondered if she was thinking by now that I was some kind of a jerk.

We walked to her house a little different way than we'd come down, passed by where they were starting to excavate for the new highway. They hadn't done much, just dug a big hole for something or other, but Elaine and I stopped for a few minutes to look at it and catch our breaths.

"Is that for I-44?" she asked.

"Yeah, I guess so."

"Steve tell you we're gonna hafta move?"

"What? No. What do you mean?"

"The highway's gonna take both our houses. They're gonna condemn them or something. We have to move."

"When?" I asked, "When do you have to get out?"

"I dunno. We've got a while, I think."

"You know where you're gonna move to?"

"No," she said, "Mom and Dad are trying to figure it out. We've been in that house a long time."

"Doesn't seem right," I said, "Making people move just to put in a road."

"No, it doesn't," she said, "My folks are pretty upset about it. I just hope we get to stay someplace close."

"Yeah," I said, looking into her eyes for the first time since we'd left the riverfront, "So do I."

Then Elaine got this funny look on her face. "Tom," she said, "Do you think this is history?"

"Whaddya mean?"

"Well, all this tearing stuff down. All the people moving, leaving the old neighborhoods. Moving out to the county."

"I dunno," I said, "But if it is, if this is history, I bet they get it all wrong. Fifty years from now some guy from New York'll come out, spend a coupla days here and think he knows St. Louis. Probably won't know about Happy-Land. Probably won't even get the names of the rivers right."

"Yeah," Elaine said, "Then he'll put it in some book and people will think cuz it's in a book it must be right. That's what kids'll learn and it'll be all messed up."

"Yep."

"Hey, maybe you oughta write a book about it."

"Me?" I said, "Yeah, right."

"No. You could," she said, kinda getting all excited, "You could write the book."

"Well, I dunno. Maybe when I'm old and gray. If I live that long."

I walked her the rest of the way to her house and I was glad to see Steve wasn't around when we got to her front porch. Elaine's mom was sitting out on the porch when we got there, but she was cool enough to go inside after chatting with us for a couple of minutes. I was grateful. I had to find out what was going on.

"Elaine," I blurted out, "I gotta ask you what you think of me."

"What I think of you? Tom, what do you mean?"

I couldn't look at her. I looked down at the ground instead and then, at the last minute, caught her eye and then looked away again. "You know," I said, "I mean, you don't think I did it, do you?"

"Did what?" she began, then figured it out, "Oh, Tom, you're not talking about the fire are you?"

"Yeah, the fire and that whole thing."

She took both of my hands in hers. "Look at me, Tom," she said, but I still couldn't. "Look at me," she repeated and I looked into those eyes.

"Tom," she said, "I know you didn't do it. I know you couldn't do a thing like that. Don't you understand yet how I feel about you?"

"Well," I said, "It's not like I'd blame you or anything. I mean people are sayin...."

"I don't care what people are saying," she said, "They don't know you. Not like I do. And I want to know a lot more. I want so much for us that I can't even tell you."

"Well, just in case," I said, "I mean just in case you ever wondered, I didn't do it. I didn't have anything to do with it, Elaine."

She smiled. "You didn't have to say that," she said, "I never had any doubts. One more thing - you know how sometimes you hear a song and it makes you think of someone?"

"Yeah," I said, "I guess."

"Well, you wanna know what song makes me think of you?"

"Sure," I said, "Which one?"

"It's 'You Send Me.'"

Wow.

Sam Cooke. 'You Send Me.' I was flying.

We had a front porch type of goodnight kiss then and I headed out through the front gate. "I had a nice time, Tom," she called after me, "Thanks for showing me about skipping and stuff."

"See ya," I said and waved.

"And I'll save our penny," she said, returning my wave.

153

It was half as far back from Elaine's house to mine as it was all the way from the river to her place, but it didn't seem very far at all, because I was feeling pretty good. You Send Me. It had worked out okay. She was such a neat girl, and I kept thinking about the way those kisses were, how she felt in my arms, how her hair smelled and everything about her. And it felt so damn good to know that she really liked me and didn't believe any of the stories that were going around. Made me feel like I could get through it, could figure it all out, could make them see I was innocent and get on with my life. A life that would for sure have Elaine in it, no matter what.

It was twilight and the sun was going down. Seemed like a great time of the evening as I walked the last few blocks to my house. I was really happy for the first time in a long time and I guess that's what a girl, a special girl like Elaine, can do for a guy.

I walked down Victor Street and when I rounded the corner at Eleventh I saw my Old Man's car part way up on the sidewalk in front of our house. Freddie and his gang were behind it, pushing it further up on the sidewalk and laughing their asses off.

THIRTEEN

"In the end, the maw of the sea-hag gets us all."
James Thurber

My Old Man's car wasn't really a car at all. It was a grey 1954 Willys Jeep station wagon, three (plus overdrive) on the tree, a little four-banger under the hood that provided excellent gas mileage and went from zero to forty in - well, forever. In a headwind, forty was about the top end, too. One vacation we drove all the way from St. Louis to Chicago, never once getting over forty miles an hour. Boy, was that a drive. Windows down in the summer heat, watching three hundred miles of corn fields going by so slow you could count the stalks, while sleek, chromed-up Chryslers and Cadillacs zipped by us like we were standing still.

The Willys was my Dad's baby, though. He'd wanted a jeep ever since he got back from the war, and when one of my uncles put his up for sale, the Old Man jumped at it. It was already old when we got it and I don't think my uncle had taken very good care of it, but Dad forked over $800, his dream come true at last.

I disliked the vehicle from the moment I laid eyes on it. It was too different. There were some things it was cool to be different about, but your car was not one of them. The Willys was boxy when everyone else's car was streamlined, it had no chrome whatsoever, and instead of that big, deep throated V8 roar, it went putt-putt. Really. I'm not kidding. The rear windows on the thing didn't even roll down, but slid open to the side, and the rear seat was up high so all your friends had a really good view of you riding around town with your folks in the dorkmobile. For a kid, especially for a teenager, the Willys was a nightmare.

But it was our nightmare. Nobody else, especially Freddie and his bunch, had any business screwing with it.

When I came around the corner that evening and saw those guys laughing as they pushed the Willys up on the sidewalk, it was like the final slap in the face from a world that seemed focused on making my life miserable. I mean, they weren't just insulting me, they were insulting my Old Man and my whole family. Some little fuse in my head blew, or maybe a whole bunch of them. I yelled out and tore across the street.

There were four guys over there, Freddie and Jay on one side of the car and two other goons on the other side. When they saw and heard me, they all started running. I guess it must be an instinct or something, when you're doing something wrong and somebody catches you at it, or maybe it was just that I was charging at them and yelling like that, but they all took off even though there were four of them and just one of me. All, that is, except Freddie.

Freddie didn't give a damn who caught him at what or who was coming at him. Oh, he took a few steps back, but then he realized it was just me and he stopped. Just stood there and waited.

"What the hell're ya doin?" I yelled when I got up to him.

"What's it to ya?" he said with this stupid grin.

"What's it to me? That's my Old Man's car, that's what"

"So?"

"Well, what's the idea of pushing it around like that?"

By that time Jay and the other two guys had seen what was going on and wandered back. Jay had to get his two cents in. "Oh, we thought yer old man's car might get hit out there in the street," he said, "so we put it up here where it's safe."

"You smartass son-of-a-bitch," I said, "You better keep your goddam hands off our car."

"Oh yeah?" he said, "Or else what?"

"Yeah," Freddie added, "And watch out what you're callin my friends, too."

I was so worked up even Freddie didn't faze me. "Up yours," I said.

I'd already seen how Freddie worked, so the elbow coming up didn't catch me by surprise like it had Jeffrey that day on the playground. I ducked back out of range, and as his elbow came by, I shoved hard in the direction he was already going. Freddie stumbled into the side of the car and hit his head.

"Goddam it, Bonner," he said, squinting his eyes, "Now that's gonna cost ya." He came at me. I waited until the last second, then stepped aside, put my right leg out and gave him a shove. Down he went, face first.

When he pulled himself up on one knee, he was really fuming. His face was all scrunched up and scraped from the fall and he had this look of pure hatred burning from his eyes. He stood all the way up, clenching and unclenching his fists. Jay and the other two were behind me, a little surprised by what had happened so far. This time though Freddie wasn't taking any chances. "Grab him!" he yelled.

Jay and one of the other guys got hold of my arms, slammed me up against the Jeep and pinned me there. Freddie walked slowly up until he was right in my face. He was punching his right hand into his left palm, making this noise that didn't sound good at all, because it was probably the same sound my face was going to be making in a minute. Freddie was a guy who liked beating up on people.

"Awright, you dork," he snarled, "Now you're mine." Whump! A right hand to the gut doubled me over and just about tore me loose from the two jerks holding me.

When I was able to pull myself upright, I looked right at the bastard. "Too bad we didn't get to do this when Bryan was around," I said.

That earned me a shot in the side of the face. "Yeah," he said, "But O'Brien ain't around is he?"

That actually made me laugh. The stupid bastard didn't even know Bryan's name. None of the jerks did. I guess because sometimes we'd call out, "Oh, Bryan," they figured his name was O'Brien. Or maybe they'd just never heard of the name Bryan before. I mean, they were dumbshits. Whatever it was, at that moment it struck me as spectacularly funny and I started laughing out loud.

"What the hell's so goddam funny?" Freddie demanded, "You think this is funny or something?" Then he came around with a left hook to the other side of my face.

I didn't care. I was still laughing. "No," I said, "This isn't funny. You're funny, you goddam idiot!"

I got a left-right combo to the stomach that took my breath away for a minute, then a pop in the nose. Blood started flowing.

"Keep laughin," Freddie said, "Keep talkin."

Then he came at me with a flurry of punches all over the place. Something happened to me where it was like the whole thing was happening to somebody else. It hurt getting beat up like that but part of me was just watching it happen. Observing, like from outside it or something. Freddie's punches were heavy and doing a lot of damage but I could see that he wasn't very fast, and I knew right then that Bryan could've taken him.

It wasn't a good idea, but when Freddie got tired and had to take a little break from beating the tar out of me, I told him. "You chickenshit bastard," I spit out together with a lot of blood, "Bryan would have cleaned up on you."

That didn't make Freddie happy at all and he started whaling away again. I would probably have gone out about then, except good old Jeffrey came flying out of his front door, leaped into the air and onto the four of us, me and Freddie and Jay and the guy holding me. I guess he must have seen what was going on or heard it, because it was almost in front of his house.

We all hit the ground together and rolled over and over. Jeffrey was the first up on his feet, followed by Jay. The two of them squared off. Jay tried to throw a roundhouse right, but Jeffrey parried it easily. Pop-pop-pop, Jeffrey hit Jay square in the face with three quick, professional boxing-style jabs, rocking him backwards.

I pulled myself to my feet and I could see Diane standing in the doorway where Jeffrey'd just come roaring to my rescue. "Diane," I yelled, "Call Ronnie. Quick." She disappeared back inside and I ducked back to avoid an elbow shot from Freddie. I was not feeling so hot and my vision was real funny, narrowing down, like. I could only see what was right in front of me. The rest was getting kinda dark and fuzzy.

Freddie was concentrating on killing me. He charged at me and I was too tired to dodge or anything, but Jeffrey stepped next to me and popped Freddie a good one alongside the head, knocking him off course.

"Come on," Jeffrey yelled, "Come on, Freddie, you piece of crap, let's see what you got."

But Freddie wasn't paying attention to Jeffrey. It was my ass Freddie was after. Jeffrey was just a minor distraction. He came at me again, and this time Jeffrey was busy trying to deal with the other guys.

I backed away from Freddie until I was up against the Jeep again. Freddie got this evil grin on his face and charged me. It was a good thing he was right in front of me, so I could still see him. As screwed up as I was, I was still fast enough to avoid his charge. Or maybe I was just lucky. I ducked aside and he went crashing into the car. I didn't know how many more moves like that I had, though.

I looked for Jeffrey and saw that one guy was holding him while Jay whaled away on him. Ignoring Freddie for a moment, I ran and launched myself into that group, carrying all of us to the ground.

I landed on top of the guy who'd been holding Jeffrey. I grabbed the jerk's throat and smashed him three good ones in the face, making his nose look a lot like mine must have. Then Jay stood up and kicked me in the side, knocking me off the guy.

I got back up and for a minute nobody was running at me or punching me. I looked around and could see that neighbors were watching. They didn't know what to do, I guess. The weird thought occurred to me that this might be the first gang fight on Eleventh Street.

Then somebody shoved Jeffrey into me. I caught him and helped him keep his balance. He looked over at me. "Where the hell's Ronnie?" he asked, out of breath.

I didn't have a chance to answer, because Jay came running at us with a beer bottle he'd picked up out of the gutter. I pushed Jeffrey aside and ducked the other way myself. Jay slammed the bottle into the back of my Old Man's car instead of my head.

I grabbed Jay by the shirt, lifted him and kicked his legs out from under him. Down he went. I dropped into a kneeling position on his chest and punched him twice in the face. Then Freddie grabbed me under both arms, pulled me off and threw me aside. I rolled out into the street and Freddie came after me.

I got up to one knee and tried to get ready to fend off Freddie's charge, but instead of coming at me, he veered off and ran right on past instead. Then Jay ran by on. That seemed real odd but by then everything was like it was in a dream or something. It took a minute or so before I picked up on what they must have heard. Sirens. Police sirens. They sounded close. Like maybe they were up on Twelfth Street and screaming our way fast. Somebody'd called the cops.

Everybody was running. Jeffrey was heading for his house and when he got to the door he turned around. "Bonner," he yelled, "Get goin, man. Get goin! You can't get caught in this!"

I was pretty beat up. Your mind doesn't quite work right after you've been hit like that. As hard as that. As many times as that. Things don't register right away.

"Tom," Diane screamed from the doorway beside Jeffrey, "Go! You gotta go, now!"

Everything was still foggy, but I started thinking that it wouldn't be good for the cops to catch me in a gang fight. Wouldn't be good for my case on the other thing, the fire thing. The arson thing. The murder thing.

All that stuff came flooding back to me and hit my mind like cold water from a hose. Woke me up, I guess. Oh man, I thought, I gotta get outta here. Can't let the cops catch me here.

I didn't know where to go. I thought about running home, but that would be the first place the cops would go. Then I thought about Jeffrey and Diane's, but they'd already high-tailed it inside and slammed the door behind them. If I got caught running in there, it would screw them up, too.

I felt trapped. Everything was closing in, the sirens getting closer by the second. I remembered what had happened right here a year ago. Some guy had escaped from Third District and had run all the way to the house right across the street from ours. I'd seen the whole thing. The guy was just a kid, not much older than me. He was running and the police were after him in cars and on foot. I saw it. He ran down the sidewalk and jumped the fence at Mrs. Kunz's house.

Mrs. Kunz's house of all places. Mrs. Kunz, who kept her place so immaculate, the grass in her side yard always so well mowed and trimmed and green, where most of us didn't even have a lawn. That was where this kid jumped the fence and ran right up on her porch. That was where the cops' bullets found him. Where he collapsed and died.

Mrs. Kunz had to go out every day from then on and scrub that porch, scrub off the blood. But she'd never be able to scrub away what happened there.

I didn't want to end up like that kid. I didn't want my Mom and Dad to find me dead on somebody's porch. So I ran. I ran as fast as I could, down between the houses, between Jeffrey's house and the one next door, and around the corner. I stopped there for a minute to catch my breath and try to figure out where to go next. I was breathing hard and I could see the cop cars' flashing lights and hear the sirens. I was as scared as I guess I'd ever been, but something was pumping me to keep going. To not get caught. To get out of this.

I was right there by Boozer's window. I was so focused on the cops and stuff that it took a minute before I noticed him kind of whining there behind me.

"Easy, Booze," I whispered, "It's okay, Boy."

He must have figured I had something for him to eat. He was pawing and scratching at the bars on his windows, trying to get me to give him whatever I had for him. But I didn't have anything to give him.

I was trying to figure out how the hell to get away, where to go, and at the same time it was hitting me again how goddam sad this dog's life was in that goddam basement, never getting let out, living in there in the dark in a room full of his own crap because I never saw those Hoosiers shovel out that basement and everybody knows a dog's sense of smell is better than ours so it's gotta be twice as bad for a dog to be down there in that crap than for a human being, and nobody or nothing ought to have to live like that.

It had gotten dark outside. There was just a slice of moon and the sky was full of stars. I looked up and tried to find a prayer but there wasn't one for somebody like me, somebody who might be a killer and who the cops were after. Somebody who was all alone. Somebody just like that poor goddam dog down there.

"Come on, Booze," I said between clenched teeth, "We're gettin outta here."

I kicked in the grate over the window. It took three good, hard kicks before it gave and old Booze came flying outta there, knocking me over and licking my face.

"Go on," I said, "Get goin. You're free, dog."

But Booze wouldn't leave. He kept wagging his tail like crazy and nuzzling me. I tried shoving him away two or three times, but he wouldn't go. Just kept coming back.

"Okay," I said, "I guess you're comin with me, boy, but I gotta tell ya, it's not such a good idea."

There was only one way I could figure I might be able to get away without the cops seeing me. I jumped the fence behind our yard, out into the yard behind us and into the alley behind that. Booze followed right behind.

When we made it to the alley I held back in the shadows, looked both ways. Didn't see anything going on, so I headed up the alley to Victor. Boozer padded along. I looked up the street and could see the red and whites flashing on the cop cars. I didn't see any cops or anything out on the street or looking down our way or anything. I stayed back behind the building and kept Booze right there beside me. It felt good not to be completely alone, even if it was just a dog with me.

We couldn't stay there long, though. We had to get out of there. We had to get away. I looked down at the dog. "Booze," I said, "You're free, man. You don't hafta go with me. Just go on and get outta here." But Booze wasn't going anywhere.

"Okay," I said, "I guess we're in it together."

I looked up and down Victor one more time, then ran as fast as I could across the street and dived into the weed cover on Dago Hill. Boozer jumped in right after me, rolled around and started licking my face.

"Good boy," I said, ruffling him up under his neck and around his ears, "Good ol Boozer. Now where we go from here?"

We were right next to one of the stone walls there on Victor Street. We climbed up together and I laid down on top of the wall and looked up towards Eleventh Street. I could see a lot of junk going on up there, cops running around and everything and I figured they had to be looking for us. For me, that is.

Boozer laid down next to me and I petted the top of his head. He made this kinda purring sound like he was telling me, yeah, we were in it together and he was my dog now. It wasn't just me anymore, it was me and my dog.

I edged away from the wall, back into the bushes and weeds. "Come on, Booze," I said, "This way."

I pushed my way through and finally found a path. The same path that me and the gang had followed up to the middle of Dago just a few days before. It was way different in the dark, though. People said there were snakes and stuff up on Dago. I'd never seen one, but I'd never been up there at night before, so I was watching where I put my feet.

There was a little wedge of moon, barely enough light to be able to stay on the path. By the time I got to the concrete pad in the middle of Dago my face and arms were scratched up, sticky from the weeds and bloody from the fight. I was a mess. I was breathing heavy, too, so I went over to the pond and sat down on the steps to catch my breath and try to figure out what to do next. Boozer sat beside me. He was panting too. I sat there and petted him and watched the reflection of the moon in the little pond. Looking back over my shoulder I could still see the glow from the lights on the police cars over by my house. I didn't hear any more sirens, though, and if the cops were looking for me, at least it didn't seem like they were coming this way. Not yet, anyhow. I was sure though that Pearse was out there someplace and it wouldn't be too long before he came after me. They'd search all through Dago.

I needed a drink of water real bad. Even the pond looked inviting. I wished I'd taken an extra minute to get a drink from the hose behind the house. Boozer went over and began lapping up the pond water. I envied him. I wanted to at least splash some of the water on my face to cool off a little, but I was so cut up I figured I'd wind up with some kind of infection. The water wasn't very clean, and who knows how many kids had thought it would be funny to take a leak in it. I'd be splashing piss all over my face. It reminded me of Irene back in chemistry class and that made me laugh a little in spite of everything. I could picture myself kneeling by the pond splashing water on my face and Irene standing there with Jake watching me, both of them laughing and saying, "I don't think that's water, Thomas."

I guess I was getting kind of goofy there for a while and maybe getting ready to pass out or something. I closed my eyes for a little bit and it would have been easy to fall asleep right there, but then something moved in the weeds on the other side of the pond and it scared me wide awake again. I started thinking that I couldn't stay there much longer because if the cops were out looking for me, they'd for sure start combing old Dago before the night was over.

It was hard to stand up again, but I did and headed over towards the path to the sink hole. Just to do something to try and cool off a little, I waded through the pond. The water felt nice. Made my tennis shoes all squishy, but who cares, right?

Boozer splashed through behind me again and we found our way to the sink hole. It looked funny at night, though. You couldn't tell how deep it was. It might have been six inches or sixty feet. There wasn't enough light and there wasn't anything to gauge it by. One thing was the same, though. If you got close to the edge the dirt started crumbling and running down into the pit. You had to back up quick or you'd go down with it.

I stood there for a while and tried to think if there was another place I could go to hide out, but nothing came to me. I looked up at the sky, made another stab at a quick prayer and stepped onto the slope. The dirt started cascading in around my feet right away and the only thing to do was get going downhill faster.

The sink hole was so deep light from the moon couldn't make it all the way to the bottom. I ran down the shifting dirt into a pitch black pit and thought to myself this had to be like running into the gates of Hell. Going there on purpose. Then that made me think of the sign I'd put up on the door to my basement room. Abandon All Hope, Ye Who Enter Here.

I made it almost all the way down before I stumbled and fell and rolled the last few yards. The dirt was a little more solid at the bottom and I didn't get buried like I was afraid might happen. Some of the dirt piled up around me while I laid on the ground at the bottom, but then it quit running down so I just laid there for a while. It felt pretty cool down there and I realized I'd landed near to the entrance to the cave or whatever it was. Cool air was flowing up out of the cave over me. That seemed like a good sign. I got on my hands and knees and felt my way over to the mouth of the cave. It was only about three feet around, half in the side of the pit and half in the bottom. You could barely make it out. Just a blob of total black against a background of almost-total black.

I felt around inside the hole and could tell it wasn't just a sheer drop-off. The cave, if that's what it was, had a floor that sloped downward, but only gradually. I took one more look at the night sky framed by the bowl shaped pit then lowered myself into the cave on my hands and knees and felt my way further inside. It was pretty damn scary because I didn't know if the cave might collapse or if the whole damn sink hole might all of a sudden start filling in or something, but I kept moving on, an inch at a time, trying to make sure I wasn't going to go tumbling over some kind of underground cliff or something.

I'd gone maybe ten or fifteen feet like that when the cave seemed to widen out. I couldn't feel all the sides of it around me like before, but I didn't know if they were just out of reach or thirty feet away and I didn't want to go exploring any more than I had to. I figured I'd gone far enough that no cop was likely to go looking down this hole and so I just leaned back against the dirt wall and rested there. I didn't know where Boozer was, but I guess he was probably too smart to follow me down into the pit, so maybe he'd gone scavenging somewhere for a midnight snack or something. I would have liked to have had him there next to me, to pet him and maybe have him lick my hand or something, but at the same time I was glad he didn't have to be in a place like this. It hit me that Boozer and I had sort of traded places. Now he was roaming around free out there and I was the one stuck in a dark hole under the ground.

The air was still moving past me from someplace further down and it felt so nice and cool, like the air conditioning in the movies and on some of the busses. I wasn't scared or anything anymore. I was just glad to be someplace I could rest for a while. I closed my eyes and I guess maybe dozed off for a little bit.

I don't think I'd slept very long before I heard a whistle and somebody calling out. At first I wasn't sure I heard anything at all, and then there it was again. A low whistle, then "Bonner - where you at?" It was Ronnie.

I climbed out to the cave entrance and I could see him walking around up at the top of the sink hole. He had a flashlight and he was waving it around down inside the pit looking for me. "Ronnie," I said, "I'm here. Don't come down, man."

He stopped and peered down into the blackness, but couldn't see me at first. Then the flashlight found me. "Tom, you okay?" he asked, shining the beam on my face.

"Yeah," I said, holding my hand up to keep the light out of my eyes, "I'm okay, but turn off that light."

"Wait a minute," he said, switching off the flashlight, "We're comin down."

"No, man, don't. It's too tricky," I said, but by then he'd already started down the slope. Did he say "we?"

I could hear the crunching of footsteps in the loose dirt and the sound of the dirt running down the slope. Ronnie'd figured out, too, that the best way was to try to run down the hill. Like me, too, he stumbled at the end and came rolling up right in front of me.

"Damn it, Ronnie, I told you not to come down here."

"Hey," he laughed, "I love you, too, buddy."

"Yeah, me too," whispered another voice behind him. It was Diane. She'd made it all the way down without falling.

"What are you guys doin here?" I asked, "Nobody saw you come this way, did they?"

"Naw," Ronnie said, "We waited til it was quiet and checked around real good before we headed over. Diane was the one who figured out you might be over here."

"We brought you some things," Diane said.

"Well," I said, "You guys wanna see my new place?" I led them down into the cave. It was a lot easier going with Ronnie's flashlight and when we got to where I'd fallen asleep, we could see it was a hollowed out area maybe ten feet across. There was plenty of room for the three of us. Diane opened a little paper bag, brought out a candle and lit it, sticking it upright in the dirt between us.

"Save the batteries," she said, and Ronnie turned the flashlight off.

"What's goin on out there?" I asked.

Ronnie and Diane glanced at each other. Ronnie was the first to speak. "Well, the cops caught Freddie and Jay and one or the other of 'em - maybe both - ratted on Jeffrey, so they came and took him off, too."

"Yes," Diane added, "And Tom, they know you were there, too. This really nasty detective was asking about you."

"Pearse?"

"Yes, I think that was his name. Seemed like he really had it in for you."

"You got that right," I said, "Looks like I'm stuck out here."

"What are you gonna do?" Ronnie asked.

"I don't know, man, but I can't go home any more. If Pearse gets his hands on me this time, I'll never get out again."

"Tom," Diane said, "You need to get to a hospital or doctor or something. You really look beat up."

I hadn't even thought about it up to that minute. I put my hand up to my face and it didn't even feel like my face. It was real lumpy, swollen I guess from the punches and stuff. Must have been bloody, too.

I laughed a little, "I guess I do look like hell, Diane, but you know, always..."

"Yes," she said softly, "I know. Always cool."

"Tom," Ronnie said, "Listen, man, you can't stay here forever. Where the hell are you gonna go?"

"I dunno," I confessed, "I really don't know. I guess I gotta figure some way of gettin outta town. I mean if I stick around it looks like I'm goin down for that other thing."

"If you can make it down to Kennett, down in the bootheel" Diane suggested, "We've got relatives there you might could stay with."

"Thanks, Diane," I said, "Maybe I can catch a freight down by the river or something." That seemed unlikely, though. I mean you always read about that kind of thing, but how the hell do you know what train's going where? Anyway, I wouldn't stay with somebody like that, put them under that harboring a fugitive thing.

"Listen," I said, "You guys better get outta here."

"We'll stick around a while," Ronnie said.

"No, man, the longer you're around, the more likely somebody's gonna come lookin. Go on. Get your butts home."

Diane looked like she was going to cry or something, but she started crawling out. Then she turned and handed me the paper bag. "Almost forgot," she said, "There's a sandwich and a coke in here. A few more candles, too."

"Yeah," Ronnie said handing me his flashlight, "You better keep this, too."

"Thanks, guys," I said as they crawled away, "Try to get word to my folks that I'm okay, alright?"

"Sure," Ronnie said, "We'll let 'em know."

"See ya," I said, "Oh, and keep an eye out for Boozer, would ya?"

"See ya," Ronnie answered.

"Bye, Tom" Diane sniffled.

After they left I sat there more alone than ever, but at least I had the candle for some light. I ate the sandwich. Diane had even cut off the crust for me. I wondered where girls learn that kind of thing. I gulped down the Coke in about three swallows. Tasted better than anything I'd ever had in my whole life.

I sat there and watched the light from the candle flickering on the dirt walls of my cave. I wished I'd told Ronnie to try and get word to Tony, too, just in case he came up with something that might get me out of this jam. That didn't seem very likely anyway, though. I wished there was some way to get word to Elaine, too, but there just wasn't. Anyway, that girl was probably better off never hearing from me again. Yeah, maybe I was feeling a little sorry for myself.

It was just a small candle Diane had lit, a votive candle, so not a whole lot of light, but the way the flame danced around and the reflections of the light on the walls was almost pretty. Five minutes after Ronnie and Diane left, I was sound asleep.

FOURTEEN

"Everything is laid out for you. Your path is straight ahead of you.
Sometimes it's invisible, but it's there. You may not know where
you're going, but you still have to follow that path."
Chief Leon Shenandoah

A cave is a nice place to sleep in a St. Louis summer. Even if it's just a little dirt cave that might fall in and bury you. It's especially nice being in a cave if people are chasing you and you can't figure out anyplace else to go. It's cozy and cool and there's a little air movement from someplace deeper underground, deeper and even cooler than where you are. It makes you forget about your problems and not feel so much the sticky blood on your arms and face. It makes it easy to sleep. To dream.

I was dreaming about a thing that happened a long time ago with Bryan on Dago Hill. We'd found a big old turtle. A huge turtle, actually. Or tortoise, maybe. I mean one with a shell at least eighteen inches in diameter. We found it hiding under a concrete pad that must have been part of the brewery. I don't remember exactly how we came to notice it under there, but once we did its fate was altered forever.

It was me and Bryan and a few other kids, and as always, Bryan took the lead. I don't guess the rest of us would ever have thought what to do with a big turtle like that, but Bryan seemed to know right off. He found a broomstick and started poking at the turtle's head with it. The turtle was a snapper and got pretty pissed off being poked at. Whenever Bryan would poke near the turtle's head, the turtle would

169

snap and grab hold of the broomstick with that big old beak. Then Bryan would pull on it and drag the turtle out a little ways from his hiding place.

It didn't take long 'til Bryan had the turtle completely out in the open and all the rest of us kids could see how big and old-looking he was, with this wrinkled old head. Bryan dragged that turtle all the way home to his house, three blocks from Dago, just by poking that stick at him and dragging him whenever he'd snap. The turtle never held onto the stick very long, just a minute maybe, so each drag was just a few feet. Then the turtle would let loose and Bryan would have to pester him again with the broomstick to get him to snap so he could drag him another few feet. The whole time there was me and this bunch of kids watching kinda awestruck at the whole thing. Not many giant turtles like that in the middle of the city, and most of us had never seen a turtle the size of this one.

The way it was in my dream was pretty much the same, except the turtle kept getting bigger. Every time Bryan poked and dragged, the turtle grew. He grew until he was the size of some of the garages Bryan was dragging him past down the alley. Bryan had to struggle harder and harder to pull the turtle, but he could always to do it. The turtle always kept snapping at the broomstick and never just snapped Bryan's head off or anything, although he could have, as big as he got.

It was sort of a pleasant dream and not like a nightmare at all, despite the turtle getting really big and all, and in the dream I was just a little kid again, which was kind of nice, and the dream was a little like going to the movies. Something kept trying to pull me awake, though. I was fighting against it because I liked being in that dream and I didn't want to wake up to the lousy messed-up situation I'd left behind, but whatever it was kept nudging me and I couldn't swat it away and so finally I woke up a little.

There I was, back in the cave, back being the real Tom Bonner again. The candle was still flickering, but it was ready to go out. I was only half awake and pissed off that I was even that, so I didn't care about the candle. I just wanted to go back to sleep. I tried to close my eyes and drift off again, but they wouldn't stay closed, and once when they blinked open it was like there was somebody there next to me.

It scared me a little and so I opened my eyes as wide as I could and tried to wake all the way up then and I could see that there really was somebody there, real close by. I thought I recognized who it was with that look on his face and all, but it couldn't have been him.

170

I reached out to feel if I could touch him but he was farther away than I could reach. "Bryan?" I said, "Bryan, is that you?"

He got a big grin on his face. "Who else?" he said softly.

It hit me so hard that I couldn't say anything back. I tried to crawl over closer so I could put my hands on him and make sure he was real.

"Bryan," I said, "My God, are you really here? I thought you were dead." I put my hand on his arm and felt better when it seemed like I was feeling something real and my hand didn't just go right through him like a ghost or something.

"You gave up on me?" he laughed gently, "Never give up on Bryan, man. Never give up."

"But I saw you go in, and I never saw you come out again."

"Tom," he said, "There's a lot more to life than what you see."

"Oh, man, how'd you get out of there?" I asked, "And where've you been?"

Seemed like he was amused by my questions, enjoying being obscure. "That's not important, right now," he said, a half-grin still on his face, "What's important is what happens next to Tom Bonner."

"Yeah," I said, "I guess I'm in kind of a mess."

"Kind of?" he laughed, "From here it looks like a great big ol'whopper of a mess."

In a flash, the answer to my problems hit me. "Bryan, if you got out, did Lovey make it, too?"

His grin dimmed. "No, man," he said, "I'm sorry. She's gone."

I realized I already knew that. They'd found her body. There was not going to be a quick and easy solution to my problem.

"You know they think I set the fire, right?" I said.

"Yeah, I heard. People believe stupid crap."

"This stupid crap looks like it's gonna send me to the slammer."

"There you go givin up again," Bryan said, his grin returning, "You ain't in the pokey yet."

"No," I said, "But I can't stay here forever either. Soon as I show my face that detective Pearse is gonna pounce."

"Well, then we just fix it so you don't show your face for a while. You ready to get movin?"

"Moving where?" I asked.

"Just follow me, Tom," Bryan said, lighting another one of the candles and heading off towards the far end of the cave.

I followed right behind and when we got to the far wall, there was a small hole. That's where the breeze was coming from. Bryan dropped down into it, me right on his heels. We crawled fifteen feet or so and then the narrow passage opened up into a larger room again. It was different from the cave we'd just left, though. Here we crawled through a brick wall and entered some kind of underground room. A big room. The candlelight was barely enough to reach the walls. My guess was the room was at least forty feet square, and maybe twenty feet floor to ceiling.

"What the hell is this place?" I asked when Bryan paused for a minute.

"Take a closer look at the walls," Bryan said.

The walls were dark, not reflecting much of the light from the candle. I went over and touched the nearest one. It gave under my touch, felt rubbery. I picked at it and it crumbled a little. "What is it?" I asked.

"Cork," Bryan said, "The walls are lined with three inches of cork. It's an old brewery store room."

"I heard there were places like this down here, but I figured it was just a story."

"It's the old Lemp Brewery," Bryan said, "They took some natural caves, added to them and put in the cork lining. Used 'em to store beer. It goes on a long ways. Links up with Anheuser-Busch."

"All the way down there?"

"Yeah, this part of the city is full of underground stuff. I think that's why they built the breweries here. You know, before refrigerators to keep the beer cold."

Bryan was on the move again and I followed the light from the candle he carried. I was trying to remember the names of all the breweries in this part of town. Busch, of course, and Lemp from long ago, and Falstaff, and . . .

"Don't forget Griesedick Brothers," Bryan chimed in, like he knew just what I was thinking.

"Yeah," I said, "Remember that old joke?"

"Fat old guys sittin around and one of 'em pats his belly and says, 'This is what Budweiser did for me,' you mean that joke?"

"Second fat guys pats his gut," I said, "says, 'This is what Falstaff did for me.'"

"And the pregnant lady pats her belly and says, 'This is what Griesedick did for me.'"

We laughed together at the old joke we'd laughed at since grade school. Back when Bryan had to explain it to me. The whole time,

Bryan kept pushing forward and it seemed like there was an endless series of rooms joined one to the next. Some were larger and some were smaller, but they were all cork lined, with some kind of stone floor. You could still smell the stale aroma of old beer. Maybe it soaked into the cork or something. It smelled just like the corner tavern.

Bryan was always just a little ahead of me and leading the way.

"How'd you know about all this under here?" I asked.

"Bonner," he said, "I know all sorts of things. Just ask."

"Well," I said, "I wish you knew how this whole thing 's gonna end up."

"I do."

"You do."

"I told you, I know all sorts of things."

"And so....."

"And so how this turns out is that you will learn some stuff."

"Oh brother," I said, "Thanks a heap. You sound like some kinda guru or Swami or something."

"Don't take guru's lightly, Tom."

"Huh? I thought you were strictly a Bible guy," I said.

"Don't knock The Bible either."

"Oh, but now you're sayin it might not be the only way?"

"Word written by man can only limit a limitless God," Bryan said.

"Geez, you sound like a preacher."

"No," Bryan laughed, "I used to think I might be a preacher someday, maybe have a radio show like some of those guys even. Sell tickets to salvation for a few bucks."

"That's what you wanted to do?"

"Sure. It sounded like fun. A way to be an important guy. Not bad for a kid from our neighborhood, huh?"

"So what changed your mind?" I asked.

Bryan stopped and turned around and got a big old smile over his face. "You think a preacher's got any answers?" he asked.

"How the hell would I know?"

"You know by how they live," he said, then turned and started heading away again.

I don't know how long we walked and talked like that. It was a long time. Room after room and sometimes a little crawl space between the rooms, but mostly walking and talking. In a way, it was kind of fun. I didn't mind talking about religious stuff. It took my mind off other stuff. It surprised me, though, how Bryan's views seemed to have changed.

"So, Bryan, you still think I been 'Dealt With'?"

"Everyone's been Dealt With," he said, "Some see it, some don't."

There came a long stretch where we had to crawl through a pretty narrow passageway. As always, Bryan was ahead and leading the way with the candle. There were places where it got so tight it was hard to squeeze through. If I'd been there by myself I probably wouldn't have even tried, but knowing Bryan was ahead made me less scared, able to keep pushing onward.

Finally, we got through and came into this huge room. I mean it wasn't really a room. Not like those we'd been through before. This was more like a cave. A real cave. Couldn't see the top or the sides of it and the ground we were on was real uneven and hard to walk on. No cork on these walls, and what looked like little stalactites way up on the top of the place.

"Where's this?" I asked.

"Part of Cherokee Cave," Bryan said, "A part nobody's seen for a long time."

"Cherokee cave? You mean we're all the way down almost to Broadway?"

"Yep. Those old stories about how Dago connected here were right."

"Great. Now where?"

"Well," Bryan said, "This is as far as I go. From here on, you're on your own."

"Huh?"

"Yeah, I gotta be gettin back. You'll be okay, though. Just keep goin."

"Well, where're you goin?" I asked.

"I gotta head off the other way," Bryan said, "But, Tom, there's something I want you to remember."

"Yeah?"

"Yeah. You're goin on without me, but what you got to remember is that you're never really alone."

"What?"

"I mean just like I'm here with you right now, Tom, somebody is always right there with you."

"Bryan, what the hell are you talkin about?"

"Listen, Tom, this is important. Sometime or other, if you're lucky, you're gonna find a girl or a woman to love. You'll carry that love around with you and it'll be part of you every minute of your life. It'll change your life."

"Okay," I said, thinking of Elaine.

"Maybe it's Elaine, maybe it's somebody else," he said, "But here's the thing."

"Yeah?"

"The thing is, there's another kind of love. As big and important as the love is between a guy and his girl or even with you and your folks, there's another kind of love that's lots bigger and ...."

"And?"

"Well," he said, "I guess I can't really explain it. Just remember that one thing."

"One thing."

"Yeah," Bryan said, "You're never alone. And you *are* loved."

"Bryan," I said, "What're you talking about?"

"Just try to keep it with you," he said, "You're never alone. If everybody just knew that...."

"Man," I said, "I never thought you'd be talkin about stuff like this - I mean love, for chrissake."

He laughed. "Yeah, I guess it does seem a little strange, comin from me. I wish I'd figured it out sooner, but Tom, there's two things you said wrong."

"Yeah?"

"Yeah. First, it's not BS. And second, it's not for Christ's sake - it's for yours."

I was getting a little fed up with this kind of talk. "Okay, okay," I said, "Let's just get going to wherever we're going."

"Alright," Bryan said, "That was the end of me preachin', anyway, but like I said, for now at least, we're heading in different directions." He gave me the candle and pointed towards the far end of the cave. "Down that way you'll find a concrete path the Cherokee Cave people put in. Follow that 'til you get to the stairs."

"Man," I said, "Can't you come along?"

"'Fraid not. Not this time. Listen, when you get to the stairs, go on past them. The stairs lead up to the main entrance in the Cherokee Cave building. You don't want that. Keep going past the stairs and you'll find another entrance not many folks know about. Go on out that way."

"Past the stairs and out," I repeated, "Then what, Bryan?"

He was already walking away, heading back the way we'd come. The light from the candle was getting pretty dim and Bryan was fading into the darkness. "You won't be alone, Tom," he said, "Someone will be there for you."

"Hey," I yelled, "Don't you need a candle or something to find your way back?" No answer.

"Bryan?"

Nothing. I couldn't see him anymore. Couldn't see much of anything. There was just the blackness of the cave and the fading circle of light from my candle. No sound except my own breathing. I stood there for a minute looking towards where Bryan had disappeared, then turned and headed slowly off the way he'd said to go.

It didn't take long to find the concrete walkway. There was a metal rail along one side of it and I kept one hand on it as I went forward. The candle beginning to flicker and die. I had one more in reserve, but I decided to save it in case I needed it later. Here at least I had the rail and the walkway to guide me. All that time I'd spent in the caves and the underground rooms I hadn't been afraid, but now, when I was close to getting out again, it hit me that I was who knows how far underground and who knows what the hell might have happened to me down here. It made me shaky thinking about that stuff. I was glad for the rail to steady me.

The walkway went gradually uphill and took me to a metal stairway, just as Bryan had said. There wasn't enough light from the candle to see the top, but it was tempting to go ahead and climb on up out of that cave and into the light I knew must be up there above somewhere.

Instead, like Bryan said, I went on around the stairs, which were held up by four big steel columns sunk into concrete. Just beyond, the walkway disappeared and I was back onto the dirt of the cave floor. The candle was almost gone, and I was getting ready to light my last one off the dying flame when I noticed a light in the distance. The floor of the cave sloped steeply upward and I climbed towards the light. As I got closer, I could see that the light was coming from outside. It was sunlight coming in. This had to be the entrance Bryan had told me about.

I tossed the remaining little hunk of candle, put the other one back in my pocket and scrambled upward. The dirt was loose and crumbly under me, but in a little while I was standing upright at the mouth of the cave, looking out into the back lot behind the Cherokee Cave building. After being in the dark so long, the sun was way too bright. So bright it hurt my eyes. Still, I could tell from the angle that it looked to be late afternoon. I had no idea how long I'd been down there. Had to be at least a full day, maybe a couple of days, because I didn't know how long I'd slept.

I took a long, deep breath of the fresh outside air and said a silent thank you for getting me out safely. I hoped Bryan got out to wherever he was going, too.

I stood there a while waiting for my eyes to adjust and just looking around. Cherokee Cave's backyard was pretty crappy looking. The building itself had always looked kinda dopey even from the front. Just a big white cube, with no windows and just the one door leading in under the huge garish orange and red "Cherokee Cave" sign with oversized Indian arrows pointing to the door. It was just a concrete block building painted white. White didn't last too long in this area, though, so it got all streaked and dirty and looked like crap.

The back was even worse. They hadn't bothered to paint it, of course, and they used the back yard to store all sorts of miscellaneous junk that was all rusted and beat up. They must have planted grass, but it hadn't been mowed for a long time and it was pretty tall, weeds sprouting out everywhere. A ten foot tall cyclone fence surrounded the backyard, I guess so nobody could sneak in and find the cave entrance I'd just come out of.

There were a half-dozen or so battered old trash cans scattered around one corner of the building, lids scattered everywhere, and the wall behind them was all discolored where somebody must have just thrown trash or garbage or something at the cans and missed. They missed a lot.

I was still looking at the trash cans when I saw something move beside them. I dodged back inside the cave entrance, then peered out. It was a man who'd just come around the corner of the building. He was inspecting each of the cans like he was looking for something important. I watched for a while, and then I thought the old trench coat the guy was wearing looked kind of familiar.

I left the cave and covered the twenty yards or so to the corner of the building slowly and quietly. The man was intent on his search and never looked up until I was right behind him.

"Jim?" I said softly.

The guy popped upright and his head jerked around with a nasty expression forming. Then he saw me and jumped backward. It looked like he was getting ready to run.

"Jim, it's just me. From the library."

He held way back and scrutinized me, his brows furrowed and his arms in front of him like he was either going to have to fend off an attack or fight me. After a while, it seemed like he recognized me. "What the hell happened to you?" he asked in a gravelly voice.

I'd forgotten how beat-up I must have looked. No wonder the poor old bum was scared. I was sure I still had blood all over me from the fight and where there wasn't blood, there was bruises and swelling and probably mud and stuff from the cave on top of that. "A little disagreement with some friends," I said, smiling.

That seemed to calm him down a little. He put his hands down, but didn't move any closer. "Some friends," he said.

It got a little awkward after that. I mean I'd seen this guy just about every day for a couple of years, but I didn't know anything about him. Hell, he was a bum and I didn't know anything about any bums. What do you say, "How 'bout them Cardinals?"

Jim broke the silence. Pointing to the trash cans, he said, "I was just doin a little shoppin, myself."

I laughed. "Find anything good?"

"Nah," he said, "This place ain't too good. They got a little snack bar inside, though and sometimes there's a hunka hot dog or something - maybe a coupla french fries."

Jim was out there looking for his dinner. I'd never known this was how the guy lived. I guess I'd never really cared, either. The funny thing was that now a hunk of hot dog and a french fry sounded like a fine idea.

"Yeah," I said, "I could use a bite myself."

"What?" he said, "Well, why don't you just go......oh, I guess you can't, can you?"

"No, I can't. I can't go anyplace right now. You heard?"

"Of course I heard," he snapped, "I'm a bum, not a freaking idiot."

"No, no," I said, "It's not that. It's just I wasn't sure if you knew who I was and all."

"I know," Jim said, "Believe me, I know who you are, Tom Bonner."

178

It surprised me the old bum knew my name, but I didn't figure this was a good time to ask him how he came by that information. "So where can we get something to eat?" I asked instead.

"The way you look, noplace."

"Oh, yeah, I forgot again."

"You forgot," he said, "You forgot you look like you been run over by a goddam steamroller?"

"Uh, yeah. I was in the dark. Down in the cave."

"What?" he said, "You been down there all this time?"

"Huh? All what time?"

"Well, the papers said you disappeared three days ago."

Three days. I'd been underground for three whole days? I couldn't have slept that long, could I? It didn't seem possible. Aloud I said, "I guess that's why I'm so hungry."

"Bein' hungry is somethin' new for you, isn't it?"

"Well, hungry like this it is."

"Can't just have Mom fix something up, can you?"

"No."

"And you wouldn't like it much if your Mom did make a nice meal for you and just when you sat down to eat your old man threw you out in the street, huh?"

He lost me there. "What?" I said.

"Ah, never mind. Come on, I'll take ya someplace we can get a bite." He walked away, over towards the fence, and without a good alternative, I followed.

There was a place where the fence was busted up and Jim crawled through. He motioned for me to do the same. We headed off together down Cherokee Street, past Broadway and down towards the river. The sun was behind us and going down as we walked.

It was only a few blocks and didn't take too long before we made it past the few houses still standing and were at the riverbank. We hadn't spoken at all during the trek down there and so I hadn't been sure exactly where we were heading, but then I saw the shacks sitting at the edge of the muddy water and I recognized the place.

"Hooverville," I said aloud.

"No," Jim said pointing at a makeshift placard, "Read the sign."

Somebody had stuck a two by four into the ground, braced it in place and nailed a one by ten across it sort of like a cross. On the crosspiece, the name had been carved and then filled in with some kind of paint. The sign read "Happy-Land." When I looked closer, I saw another, smaller board was nailed below the big one. On it somebody painted "You are welcome if you are alright."

"Jim, is this where you live?" I asked.

It pissed him off. "I'm a bum, goddam it," he snapped, "I don't live anyplace!"

"Oh, sorry," I said.

"Well, come on, let's get you cleaned up some." He led me a few yards further towards the cobbled together huts. A single pipe stuck a couple of feet up out of the ground, bent horizontally, ending in a hose bib. A boy was drawing a bucket of water. "G'wan, get outta here," Jim said to the kid, "Go tell Tugboat I'm here."

The kid looked at us with a vacant stare, then lumbered off with the bucket, leaving the water run onto the mud. "Wash yourself," Jim commanded.

I crouched down and started splashing water on my face and up my arms, scrubbing to remove the caked blood and mud and whatever else was sticking to me in bits and pieces. The water was clean and cool and felt nice. Finally I just stuck my head under the bib and let the water run through my hair and down my back.

When I stood up again and shook the water off like a dog, I saw the kid coming back our way, a large scowling man in tow. As he got closer, his scowl turned to a smile and he waved to us. "Well, Mr. Bonner" he called out, "Long time no see."

I was trying to figure out where I knew this guy from or how he knew my name when I saw from the way he was looking that he wasn't talking to me, but to Jim.

"Tugboat," Jim said, "This is my nephew Thomas. He needs to stay with you a while."

FIFTEEN

"There are processes in the soul of which we are not immediately aware."

Thomas Aquinas

What the ...? Jim introduced me as his nephew! First I thought the old bum had lost his marbles completely. Then I thought maybe this was his way of trying to get me into this community where, if he didn't actually belong, at least he was known. Then it hit me again that Tugboat had addressed him - *him*, not me - as "Mr. Bonner." I couldn't figure out what was going on, but decided to keep my trap shut and see what developed. I wasn't in a position to ask questions.

Tugboat clasped my hand and gave it a firm shake. "Welcome, Thomas," he said, "Welcome to Happy-Land."

The man's hands, like the rest of him, were huge. My hand was lost inside his. I could feel the roughness, callus on top of callus, and I could see layers of black coal or grease or something that had worked into the skin so that if he scrubbed for years his hands would never look clean.

His voice was as rough as his paws, but there was a glint of something in his eyes that told me there was a lot more to this guy than his crude appearance.

Tugboat turned back to Jim. "You know the rules, James, young Mr. Bonner will have to work."

Jim just snorted and looked away. It almost made me laugh. He was like Maynard G. Crebs on that Dobie Gillis TV show. Whenever anyone mentioned the word "work," he'd get this panicky look on his face, repeat the dread term in a tremulous voice, like "w-w-er-rr-k?" and run the other way as quick as he could. Jim was like that only not funny. He clearly had a high disdain for labor.

"I don't mind working," I said.

"Well, that's a good start," Tugboat replied with a wink, "What can you do?"

What could I do? Good question. Well, I could play a little basketball, once in a while even dunk. I could thump a watermelon. I could steal pretzels. I usually did pretty good on standardized tests. None of these talents seemed worth much in Happy-Land. I didn't know what kind of work they needed.

Tugboat was watching me, waiting for an answer. After a moment or so, he chuckled. "Don't worry," he said, "We'll find something for you to do." He turned back to Jim. "And will you be gracing us with your presence for a while as well?"

"I think you know better than that, Tug," Jim replied, "In fact, time I got to get movin on now." He turned and started shuffling off.

"Jim, wait a minute," I called.

He paused and turned back, "What now?" he asked impatiently.

"I just wondered if it was Bryan who asked you to meet me there at Cherokee Cave."

"Who?"

"You know, Bryan."

"No," Jim said flatly, "I don't know any Bryan." He turned and walked off. Didn't look back again.

Tugboat put his big hand on my shoulder. "Don't talk much, does he?."

"Nope, guess not."

"But he does talk straight. When he's not preaching, that is."

"Jim's a preacher?" I asked.

"No, at least not a religious one. Mostly he preaches his own brand of philosophy and politics. Been doin' that as long as I've known him."

"How long have you known Jim?"

Tugboat thought a minute. "Well, since the mid-thirties, I guess. About as long as I've known your old man."

"What, you know my Dad, too?"

"Used to," he said, "We hung around together some back in the old days. Actually, I knew your Dad before I met his brother Jim."

Kaplowie! "Wow, so Jim really is my uncle?" I hadn't meant to say that out loud, but the words just came out.

Tugboat raised one eyebrow. "You didn't know that?"

"No," I said, "But how....I mean, when.....?"

"Whoa," Tugboat grinned, "I can see you need a little fillin' in on your family history, but there'll be plenty of time for that later. Right now, let's see if we can find you a place to sack out for the night."

Tugboat led me down a narrow dirt alleyway with little shacks randomly scattered along it. No two of the shacks were alike, except that they were all pretty tiny - not more than the size of a decent room, maybe eight by ten or so, and they were all obviously built with whatever was handy at the time. Mostly they were wood, made out of old boards scavenged from who knows where or stuff just found laying around - parts of an old billboard, a section of corrugated metal or even a hunk of cardboard. Some didn't even qualify as shacks, but were more like lean-to's, open at the front or along one side.

There were people living here, but you didn't see much of them. We passed maybe three men and each of them had that same kind of sidling, head-down walk. Each looked up and nodded or said a brief but deferential hello to Tugboat as we passed. Not one seemed curious about this newcomer in their midst. Tugboat made no introductions.

We'd passed a dozen of these makeshift houses when Tugboat veered off to the right and headed for one of the larger cabins. Pausing at the doorway, he said, "Well, Thomas, this is home. Come on in."

As I entered, I noticed that there was no door in the frame, just as there hadn't seemed to be one in any of the places we'd passed. There was one window on the far wall, and it had obviously been taken from someplace else, because the frame still had traces of white paint on it, while the boards around it and the rest of the walls had never seen paint. There was a floor, but it was just planks, not even as nice as the tongue and groove floor in my basement room at home. For furniture, there were five things: two old mattresses on the floor, two wooden straight-back chairs, and between the chairs a table made from one of those big wooden spools like they wind wire on. In the middle of the spool-table sat a candle, burned and melted down to only an inch or so tall. No sink. No stove. No evidence of a bathroom, and not a light fixture to be seen.

I couldn't think of anything to say to Tugboat. I mean, what could you say, "Nice hovel - Gee, I love what you've done with the place?"

Again, it was up to him to break the silence. "It's not much, I know," he said, "But we don't need much down here."

"It's fine," I answered, "I appreciate your letting me stay here a while."

"You can bunk over there," he said, indicating the mattress in the far corner, "We usually turn in pretty early."

"No lights."

"Right," he grinned, "No lights, no lotsa stuff." Darkness was falling fast, and Tugboat went over and lit the candle, then sat down heavily in one of the two chairs. For a minute I thought about asking if he had any pajama's I could borrow, but then I figured maybe my smart-ass sense of humor might be a little out of place here. I also was getting a little tickled about this man's name and started wondering how I ought to address him - Tug, Mr. Boat, or what? Fortunately, for once I managed to say nothing until the goofy mood passed and more serious crap started popping into my head.

"Tugboat," I said, "I have a lot of questions."

"Yes," he said, "I know you do, and I do as well. Let's just allow them to be questions overnight, though. Okay?"

What choice did I have? "Sure," I said, and went over and sat down on my bed.

"Thirsty?" he asked.

"Yeah," I said, "Maybe a little."

Tugboat filled a ladle with water from a bucket next to the spool-table. He brought it over and I drank it down. The water was warm, like it had been sitting out in the heat for some time, but it was wet and tasted good.

"Thanks," I said.

He just nodded and went back to his chair. The last rays of the sun were coming through the window. The glass hadn't been washed in a long time and so the light that passed through it wasn't clear and sharp, kinda fuzzy as it played across the little room, lighting the dust particles dancing in the air before it hit the far wall, illuminating it with a soft yellowish cast.

I leaned back against the wall and watched the games the sunlight was playing and how the little candle tried to match what the sun was doing. My arms started feeling really heavy. My head, too. I leaned over and kind of laid out and rested my head on my hand. My eyes were pretty tired too. Then I was asleep.

The dreams started off kind of goofy. I was there in Tugboat's shack lying on the mattress, but I was covered with the Cartoon fox tonneau from Tony's Chevy. It felt real nice, but somebody kept trying to pull it off me.

Then, all of a sudden, I was back in the fire at Gettelmans. Bryan was running back inside the apartment building and I was yelling at him and then Lovey came like floating out and she was crying and kept crying "Why? Why?" over and over again. She was waving a little scrap of paper in one hand that I knew was one of the poems I'd left there at the library and I wanted to explain everything to her but I couldn't open my mouth to say anything at all. Then Beef Butcher was standing out in the back yard laughing up at me and shaking his fist and yelling, "Gonna beat you ass, Man. I gonna whup you ass."

I woke up sweating and scared and not sure where the hell I was. I looked around and everything was dark except for a little moonlight coming through the window. The candle had gone out, but I could see that Tugboat was asleep with his head on his arm. I wanted to get up and get the hell out of there, go home and sleep in my own bed and not have anything to worry about except getting up the next day for school. But I knew that whole big part of my life was gone and wasn't ever going to come back and I was so tired that I just laid down and let the sleep slip over me.

When I woke again it was morning. Tugboat was gone, but I could hear people outside. I stumbled over to the door and looked out. There were folks out moving around and a couple of places down some guy was whistling as he hung laundry out on a clothes line strung up in front of his shack. There were three pairs of underpants in a row and they were this not-white kind of gray color, patched and tattered and almost threadbare, but this guy was whistling and happy as he hung them up to dry. It made me feel kind of funny, but I think it was partly because I hadn't had much to eat for some time.

I didn't want to go back inside, so I headed back up the pathway towards the water spigot, thinking at least I'd get a drink and splash some water in my face. When I got close, I could see a bunch of people gathered around the pipe. There in the middle, towering over them, was Tugboat. He saw me coming and that big grin spread across his face.

"Let him, through, folks," he said, "Here comes the new waterboy." Then everybody was looking at me and kind of moving aside and murmuring. Tugboat pulled me up next to him, spread his arms out kind of over me and in a loud voice he said, "Everybody, this is young Mr. Thomas Bonner, and he's gonna be staying here in Happy-Land a while."

There was more murmuring and I could see from the people closest to me that they were trying to say hello, so I smiled and waved and mouthed a hello to all of them. Some of them clapped and some just nodded and some tried to smile back, but it seemed like it was real hard for them to make their faces do that.

The formal introduction over, everyone went back to what they'd been doing. Everybody had brought some kind of bucket or pot or something up to the spigot and was filling it up and taking it back to their shack. Tugboat pulled me away from the crowd.

"You hungry, boy?" he asked.

"I could eat," I said. I was starving

He laughed. "Come on, then."

He led me up the bank away from the river where a little pavilion had been set up. It had a tent-like canvas top suspended on poles, open on all four sides. There were some picnic tables inside, with a few people sitting around eating.

Tugboat took me up to a table in the middle of the big tent where food was set out. A big wooden bowl with cereal and some dishes with fruit and stuff. It looked like there'd been more earlier, but there was still some left. There were two pitchers, one with milk and another with water.

"Help yourself, boy," Tugboat said, "I've already et."

Looking at the food made me even more hungry and I thought I could probably eat every single thing left on the table, but then I realized I didn't have a bowl or a plate or anything to put the stuff on.

Tugboat left for a minute, then came back and handed me a wooden bowl and some kitchen utensils. "Wash these out when you're done," he said, "I'll be back in a little bit."

I went after breakfast with a vengeance. There was cantaloupe and I ate two halves without pausing for breath, gobbled up a handful of strawberries, then dipped into the cereal. I don't know what it was, some kind of corn flakes, I think, but whatever it was, it was great, and it filled me up. Made me feel like a human being again for the first time in days.

I was sitting there just enjoying the satisfaction of a full belly when Tugboat came back in carrying a galvanized bucket. "Well, Thomas, get enough breakfast?"

"Wow," I said, "It was great."

"Good, then I suppose you're ready to go to work."

"Sure, what can I do?"

"Well," he said, "Seein's you're without marketable skills, Mr. Bonner, you've been elected waterboy."

"Oh," I said, recalling him calling me by that earlier, "What do I do?"

"For one thing, you get up a lot earlier than you did today."

"Okay."

"Then," he said, "You take this here bucket and you fill up everybody's water for the morning."

"Huh?"

"Well, everybody's got something they keep their drinkin' water in - might be a bucket or a bowl or a pot or anything. They'll set it outside their place at bedtime and come morning you get your bucket, get to the spigot early and go around and fill 'em all up."

"Alright," I said, "Then what?"

"That's it."

"That's it?"

"Yep," he said, "I mean, you gotta live by the rules, too, of course. If you find anything, it's for everybody, and you gotta help out if somebody needs something."

"There's gotta be more to it than that."

"Nope. We're not here because any of us likes a lot of rules or stuff, Tom, or because we wanna spend all our time gettin' ahead, right? We're not exactly success-driven here. Not on the corporate fast track."

"Yeah, but..."

"But...?"

"But where do you get food and stuff," I asked.

"Oh," he said, "We've got some gardens and we do some scrounging and then there's always the do-gooders."

"The do-gooders."

"Yeah, charity people. They're always bringin' stuff by for us. That's where most of the cereal and milk comes from. Government surplus stuff, mostly. Stuff they'd throw away if it wasn't for us degenerates."

"So all you want me to do is haul some water in the morning?" I asked.

"Yep. It's been a while since we had the luxury of a waterboy. This ain't exactly a growing community. Think you can handle it?"

"I'm sure I can," I said, "Now, about those questions from last night."

Tugboat laughed. "Yes, I didn't think they'd go away. But mine come first."

"Yours?"

"Yes, remember, I had some questions too."

"Okay," I said, "Shoot."

"Well, really, there's only one question I need to ask you."

"Yeah?"

"Did you do it?"

"Huh?"

"Thomas, did you burn the place down?"

I closed my eyes and put my head in my hands. "Oh man, no, Tugboat. Of course I didn't do it."

"I didn't think so," he said softly, "But you understand I had to ask."

"Yeah, sure."

"Because Jim spoke for you, but we still have to know who we have with us."

"Sure," I said, "I understand that."

"Good," Tugboat smiled, "You're alright. Now what do you want to know?"

I wasn't sure exactly where to start, so I just plunged in. "Well first, I guess, how do you know my Dad and Jim?"

Tugboat looked off in the distance, like he was looking back in time a long ways. "Well," he began slowly, "First, like I said before, I knew your Dad first. We worked in a shoe factory together a long time ago. Bet you didn't know your old man was a shop steward, did you?

"No, I didn't."

"Yep, and on his way to bein' head of the union Local, too, except that he took things too serious."

"What do you mean, too serious?"

"I'll give you an example. There used to be a union meeting once a month. You know, where the members are supposed to get together and talk about grievances and union business and so forth."

"Yeah?"

"Well, your old man wanted to make a rule that the members had to stay for at least fifteen minutes or they wouldn't get credit for attending and they'd have to pay a fine."

"Sounds pretty benign," I said, "What was the problem with that?"

"The problem was that for most of our guys, the meeting was just a good excuse to get out of the house of an evening and go boozing. They'd show up at the union hall, get their card stamped and then head for the nearest watering hole. That fifteen minutes your dad wanted would have eaten into their drinking time. It pissed 'em off. Next election, they voted your old man out. Like I said, he took things too serious."

"Kind of hard to imagine my Dad getting in trouble because he didn't want to drink."

"Oh, don't get me wrong," Tugboat said, "Your old man could put 'em away with the best of 'em. Man, I could tell you some stories.....but anyway, it was just that he thought the union was important. He was right, too, but it didn't make much difference anyway in the long run."

"How come?"

"The company was too smart for us. They started movin' the plants out of the city, down to the country - Potosi, Pilot Knob, Ironton, places like that where there wasn't any union, or at least not a strong one like here - like used to be here, anyway."

"Geez, Tugboat, how'd they get away with that?"

"Wasn't nobody to stop 'em. And, like I said, they were too smart. They'd whipsaw us - threaten to close our plant and then at the last minute say they'd leave ours open but they were gonna have to close the one over on Washington Avenue. Everybody at our place was happy to still have a job, so what the hell did we care about the poor devils over at the other plant."

"That's too bad."

"Yeah, and of course the poor hoosiers out in the country thought they'd died and gone to heaven when a big old shoe factory come to town and started payin' better wages than anybody'd seen down there, even if it was only half what they had to pay in St. Louis. 'Course their day is comin'. Just wait."

"Why? What do you think's gonna happen?"

"Hell. It's as simple as this: when the wages get too high in outstate Missouri, why they'll just up and move those plants to Mexico or overseas someplace where they can get somebody to work his ass off for a nickel a day."

"Hmmmm." Seemed pretty farfetched to me, moving plants across an ocean just to save a few bucks, but I wasn't going to argue. "What about Jim, did he work there too?"

Tugboat laughed. "Thomas, I've never known James Bonner to work a day in his life. I guess maybe he did sometime, but if so, it was before I met the man."

"How did you meet him?"

"At your house. It was before you came along. Your Mom and Dad were living a block down from where they are now, on Menard Street. I'd come by to pick up your Dad for a meeting and Jim was there having dinner with them. Your folks used to feed him once a week, regular-like. I guess he went around to other relatives, too. Had a pretty good deal goin' on."

"Even back then he was a....."

"A bum? Yeah. And you don't have to be afraid to use that word here. Ain't no bums in Happy-Land."

"I didn't mean anything, Tugboat."

He waved his hand. "I know you didn't, Thomas. Anyway, Jim had a pretty good deal, but he managed to screw it up that night."

"What happened?"

"He opened his yap, as usual. He was preaching up a storm there at your folks dinner table and he got into this part where he was saying that anybody who worked for a living was a damn fool. Can you imagine that? He's sitting there eating food your Dad worked to pay for and your Mom worked to prepare, and he's tellin' them they're damn fools for doing it."

"Doesn't sound very smart. What did my folks do?"

"Well, I could tell your old man was getting steamed. You know the way that one eyebrow of his goes up?"

"Oh yeah, I've seen that a few times." I'd seen it alright, most of the time directed at me.

"Well, your Dad hopped up from his seat and yelled at Jim to get the hell out of his house and never come back, and just in case he didn't get the message clear enough from his yellin', he grabbed Jim by the collar and helped him out the door."

"Geez, my Old Man did that?"

"Your Dad was a tough cookie when he wanted to be. You know when he was younger he used to hang around with the Hogans and Eagans."

The Hogan and Eagan gangs were St. Louis's Irish answer to Al Capone back in the late Twenties and early Thirties. I'd heard about them, but this was something new. "He was a gangster?" I asked.

"Nah, hold on, now," Tugboat backtracked, "I never said he was one of 'em, just that he knew some of them."

A lightbulb went off somewhere in my mind. "And what about you, Tugboat, were you in that crowd, too?"

A wistful smile came across his face. "Like your Dad, Thomas, I knew some of the guys. I had a mechanic shop for a while, and I'd work on their cars."

"You were a mechanic?"

"No, I *am* a mechanic. That's not something you ever get over being. Still make a buck at it from time to time."

"So how'd you wind up here?" I asked.

"Well, after the factories all left, I went back to working on cars. Had a little shop not too far from your house, around Tenth and Victor. Not much of a place, just an old rusty metal building. Your Dad used to come by sometimes - bring me some work or just shoot the breeze."

"Yeah?"

"Yeah, but I drank a lot then. I'd get so boozed up I couldn't work and then I couldn't pay the rent on that crappy old garage and the landlord was gonna kick me out, but the city came along and condemned the place before he had a chance to. By that time, I'd had enough. I came on down here and some folks took me in and got me off the booze and here I am."

"I'm sorry, Tugboat."

"Don't be," he smiled, "I'm not. I like it here. Listen, everybody's got a story, Thomas. Everybody has hard times, just like maybe you're goin' through right now - like your Dad went through and like maybe Jim went through some time a long time ago. Mostly, though, God don't give you more than you can handle. He does expect you to handle it, though. You can't just quit, like Jim did."

"So how come you treated Jim so nice when he came by?"

"Because as goofy in the head as he is, he's somebody I know. Somebody I've known for a long time, and I've never seen him lie or cheat or screw anybody. And besides, he's a man, and a man deserves

191

to be treated with respect, no matter his circumstances. Don't forget that, Thomas."

I nodded. "I won't, Tugboat. And thanks."

He laughed. "Thanks for what?"

"For filling me in, and for the lesson."

"Don't mention it," he said with a wink, "If you keep your eyes and ears open you can learn a lot down here. Stuff not in any book."

"I've learned a few things already," I said.

Tugboat grinned, pulled his big frame up off the bench and stretched. "Well, Mr. Bonner, I'd best be moseying along now. Charlie's garage up the road here's got a '51 Chevy with a bum clutch they want me to work on." He took a last gulp of coffee and lumbered off. It struck me as he walked away that he was still wearing the same overalls and shirt as yesterday. He hadn't shaved for a few days nor had he combed his hair for a while. He didn't have his sleeves rolled up exactly twice and instead of driving a shiny '55 Chevy with a Cartoon fox tonneau, he was going off to add to the burden of grease on his hands working on somebody else's old '51. For all that, Tugboat was still pretty damn cool.

I spent the rest of the day just roaming around the riverfront. I felt a freedom I hadn't known for some time. I figured if the cops were after me, Happy-Land would be the last place they'd think of looking, and that took a big weight off my mind. I knew I couldn't stay here forever, but for the time being it wasn't such a bad place to be. I had a friend here, a place to sleep, food to eat and a spigot to go get a drink of water whenever I wanted. It was warmer out here than in the cave, but definitely a step up.

The other thing was, it was kind of pretty down here. This was a part of the riverfront I hadn't seen before, other than the one time years earlier when my Dad had brought me down. The Happy-Land folks kept their area clean and picked up. Maybe that was somebody's job, just like carrying water was going to be my job, or maybe they just didn't throw stuff away. Most other parts of the riverside were full of trash. People from all over had used the riverfront for a dumping ground for just about anything they wanted to get rid of, old cars to regular trash to one time my Dad and I even saw where somebody had dumped a mess of guts - pig guts from slaughtering a hog, he said.

The Happy-Landers not only kept their area neat, but other people stayed away and dumped their crap elsewhere, so this part of the riverfront, aside from the shacks, must have looked the same way it did a hundred years earlier. There were tall stands of prairie grass growing everywhere and waving in the wind, and a few trees here and there for shade, and a full view of the Father of Waters flowing by all day long.

I spent a big part of my first day as a Happy-Lander just watching the river go by. It does something to you to spend time like that. The river slows you down to its pace and you start breathing slower and deeper. Your eyes open up wider and something else in you opens up, too. The river gives you time to think and it makes you think in a different way - a way that brushes aside little stuff and makes you see real clear what's important and what matters.

It's like a river, especially a big one like the Mississippi, always knows where it came from and where it's going. It picks up a lot of stuff that floats along with it for a while and gets dumped off here and there or sinks of its own weight, but always the river keeps going where it's going. You know it was doing that long before you got there and it'll still be doing the same thing when you're not even a memory left in anybody's mind.

If you sit there long enough, and if you're ready, you kinda get to be part of the river. It takes you in with it and you start to see where you came from and where you are and even a vague dreamy feeling comes about where you're going, even though it might be miles downstream.

SIXTEEN

"I've known rivers
Ancient, dusky rivers
My soul has grown deep like the rivers."

Langston Hughes

There was a big difference between days and nights in Happy-Land. Almost backwards from the way it's supposed to be. My days were mostly slow-moving and peaceful times, almost drowsy, but at night if the fire wasn't chasing me around in my head, it was Detective Pearse. Or over and over it was Lovey's face floating in front of me asking "Why?"

I didn't mind the days. Even the work part wasn't bad. I got up early - how early I was never sure, because nobody in Happy-Land had a clock or watch or really much cared about time, but whenever it was, it was before most other folks were up. I took my bucket to the spigot, filled it and brought water to the shack furthest away. Then back to the spigot and off to the next shack. I worked my way down from the longest trek to the shortest.

Everybody had some kind of container out for the water. Mostly, it was just another bucket, but some folks had a tub, while others just had a few coffee cans. Whatever the container, the rule was they got no more than one bucket of water to start their day. That was the contract with me. That was my job. Water-bearer. I came up with that title, liked it better than water boy. In return for my labor, I got part of whatever was brought into the community. It meant I got a couple of decent meals just about every day. It also meant I got to know the little village and the tribe that inhabited it.

There were exactly thirteen dwellings in Happy-Land, arranged pretty much in two rows along a central street or alleyway that ran parallel with the river. The shacks weren't exactly in a row, but there was evidence of order, though no zoning board or planning committee had ever approved a plat.

At one end of - well, I'll call it "town," was the open tent we used for meals and meetings with the water spigot nearby, and at the far end were two outhouses. Between the shacks and the river was a small plot of ground where crops were grown - corn, mostly, but some other stuff like watermelon, lettuce and cabbage, as well. A rough fence surrounded the plot to keep animals out and a scarecrow had been set up for birds. Neither worked particularly well so we shared our produce with the wildlife of the area. Nobody seemed to mind.

There were more kinds of animals roaming around by the river than I would have thought. I mean, my Dad and I had taken a lot of walks to the river when I was younger, but I never noticed how many creatures were around. Maybe I was too little then or maybe you have to live there or maybe it was just because this was a different part of the riverfront, but it became a game to try and find as many different species as I could.

The first thing I saw that kind of amazed me was that there were chickens roaming around down by the river. Wild chickens. They weren't the big, white chickens like you'd see at the market, but smaller and brown. Tugboat called them range hens or prairie chickens. There was a whole bunch of them down there and they were fair game for supper. It was a big deal in Happy-Land to catch a range hen.

We had competition for the chickens, though, because there were also coyotes running around out there. Not many, I don't think, but definitely a few, because you could hear them at night with that weird crying howl of theirs. When you hear that for the first time or the first few times it wakes you up. If you've been dreaming, for a minute or so you don't know if you're better off asleep or awake. After a few nights, though, you get used to the howling. Then it's just the dreams that are troubling.

One thing there wasn't much of, fortunately, was snakes. You might see an occasional blue racer or a green snake, but I never saw a copperhead or a water moccasin.

Helping keep the snakes down to a minimum, the waterfront had a good supply of hawks. There's more than one kind of hawk, which is something I didn't know until I saw for myself. There are hawks that hunt from the sky, circling and circling up there until they spot a mouse or something and then they come barreling in like a dive-bomber, snag it up and zoom off again. The dive-bomber hawks are fun to watch, and it seemed like there were always a couple of them overhead circling and watching.

The other kind of hawk has a little tinge of red on his feathers up around his shoulders and what he does is just perch somewhere - in a tree or a fence or a light-pole - and wait for something to move. He sits perfectly still, I guess so he doesn't scare away a potential meal. Then at just the right moment, he strikes.

I watched a red-shoulders for twenty minutes or so one afternoon. He was sitting on a little stretch of barbed-wire fence a half-mile down from Happy-Land. They're pretty good sized birds, maybe a foot tall, and at first he was sitting so still that I didn't know what it was. Then I got a little too close and he ruffled up his feathers like either to scare me away or getting ready to fly off. Once I saw what he was, though, I backed away and sat down to watch him.

There really wasn't much to watch, him being so still and all, and I guess some people would think it's kind of a boring or dopey thing to do - like I might as well have been sitting there watching a bowling pin or something - but there was something kind of neat about it. Just me and him out there and each of us knew about the other. I kinda figured what he was up to, but the grass was so tall I didn't know how he could spot anything scurrying around down there. Didn't have anything else to do, though, so I sat and watched.

It was a pretty day. The sky was a pale summertime blue. No clouds. All that was up there was one of red-shoulder's dive-bomber cousins circling around. That and once an airplane droned across from horizon to horizon, the drone of its distant radial engines nearly lulling me into a lazy afternoon nap.

I still had an eye on red-shoulders, though, and the only part of him that ever moved was his head. Seemed like he could turn it almost all the way around, like an owl. The grass under his fence was waving in the wind and I was just thinking that had to make it even harder for him to see anything in it but then, wham! He was off the fence and down into the grass. He was hidden for a second or two and then he popped right back up into the same spot, a snake in his beak.

It was so fast, it was almost like you didn't really see it, but there he was with this damn snake writhing around, caught right smack dab in the middle of this hawk's beak and trying to get away. I couldn't tell what kind of snake it was, but it was a couple of feet long.

I don't know if you've ever thought about what a hawk eats or if it eats snakes, how it could eat a snake. I mean, I don't think I ever thought about that until the exact moment I saw that snake in his beak. Think about it a minute. Doesn't it seem like the only way that could work would be for the bird to like start at one end of the snake and kind of gobble him down that way, working from one end to the other?

Well, that isn't the way a bird eats a snake. At least not this bird and this snake. Red-shoulders had that snake right in the middle and that's the way he ate him. He'd wiggle his beak and work a little more of the snake into it each time, swallowing him. It took him quite a while to eat the snake that way, but he knew what he was doing and wasn't in a hurry. Watching, it was like the snake was shrinking from both ends. Shrinking, shrinking, being gobbled up, and then he was gone and it was just red-shoulders sitting there on the fence. And me watching.

I thought about Tugboat telling me "You'll learn a lot down here if you keep your eyes and ears open. Stuff that's not in books."

I wondered if there was a book someplace that told how a hawk eats a snake, and if there was, how you'd go about looking it up and how it would describe it. Probably there isn't a book like that. I don't know, maybe I'm the only one who cares about that kind of thing. Maybe it's one of those things you have to actually see before it means anything. Before you care about it.

I mean it's funny. You live in the city all your life, just a few blocks away from this place and you don't have any idea there's all this stuff going on down here. Life and death stuff. Creatures you didn't even know could be here are here and they're always hunting for their supper or else they're trying to escape being something else's supper.

You get up in the morning and wash your face and go off to school or maybe to work and you never even think about all the other things that are going on so close to you. You're so worried about a test or a promotion or who likes you or doesn't like you that you don't see everything else that's everyplace. It's like you're blind. When you think about that, about all the stuff you miss all the time, it makes you sad. You open your eyes and you see it for the first time and then you're sad because of all you missed. All the hawks and the snakes and the people you didn't know were your uncle.

It took a while, but I did figure out how Jim fit in to this community. Besides being an old friend of Tugboat's, that is. He brought them books. Jim would swipe books from the library - actually, not swipe, but just borrow without benefit of a library card - bring them to folks down here. In return he might get a meal once in a while. He didn't come by very often, maybe once a month or so, but if you asked him to bring you a particular book, he'd try to get it for you. I don't know how he snuck them out of the library, inside his clothes I guess or maybe old Snotnose helped and put them in his sacks or something. Far as I know, the books were always returned, too.

I also don't know why it had to work that way. I mean, anybody from Happy-Land could have gone up to the library if they wanted. They could have gotten a library card and, for that matter, so could Jim. They just didn't. I don't think it was because they were lazy or anything. They just had this system set up and they liked it the way it was. I had the feeling that if Jim died or just went away and never returned, they still wouldn't go up to the library. They just wouldn't get books anymore. Happy-Land folks were a little different.

There were about twenty people who lived in Happy-Land. Mostly men, but a few hard women as well. It was never the same number of people from one day or one week to the next, because folks were always coming and going, but there was a core group that was almost always there. For them, Happy-Land was both a refuge and a prison. They were safe from society there, but they could never go into society, never go up to the library, over to Soulard Market, or anyplace regular people might be. And the reason was, they were afraid. They would never say it, but after a while I could tell. They were beaten down and humbled and afraid.

They'd been kicked out by society, just like my Old Man had kicked Jim out, and maybe for as good a reason or maybe for no reason. Maybe just because they had bad luck or bad timing or were just too timid to fight back. Too gentle, maybe, to take the hurt that comes with the way most of us live.

During the Depression, there'd been a lot more of them. Tugboat told me Happy-Land used to have hundreds of people back in the thirties, and there were other Happy-Lands or Chickentowns or Hoovervilles up and down the river and in other cities around the country. He said you could hop a freight train and go all over the country, from city to city and never have to go into the city itself, but just stay in a Hooverville where they'd always take you in. When he told me that, he got kind of wistful, like the Depression was the Good Old Days or something.

"For a while, back then," he said, "It was lookin' like everybody in America was gonna end up in a Hooverville."

Tugboat was like the unofficial leader of Happy-Land, and their main contact with the outside world. Like Jim was for books, Tugboat was for everything else. He was the only guy who actually worked at a job once in a while. The only guy who had any money, although never much and sometimes none at all, He was the only guy who could go out and get something if it were needed. If somebody was sick and needed medicine, Tugboat was the one who had money to pay for it and could go up to the Globe Drugstore on Broadway to pick it up.

In some ways, and especially to some people, Tugboat was more like a Dad than anything else. He kept them in line, kept them from getting too wacky or too far away from the way regular people ought to behave. Like there were two or three people who would just let themselves go and either forget to bathe or otherwise just not want to, and when it would get to where you could smell them coming, it was Tugboat who'd gently remind them that they needed to take care of themselves.

One thing I really missed is that there wasn't any way to take a bath in Happy-Land. I remember my Old Man talking about how when he was overseas in the Marines they'd have to take a bath in their helmet, and that's what we did in Happy-Land, too, except instead of a helmet it was a bucket or a basin or whatever happened to be handy. I didn't like it too much and one day I complained about the situation to Tugboat.

"You know, Thomas," he said, "The way things work down here is, if there's something you don't like, you've got three choices."

"Yeah?"

"Well, you can either put up with it, leave and go someplace else, or fix it."

Hard to argue with logic like that. So instead of arguing I thought about the problem. After a couple of days, I came back to Tugboat with a suggestion. He listened thoughtfully, then agreed it might work and said he'd try to get the parts we'd need. I'd already found the main component, a sixty gallon drum.

What me and Tugboat did was, we built a shower.

There was always plenty of scrap lumber around, from other shacks that had been torn down as the population of Happy-Land shrank or that washed up from the river or from I don't know where. You could hammer the nails out of the lumber, straighten them out and re-use them. This was how we built a platform about six feet tall with a ladder on one side. Put the drum up on top of the platform after using nails to hammer a dozen or so holes near the bottom of the drum.

That far, it was my idea. Tugboat came up with the plan to make a little plywood and leather gate over the punctured area. The idea was to be able to turn the water on or off.

The way it worked was pretty simple. You filled the barrel with water, stood under it on a small wooden platform we'd built so you wouldn't always be standing in mud, and with a long two-by-two, pushed the gate open, turning on the shower. There was a nail hammered partway in, near the end of the two-by-two, so when you were done, you could use that to pull the gate back down, shutting off the flow.

The thing that was nice, too, was that because it was summertime, the water in the barrel would heat up during the day, so at least by afternoon you got a warm shower.

There were two things that maybe weren't so nice about the setup. First was that as Water Bearer, it got added on to my job to keep the barrel full. To be honest, I didn't mind it that much. The shower was close to the spigot, so it was just hauling the bucket up the ladder to the platform and dumping it in. I mean, I could have said I wasn't going to do it, but hell, the whole thing was my idea and as soon as it was up and people saw how it worked, they liked it a lot so how could I complain about keeping it up?

The other thing, though, was that there was no privacy. I hadn't thought about that when I figured out the design. This didn't bother the Happy-Land folks at all, though. They didn't care if anybody saw them naked. I thought it was real strange. I mean they were so shy around outside people, but here in Happy-Land, it was somehow okay to be naked in the shower where everybody in the world could see you. I guess they were just glad to have the shower.

In fact there was like a little celebration or ceremony or something after it was up and working. It was after we'd gotten together in the tent for the evening meal. Kind of a crappy meal, really. Nobody'd caught anything and the charity people hadn't come for a while so what we all had for dinner was corn. I mean, I don't mind corn, but I like it best if it's with a big steak or something. This was just corn though. There wasn't even enough of it to fill you up.

After most people were done eating, or almost done, Tugboat stood up and raised his arms. Everybody looked up at him.

"We have a new gift in Happy-Land," he announced in a deep and serious voice, but with a broad smile, "We have a shower."

Everybody clapped and whistled.

When the noise died down, Tugboat continued. "Everyone who comes to Happy-Land brings his gift. Our shower is the gift of Thomas." He nodded towards me and everyone clapped again. I was a little embarrassed, but also proud.

"And, of course," Tugboat went on, "Our shower is, as all things are, the gift of God. Let us thank Him."

Everybody in the tent got real quiet and bowed their heads like they were praying. Nobody said anything, or even moved for a full minute.

Finally, Tugboat said, "Amen" and everyone started talking and moving around again. After a while the tent cleared out except for me and Tugboat. He sat there a few minutes, then looked over at me.

"You did a good thing, here," he said, "I think you will be a good man, like your father."

"Aw," I said, "It wasn't anything."

"Yes it was," he said, "Do not make light of your accomplishments, Thomas, especially if they are in the form of a gift."

"Nuts," I said, "I was just tired of bein' dirty. You know that. Besides, it was your project, too."

He smiled. "Yes," he said, "You made it for your need, but you made it for all of us, and so you made things better where you live. Many people live their whole lives without making anything better for anyone."

"C'mon, Tug," I said, "It's a shower. You make it sound like holy water."

Tugboat laughed at that until his whole huge frame shook. "Yeah," he grinned, "Guess I get carried away sometimes."

It made me feel good, what he said. Like I wasn't under his wing anymore. Like we were equals. Seemed like a big change and something more to be proud of than building a stupid shower.

It was funny how Happy-Land changed things, how things that wouldn't amount to anything at all anyplace else were such a big thing here. The other way around, too. I was getting to really like this place.

My job, instead of getting harder with the shower and all was actually getting easier. First, it was getting easier to carry the water and second, Tugboat had found me a second bucket, so I could carry two at once. At first that was kind of tough. I mean, two buckets of water are pretty heavy, but after a while, I didn't notice it so much and it cut in half the time it took me to make my rounds.

After a while I got to where I could even carry two buckets of water at once up the ladder to the shower platform, just by balancing and not using my hands on the ladder. Every once in a while I'd lose balance and tumble off, but not very often and it was a fun challenge.

With things getting easier like that, I had more time on my hands and I got tired of just roaming around, so I asked Tugboat to bring me some tablets and a pen or pencil. I started writing stuff. I'd just go down the river a ways and sit by the bank and write whatever came into my head.

I wrote about whatever happened that day, or what I'd seen, or the way the sky looked or the way the Mississippi made me feel. I wrote some poems. Maybe that's what most of what I wrote was, because none of it made a whole lot of sense. I don't think it was very good poetry, but I didn't care. I think everybody ought to write their poems and not care if it's good or if it's lousy. Because it's theirs. If it makes sense to you, who gives a damn if it's good or great or lousy to anybody else?

Another thing I did was put together a kind of prayer. At least a draft of a prayer. I thought about it a lot. I thought about the old priests at Assumption and about the Zoroastrians and about Ronnie the Jewish-B'Hai or whatever he was. The prayer I wrote was this:

Nameless god, thank you for the gift of life.
I pray that my thoughts, words and deeds in this day
May be worthy of me
And thus acceptable to you.
Amen.

It wasn't very good, I know, but I said it in the morning and laying in bed at night like it was an Our Father or a Hail Mary and at least it was my own and not some words somebody had written a thousand years ago or so. It copied too much from the Zoroastrians, though, and I always figured I'd work on it more some time, but at least it was something. A place to start.

I got the idea from Tugboat. Some mornings I'd see him just outside our shack doing some kind of slow-moving exercise or something - maybe yoga or tai-chi or something. He was like talking to himself as he moved. It took me a few days to get it all down. To get down what he was saying. It went like this:

> *Spirit of blue sky and cloud*
> *Spirit of mountain and tree*
> *Spirit of stone and water*
> *Spirit of the crisp morning air*
> *Come now - be with me, let me walk with you*
> *Silence my fears and foolishness*
> *Heal my body and my soul*
> *And open my eyes to what is real*

I thought that was pretty good. I wanted to ask him about it, but then I figured it was a private thing and none of my business. Being nosey about other people's private stuff was a serious breach of Happy-Land etiquette.

So I let it be. Instead, I made an island.

There was a place along the bank of the Mississippi that stuck out like a little peninsula into the river and I figured I'd turn that peninsula into an island. I don't know why I wanted to do that, but in Happy-Land you didn't have to have a sensible reason to do stuff like that, so I just started trenching out along the bank, making an island.

There was no shovel to dig with, so I used a stick to poke in the dirt and then the water would come in and soften it up and I'd poke some more. It was a dopey thing to do, I know, but it was a way to occupy some time and not think about the big thing that was out there that troubled my sleep. So I dug in the dirt by the river.

The island I was making wasn't going to be a big one. If it worked at all, it was going to be a couple of square yards, with some kind of goofy bush on it. It was something you might do if you were ten years old instead of my age, but I didn't give a damn, I was digging an island.

People would come down and ask me what I was doing and I didn't know what to tell them. I couldn't say I was making an island. I mean I guess I could have and the way they were they wouldn't even have laughed or anything, but I just didn't want to. So I just didn't say anything, but kept digging. You could do that down there. You didn't have to explain anything in Happy-Land.

So I carried water and wrote poems and prayers and watched the river and dug away at my island and time went by like the river and I didn't care and nobody cared.

Except that I worried about my Mom and Dad and the name I'd left behind as maybe a killer and how that had to hurt them and how I missed them, too. I knew I had to figure some way to clear myself. I just didn't know how.

I talked to Tugboat about it, and together we figured maybe I ought to go back up to where the fire was and maybe try to find some clues or something. What kind of clues, neither of us knew, but it did seem like maybe it was the only thing that could be done.

Then one morning when I was out doing my water rounds, I noticed something going on upstream a ways. A bunch of people were up there working on something or other. I sneaked up and watched for a while as they put up a big tent. I mean a *big* tent. One that made our tent look pretty small. Then they put in rows of benches, enough to hold ten times the people that lived in Happy-Land.

I went back and told Tugboat what I'd seen. "What do you think it is?" I asked.

"Revival," he said simply, "It's the Holy Rollers. They come down once a year or so. Usually they got a good preacher, too. Folks from all over come."

"You ever go?" I asked.

"Sure," he said, "Everybody from Happy-Land goes to the revival. It's a good show. You get The Spirit and usually they serve a hot meal after, too."

"When will it be?"

"Don't worry," he said, "They'll bring around flyers. They'll talk it up. You oughta go. You might get saved. Sometimes they baptize people in the river, too. It's something to see."

"They baptize people in the Mississippi," I said, "Isn't that kinda dangerous?"

"Ain't seen 'em lose one yet," Tugboat said simply, "Seen some that was lost get found."

SEVENTEEN

"We all have a closetful of crap . . . and your closet ain't no more full than mine."

Robert Revland

C ame a time when I couldn't keep running away. Couldn't keep hiding from the fact that I was accused of setting that fire and killing two people. It kept after me. It filled my dreams and no matter how busy I tried to stay during the day it was always there in the back of my mind, banging on the door, trying to get out. Trying to take over.

Tugboat and the rest of them in Happy-Land were real good about the whole thing and after that first time Tug asked me if I'd done it, nobody ever said a word again. I'm sure they all knew about it, knew I was a suspect and all, but nobody ever even asked me anything. Not because they didn't care, just that privacy was a big thing in Happy-Land. Once you were accepted in, nobody asks anything about where you'd been or what you were before you got there. You want to talk about it, that's okay, but nobody's going to pry. Your business is your business.

So it wasn't the Happy-Landers. It wasn't that anybody was looking down on me or anything. It was just after a while I couldn't stand myself. I had to get this off my back and so I decided it was time to try to find some answers.

The Holy Rollers had come around and passed out their flyers and talked to everybody about coming to the Revival. The Revival had

207

been going on for almost a full week and was building up for the grand finale on Saturday night. A couple of Rollers had come around and cornered me once. Tried to tell me about how much I needed to be saved. I was polite, but I stayed away from the big tent. I didn't think they'd look too favorably on a guy who was writing his own prayers.

Maybe their message got through in some way though, because I figured maybe it was time I tried to save myself. I waited until Saturday evening. When everybody was heading over to the Revival, I tagged along part of the way but started lagging behind. Before we reached the tent, I veered off and started heading away from the river.

It looked like a real nasty night was coming up. Big, heavy clouds all over. You know the kind that hang down real low and then there's other clouds higher up. You see two or three different layers of them moving past each other, not quite in the same direction. It was sticky out, too, the way it gets in the summertime in St. Louis before a bad storm. The clouds were getting pushed around by some strong winds up there but down at ground level nothing was moving.

I mean nothing was moving. No breeze at all. The trees were still, their branches and leaves drooping down with the humidity. People who'd been through weather like this knew what was coming, so they stayed inside unless they had to be out for some reason. Not many people would be out on the streets.

I figured that was probably good for me. I didn't know what kind of news stories were circulating about me or if my face might even be plastered up in the Post Offices or something. I didn't want people to see me and call the cops.

I got up to Broadway and headed north. I had to pass by Globe Drug store and Miller's Dry Goods. Those two and a few other little storefront places were still trying to hold out and stay in business where most had moved on. Moved out to the county. To one of the new malls.

When I was a kid, Broadway was lined on both sides with shops, all the way from Victor Street up to Soulard Market. Then the redevelopment thing had come in and taken away most of their customers and tore down a bunch of the stores to make way for freight terminals and warehouses and stuff.

Then, too, there were starting to be shopping centers out in the county, like Crestwood Plaza way out on 66. More people were going there and big name stores like Sears and Penneys were taking over from the little shops like Millers where they used to keep underpants and t-shirts and stuff in big cardboard boxes on the floor and you could just rummage through, find what you wanted and then dicker with the owner over what you'd pay. Now everything was all packed up in plastic with the price right on it. You pay the price and that's that.

I mean, it was kind of embarrassing when your Mom or Dad argued over the price of your underwear, but they seemed to like doing that. The store guy seemed to expect it, too. It put you all on the same level. Now the big stores make the rules and you go by their rules or you don't get anything. I didn't like that much and I knew my folks didn't either. They didn't like the way Broadway was fading away. Didn't like not being able to walk to a store close by. A store where you knew the owner.

This time though, I was glad that there weren't a bunch of people out shopping. I walked along fast with my head down and didn't look at the few people who were out. I was lucky because I didn't see anybody I knew. Nobody spotted me. I guess I could have gone through the alleys but that seemed like more hiding. I was through hiding.

I got to Lafayette Avenue and headed up towards the market and the library. It was Saturday but because it was getting late and because of the weather not many folks were there. Most of the farmers had closed up and headed home.

It felt strange seeing the library again. Seemed like a year since I'd been there even though it was only a few weeks. I wondered what Miss Walker and the rest of the library staff thought about me. If they thought I was guilty. I didn't figure Miss Walker would think that but some of the others might. I wanted to go in and explain everything to them, to Miss Walker mostly, and make sure they knew I hadn't done anything wrong.

Instead though, I just walked right on past the marble stairs. Got pulled up short when I saw what was on the far side of the library. It was the first time I'd been back to the - well, The Scene Of The Crime, I guess - and it hit me pretty hard.

There wasn't anything there. Gettelmans was gone and the house behind it was gone, too. Whatever was left after the fire had been bulldozed and leveled. The debris had been hauled away and now there was just a vacant lot running all the way from Lafayette back to Soulard street.

I sat down on the library steps. Sat and stared at the place where Gettelmans had been. I'd hoped to poke around in the wreckage and maybe find something, some clue that might show how the fire really started and maybe who really did it. If somebody really did set it deliberately.

I know it was a dopey idea. The cops had probably already gone over the place but it was the only thing I could figure out to do. Now even that was gone. It was too late. I was too late.

I sat there on the steps with my head in my hands and tried to think what to do next. Trouble was, I couldn't think of a damn thing. So much for being smart. So much for a big SAT score. After a while I figured as long as I was there I might as well look around some. Maybe there'd be something left to find, something that'd been overlooked. Maybe I'd just get lucky.

By then it was starting to get pretty dark. Starting to sprinkle, too. I walked the lot from one end to the other and from side to side, and I knew it was hopeless. Nothing there but the remains of the rubblestone foundation walls, flat level with the ground, the basements all filled in. There was a little bit of grass left in what had been the backyard of the house and it made me think back to that night. How I'd jumped and landed there with Diane.

I wondered again about how Bryan had gotten out of the building. Started wondering why he hadn't come down to Happy-Land to see me. See how I was doing. He had to know I was down there. No matter what Jim said I thought for sure it was Bryan who'd had him meet me by Cherokee Cave. Bryan said there'd be someone there, and sure enough Jim shows up. Coincidence? I don't think so.

Then I thought, well, maybe Bryan's on the run, too. Maybe the cops thought he and I were in the deal together. Everybody knew we were friends and all, so that might have been it. Bryan might even be down in the country with Cathy and her people by now.

I would have liked it if I'd looked around and Bryan had been standing there right behind me. He'd have had the answers to everything and life would go back to the way it was. The machinery that keeps everything making sense would start up again. But when I looked around there was nobody there. Things weren't ever going back.

I spotted something on the ground, half buried in the dirt and picked it up. It was an old brass skeleton key, like for my folks back door only bigger and heavier. It was all crusted over with mud and stuff. I picked off as much as I could and stuck the key in my pocket. I knew it wasn't a clue, but it was something. It was something from that place. I was going to keep it.

Where to go next was the question. I thought about heading over to my house, to check in with my Mom and Dad, but for sure Pearse would have my house staked out. My friends' places, too. I was still trying to come up with a place to go and kinda singing Chuck Berry's "No Particular Place to Go" to myself when I saw a shiny black convertible cruising slowly up Lafayette. The top was up because of the rain but the windows were down.

"Tony," I called out and waved.

The car slowed further, then stopped. I could see Tony peering out, looking right at me, a puzzled expression on his face. It was like he didn't know who I was or something.

Then it hit me that he probably didn't know who I was. I hadn't shaved since I'd arrived at Happy-Land. I didn't have much of a beard but it had grown out some and I guess my hair was pretty long and messed up, too. Used to be, I'd wash my hair every day and try to keep it looking OK, but not in Happy-Land. There was nobody to look good for, so you kind of forgot about that kind of stuff.

My clothes didn't look so hot either. I walked over to the driver's side of Tony's car and it wasn't until I got closer that he finally figured out who I was.

"Bonner," he said, "What the hell happened to you?" He wasn't smiling.

"Long story," I said.

"Well, you look like hell."

"Thanks," I said, "Maybe that's where I been."

"Guess that's why I couldn't find you. I been lookin' all over, man."

"You have?" I said, "Like where?"

He acted like he was pissed at the question. "You know, around. Everywhere."

I got the feeling he hadn't looked anywhere for me, but I decided to drop it. "Tony," I said instead, "Have you found out anything about the fire?"

His eyes got kind of shifty all of a sudden. "No," he said, "Nothing new. Nobody seems to know anything. The guys have been asking around, but nothin's turned up."

A month earlier that would have disappointed me. Now it was only what I expected to hear. Didn't affect me at all. I just smiled and gave him an out. "Well, listen," I said, "Keep tryin', okay?"

"Sure," Tony said, "You bet. We'll keep checkin' it out." He was getting kind of nervous, and I decided to have some fun with him.

"Hey, Tony," I said, "Can you give me a lift?"

He got real fidgety behind the wheel. "Well, I'd like to," he said, "But the thing is, I gotta be some place in just a coupla minutes."

Bull! Tony didn't have to be anyplace. He just didn't want this bum-lookin' guy in his car. Might get the seats dirty. Might make Tony look uncool to be seen with him. Didn't go with the upholstery. Didn't fit in with the sun tan and the expensive clothes. Tom Bonner wasn't cool anymore. Unforgivable.

"Oh, yeah, sure," I said, "I mean if you gotta be somewhere..."

"Yeah," he said, "I gotta. Otherwise, I'd run you over to...well, wherever you're goin'."

"Tony, you'd better get movin', then, huh?"

"Oh. Yeah. I guess so. Listen, I'll see ya, huh?" He started pulling away, then stopped and looked back. "Where ya stayin' anyway?"

"Here and there," I said with my best Brando half sneer half grin, "Here and there, Tony. Go on, man, you're gonna be late."

"Yeah." He hit the gas and sped off into the darkening evening and I didn't care if I ever saw the SOB again.

I turned and started walking down the alley. Half a block and the rain changed from a light drizzle to a downpour. A month earlier I'd have looked for a place to get in out of it, but now rain was another thing I didn't care about. Didn't matter if I got wet. Didn't matter if I got soaked through. I just kept walking. I wasn't sure where. Back to Happy-Land, probably.

It was going to be a good storm. Lightning was snaking skinny florescent veins across the sky and the rain was pelting down so hard it almost hurt when it hit you. Then it got worse. Raining harder than I ever remember. Lightning hit a transformer half a block up with a crash so loud it made me jump. Sparks showered all around and lit up the street in a funny sick green glow. The street lights went out and it got real dark.

I headed down Soulard towards Broadway. The gutters were already full of water rushing down to the river. Streets in this area slope downhill pretty steep, then level off a little at Broadway before a gentler incline takes them to the river.

When I got to Broadway I headed south. Before I'd gone a block I started hearing these loud "Whump! Floom!" noises and then something heavy and metallic hitting the ground. I heard one, then another, then a whole bunch. I didn't know what it was until one of them went off practically right next to me.

The pressure of all the water in the storm drains rushing downhill so quick was blowing manhole covers off. It was pretty scary. The one that went off beside me must have blown ten feet in the air, followed by a geyser shooting up out of the manhole. Then the sewer plate came crashing down a few feet away. Those things are cast iron. Heavy. If one hit me, I'd be dead. Never saw anything like this before.

I kept moving though, staying close to the buildings to avoid the wind and rain and to keep out of the way of falling sewer plates. It was a weird thing, watching those big metal disks explode up into the air and then bang down on the pavement. I thought to myself it was like a horror movie or something, except then there'd be some kind of monsters or zombies or something crawling up out of the storm sewers to chase you. I kinda went with the idea, thought how great it would be if Tony was still cruising around down here and one of those sewer plates came crashing down on the hood of his precious Chevy. Then one of the monsters could come up, drag his ass out through the window and haul him down into the sewers. He'd have a tough time trying to figure out how to be cool down there.

The mental picture of that made me laugh out loud and then I felt really stupid being out there in this world-class downpour in the first place and then being out there laughing like a crazy guy or something.

I was the only person on the streets. Maybe the only living thing. There weren't even any cars on Broadway, which was good because they might have hit one of those open manholes and had one hell of an accident, maybe lost control and crashed into a building. Somebody could have been hurt pretty bad.

The sewers couldn't handle the water and the street had turned into a shallow creek from curb to curb. In some places the water was even up over the curb and I had to wade through it even up on the sidewalk.

One thing, though - it wasn't hot and humid anymore. The rain was cold and the air had cooled down a lot. Of course my clothes were soaked and it would have felt good to have been inside next to a fire. I could see lights in the windows of houses as I walked past and it looked all warm and cozy inside. I wished I could go up to a door someplace and know somebody inside and they'd let me in and give me a towel and let me take a hot bath and give me some different clothes to change into. Let me rest up and maybe spend the night there. But none of that was going to happen.

I got as far as Arsenal street and then started heading down below Broadway. I'd walk a street down and then a street across, making my way back to the only place I knew to go. Making my way back to Happy-Land. The rain let up some and only then did I realize how I'd been walking - all hunched-over against the rain. I straightened up and my back and shoulders ached from being scrunched up so long. I had to arch my back and reach my arms up over my head to try and stretch out.

I had both arms up like that and was looking up into the night sky and it struck me that it must look like I was saying some kind of desperate prayer or something. Like I was pleading with God. Like I was some kind of rain-soaked, out-of-work, out-of-luck bum hoping God would save him.

That didn't seem like a very funny picture and the other thing was that it didn't seem very far from what was really going on. I didn't know what kind of prayer to say, though. The one I'd made up myself didn't seem very good anymore. It sure didn't seem to fit here at all.

I ran through an Our Father and a Hail Mary and they seemed better, but not enough and I wasn't going to just keep doing them over and over like a rosary or anything, so I just kind of tried talking to God as I walked along. I told him I was sorry for all the crap I'd pulled. Said it just like that, "God, I'm sorry for all the crap I've pulled."

I didn't know if it was OK to talk to God like that, saying "crap" and all, but that's just the way it came out and there didn't seem much point in going back and cleaning up my language once it was said so I just kept on the same way. I told Him He knew I didn't set any damn fire and I sure as hell didn't kill anybody and I said I hoped He'd help me get my ass out of this jam. I told Him I knew I'd been kind of a lousy kid sometimes and a smart-ass and that if I could just get out of this I'd try to do better from then on.

I talked to Him a little about Lovey, too, and told Him I hoped that nothing I did had anything to do with her dying. I said I wished I'd been able to go back in with Bryan to try and get her out. I told God I didn't think I could have gotten back in, but if that was what I was supposed to do, then I was sorry for being such a chicken not to try.

Then I said I hoped He'd set up a nice little place in Heaven for Lovey because she was a good kid and she deserved something nice. I hoped she was happy up there.

I don't know, I talked to Him about a whole bunch of stuff and I kind of ended by saying I hoped I wasn't just talking to myself and that made me feel so damn sad and lonesome that I almost started bawling like a goddam kid. Only thing that stopped me was I could see myself walking along in the dark and the drizzle and sniffling like a two-year-old. That's me. That's Mr. Always Cool. Nope. Don't think so.

So I held it together and kept shuffling along, pressing on towards Happy-Land. When the little village came in view, it wasn't good. The river was up. Way up.

The storm that came through must have blown down from up north, and it must have dumped as much rain upstream as it had on St. Louis, because the Mississippi was out of its banks and rising.

I got as far as the welcome sign and I could see the water was within a few feet of the shacks on the far side of the road. Nobody around, though. Not a soul anywhere. At first I thought maybe they'd evacuated, taken what little they had and gone to higher ground somewhere. Then I heard the music in the distance and I remembered - the Revival.

Got to get up there and warn them, I thought. They're about to lose their town.

I headed towards the music. Just over a small rise the tent came in view, all lighted up from the inside and kind of glowing in the darkness. They'd strung up Christmas lights all around the tent and it looked pretty. Odd, too, though. It didn't look like Christmas. More like a carnival or a used car lot or something, especially since there were a bunch of cars parked around the tent. Still, in the cold rain, the tent looked warm and inviting.

Getting to the tent was tough, though. The ground was muddy from all the rain. Slippery, too. My feet sunk in some places and when I'd pull them up they came up with five pounds of mud stuck to my shoes. Felt like I was walking with weights on. Other places there'd be a little bit of grass and my muddy feet would slip and I'd have to struggle to keep my balance. I fell more than once. I was covered with mud by the time I reached the tent.

I came up on the tent from the back and everybody was so intent on what was going on up front that nobody even noticed me. I hung back outside until I spotted Tugboat sitting halfway back on the far side. I circled around outside, but I didn't want to go in. Didn't want to cause a big commotion. I figured the best thing would be to let Tugboat know what was going on and then he could get everybody down and start sandbagging or have them get their stuff out or whatever they thought was best.

I edged over a little in front of Tugboat and started waving at him. He was watching the show and didn't see me. I whistled softly and waved some more and finally he looked over. His eyes got real wide and his brows furrowed and then he waved for me to come in.

I shook my head no and waved for him to come out. He looked back up front and then slowly got up and, crouching over the whole way so he wouldn't get in the way of folks behind him, he came outside.

"Thomas," he said softly, "Where have you been...and what's happened to you?"

"Never mind that," I said hurriedly, "Tug, you gotta get everybody out of here."

"What? Why?"

"It's Happy-Land," I said, "It's gonna flood. The water's way up. You gotta get everybody back there right away."

Tugboat just smiled. "Thomas, don't worry about Happy-Land. The river's visited us before."

"Tug, you don't understand. The water's way up. The whole place is going under. We gotta sandbag or something."

He shook his head. "Calm yourself. There's no need. Every one of those shacks has seen water before. You don't live on the river and not get wet from time to time."

"But there'll be no place to stay," I protested.

"There's always a place. If the water doesn't get too high we can stay in our homes by just raising the plank floors some. Put some planks in the street to get around, too. We've done it before. Kinda fun fishing out your front door, or even right inside your house."

"I don't understand," I said.

"It's alright, Thomas, it's just another thing you'll know about once you've been through it. And if the water gets a lot higher, I bet the Holy Rollers let us stay in the tent here on high ground."

"Well...."

"Believe me," he said, "It'll be okay. Now come inside here. Let's get out of the rain." He put his hand on my shoulder and nudged me in under the tent to a folding chair next to him.

I was starting to feel kind of dizzy so it felt good to sit down. I closed my eyes for a minute and rubbed the rainwater out of my hair and off my face. There was some huge black lady up in front just wrapping up a gospel song. "Didn' it rain, children, rain all night long?" she wailed, "Rained 40 days and 40 nights without stoppin; didn' it rain, children, rain all night long?" The lady had a great voice and the song was a rocker, had everybody clapping to the beat. There was another lady playing piano and even though this was gospel music, the way she was pounding the keyboard reminded me of Jerry Lee Lewis.

The song finished up and the preacher, who'd been sitting in a folding chair on the other side of the stage came over and put his arm around the black lady and waved to the audience with the other arm. "Ladies and gentlemen," he said, "Miss Millie Jackson."

The black lady smiled and closed her eyes and did a little bow and everybody clapped for her. She was a good singer. Every bit as good as Tina Turner. People clapped some more and Millie took another little bow and then lumbered over to the side, leaving the preacher alone in the middle of the stage. I don't know what kind of preacher he was, other than Holy Roller. He wasn't a priest. He wasn't wearing a smock or gown or anything, just a regular suit. Didn't even have his collar backwards. He was a skinny guy, but tall and he wore his gray hair in a big pompadour, which made him look even taller.

He waited until the crowd quieted down some, then he spread his arms out and looked from one side of the tent to the other. "Yes," he smiled and intoned in this powerful bass voice, "Didn't it rain, children?"

The audience clapped and chuckled and I heard some shout "Amen."

The preacher's expression turned more serious. "And how long will it rain, children?" He paused as if waiting for someone to answer, but there was just murmuring from the crowd.

"I'm askin' does any-body know how long it's gonna rain?" Again he paused and again no reply. "And how much rain have you already had in your life?"

He was pretty good. I'd heard the preacher up at the Holy Roller church near my house and this guy was just warming up and already he had folks fidgeting in their seats. I was still feeling tired and a little dizzy, but the guy's preaching was starting to wake me up a little. I forgot about the flooding. I figured Tugboat oughta know what he was talking about. If he wasn't worried, why should I be?

I started looking around the tent. It was pretty full, which was surprising, the weather being so nasty and all. It looked like everybody from Happy-Land was there. A whole bunch of folks not from

Happy-Land, too. I drew back a little when I noticed that there were cops in the tent. Two in front and two in back, plus one on each side. They were just standing there, though. Didn't look like they were searching for anybody, like they were searching for me, so I figured they were just there for crowd control or maybe to direct traffic for the folks not from Happy-Land.. I relaxed a little, but kept glancing around at them.

The preacher was getting pretty fired up, getting to the hellfire and damnation part. I didn't have any place else to go. It was dry in the tent and it was warm from the crowd. I didn't know where I'd go after the Revival was over, but my life seemed like I was just living it minute to minute anymore anyway, so I just sat there next to Tugboat and listened to the preacher.

Not like Assumption Church, but nice. Real nice. At least you could understand the guy.

EIGHTEEN

"Always remember: no-one escapes The Dunderbug."
Porky Pig

"There never was a perfect world. There was only death and the language of happiness. People who tried to tell the truth and people who tried not to."
John Straley

Turned out it wasn't such a bad night. I mean I was wet and muddy, just back from a fruitless journey to save my young ass from the slammer, and my new home was about to flood, but you had to look on the positive side. I was in out of the rain and what had been a steamy, muggy St. Louis summer evening had turned into a nice, cool night. I was around friends and there was a show going on to keep me entertained. Maybe I'd get something to eat afterwards. I wasn't in jail and nobody was getting ready to beat my ass. At least not in the next few minutes. Gotta take life's little pleasures as they come.

The preacher was really warming up now. I hoped maybe he'd do some healing. That was always fun to watch. At least it had been at the little storefront church up on Eleventh Street, and this guy seemed like he might be able to do it even better. For now though, he was at the part where he was telling everybody how bad they were and how there was no question but every one of them was going to hell.

"You think you're a good person?" the preacher asked, "Been a good man or a good woman, do ya think?"

Lots of folks shaking their heads no. A few holdouts, though. Preacher zoomed in on them.

"Oh," he said, pointing at a man in the second row up front who'd failed to own up that he was a sinner, "You been a good man, have ya?"

Poor guy. Some middle age overweight fellow in a shirt buttoned up way too tight around his neck. He didn't know what to do, so he just sat there. Got real red in the face.

"Here a good man, ever'body," the preacher said, keeping his eyes on the victim, "Here a man never did nothin wrong, a man never ever did nothin wrong in his life."

The man squirmed in his seat.

"Here a man kept all the Commandments, my friends. Here a good man."

A few people in the audience echoed back, "A good man."

"Here a man never stole nothin his whole life," the preacher went on, "Never lied, never cheated nobody, never drank, never even thought a bad thought. Here a good man, ever'body."

"A good man," more folks chanted back.

"Good man," preacher said, "Man always done right, man go to church ever' Sund'y, man who tithe to his church, man who he'p his fella man. Yay, here a good man, my friends. Gimme Amen."

"Amen," the crowd responded.

"A good man," the preacher said.

"Good man."

The preacher turned and walked towards the back of the stage. He stood there a minute, just stock still. Then he turned around and sort of roared back to the front of the stage. His face was all red and mad-looking, and he pointed to the guy in the second row again.

"This a good man?" he demanded in a loud voice.

"Good man," the crowd cried back.

The preacher gave the audience a long, slow look, scanning the tent from one side to the other. Then he asked in a softer tone, "This a good man like alla ya?"

They weren't sure how to answer that one. Some people tried "Good man" again, but it kind of petered out. Others reverted to an "Amen." That sounded weak, too. Most just murmured something you couldn't make out.

Preacher stood there in the middle of the stage and didn't say anything until the tent got real quiet. Then he looked right in the eyes of the man in the second row. He raised one hand up like he was asking God to pull him upstairs right then and he put his other arm out, palm up, toward the man. He raised his face to where he was looking up at the top of the tent or maybe up to God or something and stood like that a minute and then looked back at the man. "Before God," he said in an even, but powerful voice, "Tell us have you done no wrong in your life?"

Good question. Not too many folks could answer that one with a loud "Damn right!" The second row guy just sat there a minute looking real uncomfortable, then started to blubber. He broke down. A woman next to him, must have been his wife, put her arm around him, but he was really having a hard time. He was sobbing and shaking all over. Put his head down, almost in his wife's lap.

The preacher watched and waited for just the right moment. "In Jesus' name," he yelled.

The overweight guy looked up, startled.

"In Jesus' name," the preacher yelled again, "Have you sinned?"

The guy reached an arm out towards the stage and his eyes were streaming. "I'm a sinner," he cried, "God help me, I'm a sinner."

"Oh yes," the preacher beamed, "You are. You're a sinner among sinners, gimme amen."

"Amen," the crowd roared.

"Come on up front, sinner. Confess your sins."

The man kind of rocked back and forth a minute, then pulled himself heavily up out of his chair and lumbered forward, stopping in front of the preacher. The man's wife had come with him, her arm around him the whole way.

The preacher knelt at the edge of the stage and put his hand on the sinner's head. "Confess now," he said, "Confess your sins and be saved."

The man started mumbling something.

"Speak up," the preacher demanded, "Confess your sins before God and man. Save your eternal soul."

"Adultery," the man said abruptly, "Forgive me, God. Oh God, I done laid with a whore."

The wife's head jerked back on that one. She took her arm from around her husband's shoulder. Didn't look happy. Not even sympathetic. Looked pissed. This was one guy definitely wasn't getting any that night. Probably not for a long time. The preacher saw the reaction, though, and put his free hand on the wife's shoulder, pulling her back next to her husband. Then he moved his hand to her head, saying "Judge not, woman, that ye be not judged." The wife bent her head under his hand. Looked like she might be crying too.

"Forgive," the preacher said gently, "Forgive as the Lord forgives sinners." He let his hands drop down from their heads and onto their shoulders, pressed husband and wife together. "Go now and sin no more," he said. Then, looking out at the crowd, he raised both arms and shouted "Amen. Amen, my friends, the Lord has done his work here."

"Amen," the crowd shouted back.

"And who else among ye got sins to confess? Come on forward now."

A few folks came up to the front of the tent and confessed in tears they'd done one thing or another to deserve eternal damnation. It was a pretty good show, but after a while I got a little bored with one confession after another, especially since none of them were as good as the first guy. I started looking around the tent and I was surprised to see a row of guys in shiny silk jackets sitting across the aisle and a few rows up.

I nudged Tug and pointed out the guys. "Aces?" I whispered.

Tugboat looked over at me. "Sure," he said in a hoarse stage whisper, "Those guys come down sometimes. Mostly a good bunch, they are."

I looked down the row of Aces again and in the middle, I could see the shortest one of the bunch, the one without a neck. Couldn't believe a guy like that would be sitting at a revival.

Again I poked Tugboat and pointed. "You know Beef Butcher?" I asked.

"Beef Butcher? You mean Manuel?"

I answered with nothing more than a puzzled look.

"Beef Butcher, Manuel, same thing," Tugboat said with a grin, "Tough Mexican kid, huh?"

"Yeah," I said with raised eyebrows.

"Seven cops, huh?"

"Yeah."

"Bunch of crap," Tugboat whispered, "Manuel's a pretty decent guy, really. Used to hang out at the repair shop when he was younger."

"The Beef Butcher hung out at your place?"

Tugboat laughed. "Beef Butcher my ass. I dunno how that whole thing got started. He's just Manuel. Kid I used to have to cuff around once in a while to keep 'im in line."

It was a little hard to figure at first, the Beef Butcher being the legend he was and all, but after I thought about it a little, I could see Tugboat, big old Tugboat, shoving a little Mexican kid good naturedly around, giving him a hard time, teasing him. I mean Tug was a good foot or more taller than the Beef, and he looked like he'd been able to take care of himself pretty good when he was younger, even against the likes of a Beef Butcher. At least a kid version of a Beef Butcher.

Almost as if on cue, Beef turned in his seat and spotted Tugboat. Then he did something I bet nobody'd ever seen before. He gave old Tug this big, goofy-ass grin and waved at him. Tugboat smiled and waved back, then pointed up front. The Beef nodded, turned back around to listen to the preacher.

It was a strange evening. I glanced around the crowd to see who else I might know there and sure enough, who do I see a few rows back but my bum friend Jim, old Snot-nose sitting right beside him. It didn't look like Jim was getting much out of the service. He had his usual pissed-off scowl and it looked like he was mumbling to himself, too - probably debating the preacher, I figured. Probably arguing about religion being the opiate of the masses or something.

Snot-nose, to his credit, was at least not asleep. His face was clean, too, and he actually looked like he might be aware of what was going. He and Jim were both there for the food that would come after the service, of course. Jim must have dragged his friend down here. Seeing to it that the old guy got a decent meal once in a while must have been part of the odd relationship between these two bums. I wondered what would happen to Snot-nose if Jim died or something. Probably he'd die, too, starve or get the crap kicked out of him or drown or wander into some construction site and get hit with something or buried in debris or who knows what? Either that or he'd get put away in some funny farm. It was kind of weird thinking that Jim, my uncle Jim, a nutty old bum, was actually somebody's lifeline, his guardian like, and probably the only reason Snot-nose could survive outside of an institution.

Then I saw something even goofier than that. About three rows back from the front, on the other side of the tent near the center aisle, were old Jeffrey Deems and his mom. It almost made me laugh out loud. She'd dragged him down here just like Jim dragged Snot-nose, but for a different reason. It just like my Mom dragged me over to Assumption on Sundays.

Jeffrey looked real uncomfortable. He was fidgeting and looking around like he was searching for a way out. For a minute I was afraid he might spot me, but then I realized even if he looked right at me, the way I looked, all wet and muddy and unshaven and everything, he probably wouldn't recognize me.

Meanwhile, the preacher was really hitting his stride, pacing back and forth on the stage letting everybody know that if they didn't confess and get right with God, they were going to have a rough time in the next world.

"Do you know, my friends," he shouted, "What Jesus love?"

"We know," the crowd called back.

"Askin' if you know what Jesus love," preacher fed them back.

"We know what Jesus love."

"If you know what Jesus love," preacher paused and looked around, "Will ya tell me what Jesus love?"

"Truth!" the audience yelled.

Preacher put his hand to his ear. "Don't hear what you tol' me. I don't hear what Jesus love."

"The truth!" they cried again.

"Is it truth that Jesus love?" Preacher asked with eyes wide.

"The truth!"

"Is it the truth I hear tonight?"

"The truth!"

"Is it the truth Jesus hear in your heart?"

"The truth!"

Preacher got a troubled look on his face. A real troubled look. He cocked his head to one side and frowned. He walked from one side of the stage to the other, looking out at the audience and up in the air.

"Don't think I hear the truth," he said softly.

Some of the people tried to echo back "the truth," but it faded out quickly.

"No," he said a little louder, "Don't think I hear the truth tonight." He slammed one hand into the other palm. "Not *enough* truth. Don't think Jesus hear the whole truth tonight neither!"

I looked over at Jeffrey and he was more uncomfortable than ever. Funny thing, though, was that it struck me it wasn't so much he was uncomfortable being there, getting dragged her by his Mom and all, but more that he was uncomfortable with what he was hearing. He kept putting his hands up over his ears and shaking his head. His mom was looking over at him kind of funny, too.

The preacher was looking up, had both arms up in the air. "Can you forgive a lying sinner?" he implored, "Can you forgive him what he hold inside?"

Some of the folks in the audience were getting kind of agitated, but none more than Jeffrey. He was rocking back and forth and shaking, holding his hands over his ears. His mom put her arm around him.

The preacher looked out at the crowd, then bowed his head as if he'd failed in some endeavor, failed in his intercession with God. "The Lord cannot forgive," he said sadly, "What you don't confess. The Lord can not forgive what you ain't gonna confess." He looked up and his eyes were blazing. "Lord gonna send you straight to HELL for what you don't confess. Fires of Hell gonna burn you up for what you don't confess. You gonna burn in hellfire FOREVER for what you don't confess. What I ain't got you to confess."

The crowd started picking up a chant. "Confess," a few of them murmured.

"If you know the truth you gotta confess it," preacher said.

"Confess," more people said back.

"If there's evil in your heart you gotta confess."

"Confess!" the crowd called out.

"If you wanna be saved you got to confess. Got to, GOT TO!"

"Confess!"

"To save your soul you MUST confess."

"Confess!"

People were slowly starting to get up and head up the aisle to confess their sins.

"The Lord will save you but first you gotta confess," Preacher yelled.

"Confess!" the audience yelled back.

"You gotta confess TONIGHT! You gotta be true, be righteous! RIGHT NOW you gotta confess!"

"Confess!"

Then something perfectly weird happened. Jeffrey Deems stood up, raised both hands over his head and shrieked out "I done it! I done it! I confess I done it!" Tears were streaming down his face and he was shaking all over. Even the preacher had to stop and look at him.

"Come forward, boy," the preacher commanded, "Confess and be saved."

Jeffrey came stumbling out of his row and down the aisle, his mother right behind him. She was crying, too, but more like she was happy some message got through to her son. Jeffrey fell on his knees in front of the preacher, bawling and screaming, "I done it, preacher. I done it. God, I done it!"

The preacher hopped down off the stage. You could almost hear him thinking, "Oh, boy, a show-stopper." That's not what he said out loud, of course. What he said, putting his hand on Jeffrey's head, was "What did you do, son? What is your sin?"

Jeffrey was crying these big sobs that just wracked his whole body and you could see it was hard for him to say anything. He did finally manage to get some words out, though, and the words he got out were, "I set the fire. I set the fire, preacher. God forgive me, I done set that fire."

I don't know how to say how that hit me, hearing that. I think that most people go through their whole lives and never hear words that hit them like that. Felt like somebody had poured ice water down the back of my neck or something, and then it was like I wasn't sure I'd heard what I thought I had or if I'd just made it up or maybe I fell asleep and this was just a dream or something.

I looked over at Tugboat and he was looking back at me. "Did you hear that?" I asked.

He nodded. "Yes," he said softly, "I heard. And others heard as well. Question is, do you believe it?"

"No," I said, "I don't. I don't believe Jeffrey did it any more than I believe I did it."

"How do you figure?"

"Hell, I think Jeffrey just got all caught up with this revival mumbo-jumbo. Got hysterical or something. Stick around – maybe more folks'll confess to the fire."

"Well," Tug said, "You might be right, but could also be best to keep your doubts to yourself."

"Yeah," I said, "Guess you're right."

The preacher had this puzzled look on his face, like he wasn't quite sure what was going on and like the show might be getting a little out of hand. "Fire?" he said, "You set a fire?" The two cops who'd been standing up front started closing in on Jeffrey and his mom.

After that it got more and more like some kind of dream or something. I think maybe I was crying a little bit and my stomach hurt. Tugboat was trying to talk to me but I couldn't understand what he was saying.

The two cops got hold of Jeffrey and started walking him up the center aisle. He was still crying and he had this crazy, tortured look on his face. Somehow I got over to the middle aisle, too, at the back of the tent. The cops were dragging Jeffrey right in front of me. His mom was right behind him screaming "My boy. my boy. Don't let 'em take my boy."

I was wrong, too, because when Jeffrey got right in front of me he did recognize me. He pulled away from the cops and fell down on his knees in front of me and grabbed me around the legs. "Tom," he cried, "Tom, I'm sorry, I'm sorry. I burned 'em up. Oh, God forgive me."

I bent over and gently pulled Jeffrey up. I looked in his eyes and then I put my arms around him and pulled him close. I could feel it was hard for him to even keep standing, so I was partly holding him up. "It's okay, Jeffrey," I said. I patted him on the back of the head. "It's okay, man."

He had his arms around me, too. "I'm sorry, Tom," he said, "I'm so damn sorry. I didn't mean none of this to happen."

I pulled him up straight and looked into his eyes. "I know you didn't, Jeffrey," I said. He just looked back at me and didn't say anything more. Then the two cops grabbed him again and dragged him away, up the aisle and out of the tent with his Mom right behind, still wailing away.

Everybody was just kind of milling around and buzzing and trying to figure out what had just happened and what they ought to do about it. Up front the Preacher came to his senses and figured he'd better get things back under control, especially since he hadn't passed the collection plate yet. He climbed back up on the stage and raised his arms.

"Hallelujah!" he shouted, "Hallelujah for the truth. For salvation!"

People started turning back towards the stage and remembering where they were and what was supposed to be happening.

"Praise the Lord for salvation!" the Preacher yelled.

"Praise the Lord," a few folks sang out.

"Jesus' been with us tonight, praise the Lord."

"Praise the Lord," the crowd responded.

I could see that he was getting back into his rhythm, getting his audience back into it with him, too, but I wasn't too interested anymore. Tugboat was standing there next to me and I guess he wasn't much interested either. "Come on," he said, "Let's get you cleaned up some."

We walked together down to the spigot. I turned it on and started scrubbing the mud off my hands and arms. Splashed the cool water on my face and washed away the mud and the sweat and the tears. It wasn't raining anymore. The clouds had blown away and there was a big old almost-full moon overhead. From back at the tent I could hear the piano start up again, but kind of soft and gentle, and then I could hear Millie. She was singing The Lord's Prayer. There was a little breeze blowing and it wasn't too hot or too cold out and Millie's voice and the song she was singing sounded so sweet that I almost couldn't stand it. I felt like I was free after being in prison or locked in a dark basement room like a dog, like old Boozer, and at last I was out and I was okay and I was going to be okay.

"Feelin' better?" Tugboat asked.

"Yeah," I sighed, "I'm feeling a lot better."

"Good. I'm glad. Now, how 'bout a little somethin' to eat?"

I laughed. "Yeah," I said, "That sounds pretty good, Tug."

"I think things are breakin' up in there," he said, "If we hurry, we can beat the rush."

We walked back to our chow tent where the Holy Rollers had set out a feast. There was more food than I'd ever seen before, and ladies in pretty dresses were standing ready to serve. We had beat the crowd, too, but we hadn't beaten Jim and Snotnose. They'd already been through the line and were sitting at a table shoveling food down as fast as they could. Jim looked up when we came in and gave us a quick nod, then went right back to the job at hand.

Tugboat and I went through the serving line and stacked our plates with one of everything. Before we found seats the rest of the crowd was pouring in, all boisterous and happy. They'd seen a good show. Some of them had been saved. They were hungry, too. Guess you work up an appetite getting saved.

Tugboat was sitting next to me. He leaned over so I could hear him over the noise. "I guess you'll be leaving us now, huh?"

"I don't know, Tug," I said, "Maybe. Maybe not. I don't know yet."

He gave me a kind of funny look, but didn't say anything.

After a while we were getting up to leave when two cops walked into the place, followed by none other than Detective Pearse. My stomach clenched up and my instinct was to run, but then I realized I didn't have anything to run from anymore. I didn't have to hide anymore.

Pearse scanned the crowd, caught my eye and headed towards me and Tugboat.

"Bonner," he said, "I just thought you oughta know, that Deems kid gave us a full statement - told us the whole thing was his idea. He was tryin' to get into the jewelry store and something went wrong."

"Yeah," I said, "Okay."

"Well, I just wanted you to know," Pearse said, scowling. Then he kind of looked down. "I guess maybe I was wrong about you, kid. Sorry."

I just nodded. He might be wrong about Jeffrey, too, but now wasn't the time to say anything. He turned and started to walk away. "Pearse," I called after him, "Can I ask you something?"

He turned back. "Huh? Yeah, what?"

"What about Bryan?" I said, "He's off the hook, too, right?"

Pearse looked puzzled. "Uh, well, I suppose."

"Well," I said, "Anybody know where he is?"

Pearse's brow furrowed. "Bryan's dead, kid. Didn't you know that?"

"What? What do you mean he's dead? I thought you never found anything."

"Well, not at first," Pearse said, "But when forensics went over the scene they found enough. It's official. He's gone. I'm sorry you didn't know."

"But....the cave...."

"I'm sorry, kid. Listen, can we give you a ride someplace?"

"No," I said, "No, thanks."

Pearse and the two cops strode off out of the tent, into the darkness.

229

NINETEEN

Happy-Land didn't get flooded that night. The water never got higher than what I'd seen earlier. Went back down pretty quickly. I stayed with Tugboat in his place as usual. Next morning I got up, took a quick shower, cleaned up my clothes and started in on my regular water-bearing routine. Did some thinking, too.

When Tugboat finally came lumbering up the hill to breakfast, I went over to talk with him.

"Tugboat, if it's okay I think I'm gonna stick around here a while."

He looked at me real funny. "Huh? What the hell for?"

"I dunno," I smiled, "I kinda like it here."

"Bonner," he said, "I don' never tell nobody what to do, but you're nuts."

"Maybe so," I said, "But remember, I still got the Calcatorri's to worry about on that bond money thing."

Tugboat chuckled, "Well, if that's it, I wouldn't worry too much."

"Huh? Why not?"

"Listen, you remember what I told you about me and your old man and the Hogans and Eagans, right?"

"Yeah, but..."

"Well, Johnny Eagan's still around, and he's still got a helluva lot more clout than any of that Calcatorri bunch. He's tied into that Buster Werner crew over on the East Side, too. Your old man puts in a word with Johnny and them Calcatorri's not ever gonna bother you again."

"You think.....?"

"I know!"

"Okay," I said, "But what if I wanna stick around anyway?"

Tugboat just shook his head. "Up to you, kid, but I still say you're nuts."

I stuck around.

It seemed like school and Mick, Steve, Wally, Bob and The Schwantz and even Ronnie and them were a long way away. I thought about my folks and about Elaine sometimes and I missed them, but it was like they were from another life. A life I'd left behind. A life I didn't seem to fit into anymore. Or maybe life itself just didn't fit together like before. A bunch of stuff I'd taken for granted seemed like I had to figure out all over again. Like the Holy Rollers. I used to think they were just kinda goofy. A show to watch and yeah, make fun of. But look what happened at the revival. Hadn't have been for that I might be in jail right now.

I guess every once in a while you have to re-think what you believe. Figure out why you believe the way you do. Because you just pick up stuff. From your parents, teachers and even your friends. You think like they do. I mean my old man had lots of prejudices that were easy to see through, but maybe there were others that were subtler. And the easiest ones to fall into were probably from the kids you hung out with. I had a lot of testing to do, including what I believed about God. I mean maybe He was at work in that revival. I don't know. It was all kinda confusing. It would take some time to sort out.

So I stayed in Happy-Land. It was OK there. These people had taken me in and believed that I was alright and never asked any questions. I had my job here. I was needed and I had lots of time to myself to roam around and look at the river and watch the animals and stuff. Never once had to think about being cool. I didn't even roll up my t-shirt sleeves anymore.

The next day after the revival thing, my Old Man came down and asked me when I was coming home.

"I don't know, Dad," I said, "But not right now."

He thought about it for a while and I figured I was in for a big argument or that he was going to try and make me come home. Instead he was a lot cooler than I expected.

"Well," he said, "I guess maybe I understand, after what you been through. You need anything, son?"

"No, Dad, got everything right here."

"Okay, then," he said, "Well, is it okay if we come down to see you sometimes?"

"Sure," I said, "Sure you can."

"Then I understand maybe you need some time to get yourself right again," he said, "And when that happens, in a day or so, you come on home, okay?"

"Maybe so, Dad," I said.

Ronnie came down once to visit me, too and he asked when I was coming back. I told him the same thing. I just didn't know.

"So whatdya gonna do, just live down here with the bums?" he asked.

I tried to explain to him that these people weren't bums, about the difference between Happy-Land people and bums and that even among bums there's differences, but I don't think it made too much sense to Ronnie. Maybe I just didn't do a very good job of explaining it all. I didn't tell him about Jim being my uncle, either. Not because I was ashamed of Jim or anything, I just didn't figure it was anybody's business.

"I'm just gonna stick around here a while," I said, "You say hi to everybody for me, okay?"

"Sure," he said, "Oh, and Diane's askin' about you like all the time, man."

"Well, just tell her I'm doin' good and maybe I'll see her sometime."

"I think she likes you, Tom."

"Yeah, Ronnie, I like her too. She's a nice kid."

"No," he said, "I mean I think she likes you a lot."

I laughed. "She's a nice kid, Ronnie. *Kid.*"

"Yeah," he said, smiling, "But nice, huh?"

I stayed in Happy-Land and carried water and hung out. One thing the flood had done was wipe out the little island I'd been making. I went down there one day and there was no island anymore. The moat I'd been digging got all filled up with silt and it was back being just a small peninsula with a bushy tree on it again. I thought about trying to dig it out, but then I figured it would just fill up again. I'd be wasting my time. Some things just aren't meant to be islands, I guess. Some things you gotta let 'em like they are.

While I was down there looking at my not-island, I got a big surprise. I spotted a pack of dogs roaming around hunting for something to eat. They were led by a big, black skinny-ass mutt. There were always dogs down by the river, sometimes alone but more often in packs. Three, four, five dogs roaming around together. I'd asked Tugboat once where they all came from.

"They come from everyplace," he said, "From all over the city and probably even beyond. The river's the low point, you know. Anything not tied down one way or another winds up rolling downhill and comes to rest at the river. Goin' downhill is the easiest way. For dogs, for people - it's the same thing."

You had to watch out for dogs in packs. They can be dangerous when they're hungry. Tugboat warned me about that when I first got to Happy-Land, but this particular pack didn't seem too bad. I was cautious and kept my distance, but something about the black lead dog looked familiar. I guess I looked familiar to him, too, or smelled familiar or something, because after a while he came trotting over. Came right over and stood in front of me and lowered his head like he wanted to be petted. That's when I saw it was Boozer.

I was real happy to see him and gave him a good petting and scratching behind the ears and everything. I was glad he was still alive and not run over or anything and that he was still free and out of that damn coal mine of a basement room he'd been trapped in for so long. I figured maybe I'd keep him - feed him and take care of him. He'd be my dog. Tugboat said he didn't think that would be a good idea, though.

"Got a few problems, there," he said, "First, there's them dog-ass fleas."

"Huh? Dog-ass fleas?"

"Yeah," Tug chuckled, "You know, you'll see a cloud of fleas buzzin' around a dog's ass, then next thing you know they're buzzing right around your face."

"Yeah, right," I said.

"More seriously tho," Tug went on, "Where's the food gonna come from? You know there's times there ain't hardly enough for the folks here, let alone any extra for a animal. The other thing, though, is that a dog, once he gets to running with a pack like that, once he gets a taste of bein' wild, mostly he don't wanna go back bein' tame again, bein anybody's pet."

Like most things, Tugboat was right about that. About a dog needing to be free. Boozer hung around for a few days and let himself be fed and petted and stuff, but when night came he always disappeared, went off roaming with his buddies. One day he just didn't come back and that was it. I never saw him again. I missed him, but because of how Tugboat had explained things, I understood. Boozer had to go and be with his own kind.

Still, it seemed like I was getting left behind again. First Lovey and Bryan and then in a different way maybe my school friends and for sure that jerk Tony. Then Jeffrey and now even Boozer. When Boozer went off like that it made me think that maybe part of the reason I'd decided to stay in Happy-Land was that I was tired of people going off and leaving and I thought maybe that wasn't going to happen here because this was the last place anybody could go. No place left to run off to after that. Now it turned out even that wasn't true. You get left behind even in Happy-Land. Nothing stays the same, not anyplace.

Even the weather was changing. Summer was coming to an end and what little was green along the river had started turning brown. There were more cool days and the sky got that clear, pale blue color it gets when Fall's right around the corner. There were still some hot, sunny days and some rainy days, but not quite so hot and never any rainy days like that sewer plate blowing one. No floods and no revivals.

After a while it started feeling funny still being there in Happy-Land. The time of year or something. It started feeling like I ought to be getting ready to go back to school. I ought to be doing what I'd done every year at this time, in this season.

My Dad came down again, told me it was time for me to come home. Said my mother missed me and needed me to come home. He grabbed me and hugged me and told me that he missed me and wanted me to come home, I didn't put up much of a fight. He'd gotten to Tugboat, too, and had him talk to me.

"Thomas, you don't belong here anymore," Tugboat said, "This is a place for people ending up, not kids like you just startin' out. It's time for you to get goin'. This ain't *your* Happy-Land."

If this was a movie or TV program or something, the Happy-Land folks would have put together a big party to send me off. There'd be a big cake and a celebration and a bunch of happy folks wishing me well and telling me to be sure to come back and visit and not to forget to write and not to forget them ever. It could have been a musical with Doris Day or somebody singing and maybe Gene Kelly or Donald O'Connor dancing down the middle of the dirt street, everybody clapping and singing and just having a helluva time.

It wasn't a movie, though. I was just another guy moving on. I wanted to think I'd made a little bit of a difference in Happy-Land, done something good for these people, even if it was only making sure they had water in the morning and could take a shower when they wanted. I guess what I really wanted was to have them - some of them anyway - ask me not to go. I wanted them to tell me they needed me and that I was important there and that the place was going to fall apart without me. I wanted them to hug me and cry because I was going.

But that wasn't the way it was. I was just another guy moving on, like lots of guys had done before, and in the long run it didn't make a damn bit of difference. In two weeks, nobody would remember I'd been there.

Except Tugboat. We ate our last breakfast together the morning I was heading out. Drank a last cup of coffee together. Said our goodbye's.

"Been good knowin' ya," Tugboat said, "Ya done good here."

"Thanks, Tug. I'm gonna miss this place. Miss you, too."

"Nah," he said, "Don't miss us, just get on with things." He paused a minute and looked around. "There is one thing you could do, though. Something somebody ought to do, and maybe you're the one to do it."

"What's that?"

"Tell folks about this place," he said, "Happy-Land is dying. Five years from now it'll be gone. Ten years from now nobody'll remember it was ever here or even what a place like this was. Nobody'll know about Hoovervilles. Nobody'll know how people lived, how poor people lived. People with nothing. People who just didn't fit in. Maybe you could tell 'em. Not now. Not right away, but sometime."

"I will, Tugboat. I'll tell 'em."

"Good," he said, "I think maybe you will, Thomas. Oh, I almost forgot - I got something for ya." He reached in his pocket and pulled out a little package wrapped carefully in a scrap of newspaper.

"What's this?" I asked.

"Just a little going-away present. Go on, open it up."

I tore open the wrapping. It was my key. The brass skeleton key I'd found the day I went searching for clues at Gettelmans. I guess I must have left it out somewhere at Tugboat's place and he'd found it. He'd polished the brass all shiny & made a necklace, stringing the key on a leather thong.

I put it around my neck. "Thanks, Tug," I said, "Thanks a lot."

"It's to remind you," he said.

"Yeah, I'll always remember this place."

"No," he said, "That's not what I mean. It's to remind you that you hold the key."

I chuckled. "Yeah, but I don't even know what it's for."

Tugboat's face stayed pretty serious. "Doesn't matter," he said, "You will someday." He stood up and grinned and winked at me. "Now get the hell out of here."

I got up, too, and we shook hands, firmly and solidly. "So long, Tug," I said.

"So long, Thomas. You're a good man. Like your father."

I turned and headed up and away from the river. Away from Happy-Land and Tugboat and Boozer, wherever he was. I walked all the way back to Eleventh Street, walked back to all the stuff I'd tried to walk away from but found out I couldn't.

At first it seemed real strange being back at home and I wasn't sure I was going to be able to do it. I wasn't sure I was going to be able to get up and go to school every day and come home and study and see my friends - the guys I thought were my friends - and play basketball and goof around and stuff like that. It felt like maybe I'd gotten a lot older over the last few months and I wasn't a kid anymore. Doing kid things seemed pretty stupid. Childish, I guess. After a while, though, things kind of faded in my mind and I was able to pick up again and go on.

Some things, though, were different. For one thing, I wasn't the same guy anymore even in the way I looked. When I got back from Happy-Land and got cleaned up, really cleaned up, got some new clothes on and saw myself in a mirror for the first time since all that stuff had happened, I was surprised at what I saw.

First, I wasn't so goofy-looking anymore. It took me a while to figure it out, but finally it came to me that it was carrying those buckets of water every day. You've got these muscles in the back of your neck, trapezius or something, and carrying that water had made them bigger. My shoulders were broader and more powerful looking and so I wasn't so gangly anymore.

The other thing was that for the same reason my arms had gotten a lot bigger, too. And that big old pulsing vein that Bryan had running across his bicep? Now I had one of those, too.

It wasn't just me that noticed it. I saw old Freddie once in a while, and he and Jay and that whole crew left me alone. I mean, they'd nod and say hi or something if we passed or saw each other on the street, but there wasn't any more messing around. Partly, I think, it was the way I looked now, but partly, too, it was the way I was. I wasn't afraid of those guys. I really just didn't give a damn about them. In some ways, it would have been neat to have faced old Freddie down and beat the crap out of him, which I think I had a pretty good shot at doing now. But it just wasn't important anymore. It didn't mean anything. My Old Man's car never wound up on the sidewalk again, though.

So I went to school and I came home and I hung out and did most of the stuff I used to do and it was almost the same, but not quite. The Old Man and I never talked much about what had happened. He tried to get me to open up a couple of times but I told him it was all water under the bridge and we ought to just forget the whole thing. He didn't push. There was some kind of new respect between the two of us that went both ways. We got along better than we had for a long time. We didn't have to say that much. We just understood each other a lot more. We were two men who happened to be father and son.

I saw Tony a few times cruising around and he pulled up and acted like nothing had happened. Tried to be my friend again, but it was way too late for that. When the friendship bit didn't work, he tried to pressure me some about the Calcatorri deal. I told him about Johnny Eagan and he shut up pretty quick. After that, we just stayed away from each other.

I went back to picking up Mick on the way to school most days and before long we were buddies again and even talked about going to college together. I'd pretty much decided that was what I was going to do if I got the chance, since Tony's union deal didn't sound like such a hot idea anymore.

I went back and played basketball and didn't say anything to Coach about what Steve had told me he'd said about not letting me back on the team. People say stupid stuff all the time. Stuff they don't mean or know anything about and sometimes you just have to overlook it. You have to look at the person instead of the goofy crap that comes out of their mouth.

As far as Ronnie, I still thought of him as a good friend, one of the ones who'd stuck by me when things were sticky and lots of people were looking the other way whenever I came around. You don't get many friends like that. If you get one, you ought to hold onto him. We played a lot of chess and talked a lot about all sorts of stuff and helped each other figure things out. He was an okay guy. Like they'd say in Happy-Land, he was alright.

Diane and her family moved away. The shame of what Jeffrey had done was just too much for them to stay in the neighborhood, so they moved back down to the boot heel someplace. I saw Diane the day they left and she cried a whole lot. She said she was going to write me every day and that someday they'd come back, or if her family wouldn't, then she'd come back by herself. She gave me a big old kiss that was real salty from her tears. She was trying hard, I think, to make it passionate, but it seemed like a kiss I might have gotten from my sister, if I'd had a sister. I think she felt that, too, and it made her cry even more.

Elaine and I started hanging out together more and more. I never really asked her, though, what she thought about all the stuff that had gone on. I never asked if she got to believing I'd done it or anything. I mean what was she going to say? What would have been the point in asking something like that? So we went to a few parties and dances and stuff together and had a good time and I was glad she was around. I still had a special feeling about this girl, but the truth is that even that wasn't like it was before. I don't know why. I didn't think any less of her. I didn't resent that she didn't come down to see me or try more to find out what was going on with me when all that mess was going on.

I think it was this: there was a time when she could have been everything, could have filled me up like you fill up a glass with milk or coke or something. Now, though, there was a big part of me that maybe nothing was ever going to fill up. Something got emptied out and sealed off and closed up and maybe nothing was ever going to get in there again. I don't know what you call that part, maybe trust or simplicity or just being naive about people. Maybe it was the part that makes you a kid and it's like when you get to a point where the ends of your bones seal off and stop growing, except instead of your bones it's part of your spirit or your soul or something that gets sealed off. I don't know if it ever opens up again.

One good thing was that I did get the National Merit thing. Old Man Conklin announced the results. Bob Lee and I finished 1-2, with

Agnieska third and Thor Berkle a distant fourth. Nobody knew what happened to that Martin kid, who'd probably have won if he hadn't dropped out of school. Thor was pretty good about losing, came over and congratulated me after the results were in. He could afford to be generous, I suppose. He was going to Harvard anyway.

I got scholarship offers from a bunch of colleges. The best of them was Washington U. right there in St. Louis, but that was the last place I wanted to go. It was time for me to leave St. Louis. I knew that, so I picked a little college I'd never even heard of before, way the hell up in Wisconsin someplace. Part of the reason I decided to go there is that it was the farthest college that came in with an offer.

When it came time to go it was Elaine who drove me to the old Greyhound station downtown. I'd already said my goodbye's to my folks and everyone else who mattered.

Elaine and I were standing next to the bus. My bags were getting loaded into the storage compartment under the seats and we were right there by the door I was going to go through in just a minute. Elaine's eyes were a little red and there was one cute little tear that made its way down her cheek, but she wasn't bawling like Diane.

"I'll miss you," Elaine said.

"Yeah, me too. I'll be back in a coupla months, though."

"Will you write me?"

I told her I would and I meant it. Diane had written a few times and I'd answered, but then that had just faded off and probably she found a boyfriend down in the country more her age or something. I figured Elaine and I would go on longer than that, though. Then she said something kind of strange.

"Tom," she said, "I want you to know something."

"Yeah?"

"Yeah. Well, it's just this: I hope that you come back to me."

"What?" I said, "Of course I'm comin' back to you."

"No, listen," she said, "Maybe you will and maybe you won't. Maybe you'll find some other girl off at college and she'll mean more to you than me. But still, I hope you remember something."

"Remember what?" I said.

"Just that there was a time we might have loved each other. Even if you find somebody you love more and you get married and have a bunch of kids and stuff, still I don't want you to ever forget me, ever forget us."

"I won't, Elaine," I said. I put my arms around her and kissed her. It was a good kiss. A deep one and a long one and it didn't feel at all sister-like. We pulled ourselves apart and I got on the bus and walked back and found a seat by myself.

Funny how lonely a bus can feel.

Elaine was still standing there waving as the big Greyhound pulled out of the station, taking me away from everything and everyone I knew into a slippery, foggy future I couldn't quite get ahold of. We were heading north and the driver took us out across the Eads Bridge to pick up Highway 66 up to Chicago. Through the bus's tinted windows the Mississippi looked like something out of a movie. The river was way down below, brown and turbulent and carrying its usual load of boards and tree limbs and stuff floating along down to the Gulf of Mexico.

I twisted around in my seat and looked way downstream to see if I could make out Happy-Land, but it was too far away. I wondered how many of the people I knew were still there and what Tugboat was doing and if he ever looked up and saw busses going across the bridge. If he was looking up now and saw this bus going across. I felt the rawhide strap, reached inside my shirt and pulled out the brass key I'd worn ever since Tug gave it to me, and I made a fist around it. It was still warm from my chest or from something.

I thought about Tugboat's words - this ain't your Happy-Land. Maybe that was it. Maybe everybody's just searching for their Happy-Land. Not a shanty town, but just their own special place. A place they can be happy.

And maybe each of us has to find his own key to that place.

I thought about Bryan for the thousandth time and wondered if he was really dead or if he'd just gotten away and was someplace he wanted to be right now, having a good time in *his* Happy-Land. I thought about Jeffrey and what he must be going through, and about Jim and Snotnose and I wondered if they'd found something to eat and a place to spend the night. I thought about Boozer. I thought about Lovey and the notes we'd passed back and forth without me knowing who it was.

I wondered where she was tonight and if wherever it was they had a poet's chapel.

The Mississippi is a great, wide river. It took a long time to get over it.

241

St. Louis Globe Democrat photograph, reprinted with permission of the St. Louis Mercantile Library at University of Missouri - St. Louis.

St. Louis Post-Dispatch photograph, reprinted with permission of St. Louis Post-Dispatch.

www.ingramcontent.com/pod-product-compliance
Lightning Source LLC
Chambersburg PA
CBHW071429260626
47170CB00008B/2646